S0-AZP-729

Deadly Provenance

By
Lynne Kennedy

Also by Lynne Kennedy:

THE TRIANGLE MURDERS
TIME EXPOSURE
THE COVENANT

Copyright © 2013 Lynne Kennedy
All rights reserved.
ISBN: 1484922115
ISBN 13: 9781484922118

No part of this book may be reproduced, scanned, or distributed in any printed or electronic form without permission.

Author's Note: This is a work of fiction based on historical fact. During World War II, the Nazis appointed a group, *Einsatzstab Reichsletter Rosenberg*, or ERR, to confiscate "decadent" art from undesirables, mostly Jews. In Paris, during the Occupation, these works of art were often stored at the *Musée du Jeu de Paume* in the Room of Martyrs. Thanks to the courage of a curator named Rose Valland, documentation on the stolen art was recorded and even today, is responsible for the return of many valuable pieces to their owners (or descendants.)

To the question of whether a painting can be authenticated from a photograph, infrared, x-rays and spectral imaging techniques are moving science closer to such a possibility. In fact, scientists at the University of California, San Diego, have been uncovering paintings under paintings with such technology.

One last note: Vincent Van Gogh's "Still Life: Vase With Oleanders," is, indeed, a real painting. It has been missing since 1944.

Acknowledgments: Thanks to my critique group, Ken, Dave, Barb, Barbara and Maynard, for all your wisdom and wit, without which, I might never have finished this book.

And always to my husband John, for his wealth of historical knowledge about the time period, his insight into human foibles, and his unwavering patience with all my rewrites.

To the thousands of precious paintings lost during the Nazi Regime.
May they eventually find their way home.

Prologue

P aris, France, Winter, 1941

Klaus Wilhelm Rettke knew he could be shot for what he was about to do. Still, he would not be dissuaded. He exited the *Hôtel de Crillon*, headquarters of the German army, and set out to navigate the *Place de la Concorde*. Despite the December chill, the package he'd hidden in his inner pocket gave him a warm rush of exhilaration, a toxic blend of euphoria and apprehension.

Across the huge impressive square of seventeenth and eighteenth century buildings, Rettke's destination appeared small and insignificant. He stepped into the crosswalk. Paris's five and six-way intersections infuriated him. He half-ran, half-jogged to reach the opposite side. Horns blared, brakes squealed while the local pedestrians seemed oblivious of the din. He patted the treasure in his coat and darted across the final bridge over the Seine. At last, Rettke stood on the steps of the *Musée du Jeu de Paume* and exhaled a plume of vapor, along with a frisson of fear. He was not in the clear yet.

He gazed at the stately entry of pillars and glass. Long the premier gallery for exhibitions of contemporary art, the *Jeu de Paume* now served as a storehouse for thousands of displaced paintings from all over Europe. Confiscated from the Rothschilds and the Bernheims, the Schlosses and the Weills, to Rettke most were worthless, like the Picassos. Bah. But there were those noteworthy pieces. By Monet, Vuillard, and Degas, yes, but the most extraordinary by far, Vincent Van Gogh. Slashes of bold color, lavish, almost careless brush strokes, ethereal light, shadows within shadows. An artist meant for immortality.

Rettke glanced over his shoulder at the city. Patches of snow glittered like pearls on the winter lawns of the *Jardin des Tuileries*. Beyond, the graceful curves of *La Tour d'Eiffel* leaned against a leaden sky.

Inside, the museum buzzed with scores of staffers darting to and fro like worker bees in a field of sunflowers. They wheeled around dollies of wooden crates, their destinations stamped in black ink on the side. They scribbled on clipboards and answered phones that never ceased ringing on government-issue desks placed haphazardly in the great hall.

Rettke steered clear of them and proceeded to the rear gallery. At the entrance, a National Labour guard clicked his black-booted heels and raised an arm in salute. The soldier, barely eighteen, wore shirt and pants of olive-drab wool, a red swastika band wrapped neatly around his left arm. Rettke could feel the package burning a hole in his skin as the man examined his identification. Every day the guard saw him, every day the guard demanded his papers. Rettke was tempted to argue; however, today of all days he could not afford to be contrary.

He entered the Room of Martyrs. One of the larger galleries in the Museum, it boasted fourteen-foot ceilings, gilded moldings and rich oak floors covered with muted Persian rugs. It was aptly named, for the room was crowded with hundreds of paintings, each relinquishing its life to the Third Reich.

Dozens of easels had been consigned to display even more works: oils, charcoals, water colors, stacked one in front of another. Paul Cezanne's *Self-Portrait*, and *Woman in White* by Berthe Morisot. Colors, forms, angles, light. Every time Rettke entered the Room, his heart sped as if on nitroglycerin, a drug he sometimes used for angina.

On a large wooden desk in the far corner of the room, he unpacked the equipment that waited for him every day in that very place: camera, lenses, tripod, film packages. Rettke's official job was to photograph and archive confiscated art. And he was good at it, in fact, considered one of the finest photographers in Europe, ahead of his time in the latest technological advances.

He pulled out a log book and jar of ink from the desk drawer. As he assembled his tools, the only sound was the reassuring hum of the air filtration system. And the rush of blood in his ears.

He reached deep into his inside coat pocket and drew out a rolled up canvas, about 56 centimeters long and slender, easy to hide. Moving quickly to the aisle farthest from the door, he flipped through six paintings before he found the empty frame. As he lifted it from the stack, it slipped from his hands and clattered to the floor. He swore and glanced at the door. No sound, no movement.

With a touch akin to tenderness, he stretched out the rolled-up painting. Sweat made its way down his forehead. A drop fell onto the canvas and his lungs almost burst. He dabbed at the liquid, fearing salt might damage the paint.

Before he could fit the painting into the frame, the sound of voices reached him from the outer hall. His skin turned to ice. He fumbled the canvas and it, too, dropped to the floor. With his toe he nudged it under the easel, thankful the painting sprang back into a protective roll. Then he hastened back to the desk.

"Ah, there you are." That distinctive guttural voice made Rettke's skin crawl. "I see you have received my gift."

Rettke swung around. Gift? Ah, the new Zeiss. "Indeed I have, *Reichsminister*. It is a very fine camera, very fine, indeed."

Alfred Rosenberg curled his thin lips into a wry smile. He approached Rettke and plucked the instrument from his hands.

"*Ja. Ausgezeichnet!*" Perfect.

"I am loading it with--"

"With *Agfacolor Neu*, I expect?"

"Of course." When did Rosenberg become such an expert?

"*Sehr gut.* We shall see how this new color photography works. What better experiment than this room, eh?" Rosenberg waved an arm. "Color, color, and more color. Like a penny carnival, no?"

Rettke tightened his grip on the Contax. His eyes darted to the hidden prize on the floor.

Rosenberg clasped his hands behind his back and ambled through the aisles. "Disgusting. Fake life, grotesque forms, artificial colors," he said, pointing to a Kandinsky. "Pure filth. Don't you agree?" He didn't wait for an answer. "Like the Fuhrer, I, myself, favor the old Masters. Rembrandt, Vermeer, Goya."

"Of course," Rettke mumbled.

"By the way, the *Reichsmarschall* himself will arrive later today for inspection."

Goering here? Rettke turned to find Rosenberg glaring at him. "I am just about to begin, *Mein Herr*," he said. "Will you be needing something?"

"Ach, I am in your way?

"*Nein, nein.*" Despicable man. Rettke found it striking that most Rosenbergs he knew were Jews. This one was a Jew-hater.

The photographer forced himself steady as he shrugged the camera strap around his neck. He arranged the tripod and adjusted the lights from the last session. Next, he set the built-in meter on the rangefinder, twisted a wide-angle lens in place and zoomed in on the first painting. Concentrate. Aim, focus, shoot, record pertinent information in his logbook: artist, title, date, provenance.

When he straightened a few minutes later, Rosenberg was gone. Relief coursed through his body. At long last, he could complete his mission.

Chapter 1

Washington, D.C., March, 2004

Maggie Thornhill could barely see through the window at Pappalecco's Café. Between the steam haze inside and the teeming rain outside, the glass was all but opaque. Her chair was wedged in a corner of wall and window, her favorite spot in her favorite coffee house in Georgetown. She nursed a double mocha no whip as she waited for her friend. As usual, Ingrid was late. Since their high school days almost twenty years ago, their standing joke had been Maggie always early, Ingrid always late. Maggie always impatient and irritated. Ingrid always apologetic and contrite. Nothing changed.

Today, however, Maggie felt this nagging bite of worry. Something had been bothering Ingrid for weeks now and Maggie believed it was more than the death of her grandfather a month ago. Ingrid seemed on edge, nervous; maybe frightened was a better word. So where was she? Maggie pulled out her new Motorola RAZR to see if she'd gotten a voice message. Nothing. She checked her email on her phone. Nothing. She peered out the window again and suddenly recognized Ingrid. Her friend was hard to miss even through the fog and rain. She was six feet in flats and thin as a Vogue model. But it was Ingrid's shoulder-length platinum hair that drew eyes. And damned if it wasn't natural.

Ingrid burst into the cafe, catching the knob before the wind tore the door out of her hands. She shook her head and raindrops flew. Maggie stood and Ingrid leaned in to kiss both cheeks.

"Don't you have an umbrella?" Maggie said.

"I did, but it's turned inside out and no doubt in Baltimore by now. *Mein Gott*, what a wind." Ingrid untied the belt on her raincoat and squirmed out if it. She threw it on the nearby empty chair and sat with a deep sigh across from Maggie. They looked at each other and settled into comfortable small talk until the waitress came. Ingrid ordered espresso. Maggie ordered a second mocha.

"So what's going on with you?" Maggie said when the drinks were in front of them.

Ingrid raised an eyebrow. "You know me so well."

"Well, apart from the fact that you said you had to talk to me, yes, I think something's going on."

Ingrid concentrated on her cup and Maggie noticed a slight tremble to her lip.

"Ever since your grandfather died, you've been on edge," Maggie said. "I didn't realize the two of you were that close."

"We weren't. Klaus has, had, only been in this country for a few years."

"From Berlin. I remember," Maggie said. "Did you always call him Klaus?"

"He wanted me to. Didn't like *grandfather* or *grandpa*."

"So what did you want to talk to me about?"

Ingrid reached into her purse. "Let me show you something." She withdrew a five-by-seven brown envelope and handed it to Maggie.

Maggie opened the flap and pulled out photographs. Four total, three color and one black and white. She pushed her coffee cup to the side and spread the color photographs on the table in front of her, then lay the black and white one above them.

"What do you see?" Ingrid said.

"The color ones look like pictures of a Van Gogh painting, the same one in all three. He did such beautiful flowers, didn't he?" Maggie stopped, picked up the black and white image. "Four men circa 1940s?"

"Go on," Ingrid said.

"This is your grandfather, right? Klaus Rettke?" Maggie pointed to the man on the left. "I've seen his picture in your apartment."

Ingrid nodded.

"This man next to Klaus, the one in uniform, I know him." Maggie pointed. "God, this is Hermann Goering, isn't it?"

"Yes," Ingrid said in almost a whisper. "Hitler's second man."

Maggie narrowed her eyes at Ingrid then looked at the photo again. "The third man, also in uniform. I don't recognize him. Who is he?" When Ingrid didn't speak, Maggie examined the photograph again. "And the fourth man, he's in ordinary street clothes. He looks. . . I don't know. . ."

"He looks what?"

"He looks miserable, like he doesn't want to be there. See the third guy in the uniform is clasping his shoulder to keep him in place." Maggie looked up. "Who is he?"

"I don't know."

Maggie leaned back. "What do you know?"

Ingrid hesitated before speaking. "Very little, actually. Klaus never talked about his days in Germany, except for the times when he was growing up." She bit her lip. " Not the war. Never the war."

"He worked as an art dealer, didn't he, in Paris? Is that why he has this photo of a painting?"

"Maggie, let me ask you something. As the director of the Digital Photography Lab at Georgetown U, you would know the answer."

Maggie waited.

"Can you authenticate a painting from a photograph?"

"What? Are you serious?"

"Deadly serious." Ingrid leaned over the table. "I think that picture is indeed, of a Van Gogh painting. A painting missing since World War Two. I believe Klaus may have stolen it."

"Stolen it?" Maggie picked up the snapshot of the four men and looked at it. "As in confiscated it? For the Nazis?"

Ingrid blinked.

"Was your grandfather a Nazi?"

"I, we, I mean, no, we never talked about it. I don't know."

Maggie stared at her.

Ingrid averted her eyes. "That picture. The other man in the German uniform is Alfred Rosenberg. He was the head of the ERR, in fact it was named for him. The *Einsatzstab Reichsletter Rosenberg*. The group assigned the task of confiscating all art, artifacts, and cultural objects from, er, undesirables."

"You mean Jews?"

"Not just Jews, but yes, mostly."

Maggie waved the picture. "And the fourth man?"

Ingrid shrugged her ignorance. "The point is, Klaus was part of them, the ERR. At least that's what it looks like in the picture."

"But it's just one photograph," Maggie said. "Perhaps it has another meaning."

"I searched Klaus' apartment and could find nothing to tell me. No letters, no diary, nothing to connect him to the Nazis. Except that." Ingrid tilted her head toward the snapshot.

Maggie studied her friend's face. Skin like porcelain, elegant bones. "Now I understand why you haven't seemed yourself. You just learned your grandfather might have been a Nazi." Maggie shook her head. "And that maybe he has a Van Gogh painting hidden somewhere. My God."

Ingrid took a moment to respond, picked at her perfect nail polish.

"There's something else?"

Ingrid stared at her empty espresso cup. "Yes. I don't know, maybe I'm crazy."

"Go on."

"I think I'm being followed. I'm not sure. I walk down the street and feel someone's behind me but I turn and there's no one." Ingrid brought her hand to her forehead. "I'm scared Maggie. What if Klaus had this painting. What's if it's a real Van Gogh and now someone is trying to find it?"

"Whoa, slow down. It's easy to get spooked. Have you checked out this painting? Is it really a Van Gogh? Maybe Rudolf would know." Maggie's soon-to-be ex-husband, Rudolf Hofer, was a curator at the National Gallery of Art. "If he doesn't know, I'm sure he could locate a Van Gogh expert."

"Right now, I don't want anyone to know about this. Only you. I trust only you." Ingrid grabbed Maggie's hand and squeezed it. "That's why I asked. Can you authenticate a painting from a photograph?"

Maggie blew out a breath, held her friend's hand. "I don't know. I don't believe it's ever been done."

"Can you find out?"

"But what difference does it make? If this is a real Van Gogh, all you have is a photograph. Where's the painting?"

"That's what I'm trying to figure out," Ingrid said. "If Klaus had a genuine Van Gogh, where would it be now?"

A clap of thunder made them jump.

"Maggie, why would Klaus have these photographs if the painting was a fake? It makes no sense. No, it must be real."

"Where did you find these photos?"

"That's also strange," Ingrid said. "Not in any place you'd expect. They were well hidden in his apartment. Behind the front of a fake big screen television. It was only by chance that I happened to find them. I wanted to turn on the news and nothing worked, the screen, the remote. So when I looked closer I saw it wasn't plugged in. Then I noticed the face of the screen was tilted slightly and, well, it doesn't matter. They were behind the screen."

"Nothing else, just the photographs?"

"Nothing. Believe me, I looked."

Maggie wasn't so sure. Ingrid was never one for details. "Did he leave a will?"

"Yes, but it's very basic. Everything in his apartment and some small bank accounts were to come to me. They don't amount to much."

"No Van Goghs on the wall?"

Ingrid shook her head, not smiling.

"But if this is a real Van Gogh and he's got it hidden, it would be worth a fortune."

"Yes, it would."

"Like, how much?" Maggie asked.

"Tens of millions, probably."

"And you would inherit it."

Ingrid gazed down at her cup.

"But it wouldn't rightfully be yours," Maggie said softly. "Would it? Not if it were stolen."

Ingrid ignored the question. "Will you help me, Maggie?"

Maggie reached out and laid her hand over her friend's. "I'll find out if a painting can be authenticated from a photograph. If there's no process out there yet, well, I'll have to invent one, won't I?"

Ingrid smiled.

"That's the first time I've seen you smile in a month," Maggie said. "What will you do about this stalker? You should contact the police."

"If it happens again, I will. I think it may just be my imagination."

"Can I keep these?" Maggie held up the photographs.

"Yes. Those are the originals but I made copies. If you can find out about the painting, I will find out the truth about Klaus."

"How? There are no family members to ask, are there?"

"Not here. I've been putting together a family scrapbook and have already started looking into my German history." Her face flushed in embarrassment. "The Nazis kept exemplary documentation. I'll even go to Berlin if I must. I have a distant cousin or two there."

Maggie gazed at her friend again and this time noticed the fine lines under her blue eyes and the drawn look to her cheeks.

Ingrid stared down at her hands. "I must know about this painting and . . . the truth about my grandfather. Was he a Nazi?"

Chapter 2

The next two days kept Maggie immersed in midterms and projects for the computer science classes she taught at Georgetown University. The only living creature she found time for was her sweet Rosie, a two-year old Golden Retriever. She had even largely ignored Rosie, but the dog understood, having been through Maggie's frenetic periods before.

Each night Maggie fell into bed around midnight after reading a number of theses and project summaries and woke at 5:00 a.m. to prepare for that day's exams. On the third afternoon, she turned her attention to Ingrid and wondered if she'd found out more about her grandfather. Maggie scrabbled through her bag to find her cell and pressed the speed dial for her friend. The call went straight to voicemail. Maggie left a message and returned to her classwork.

Later that night she tried Ingrid again with the same results. She left a voice message and an email. A tickle of worry raised the hairs on her arms when she recalled Ingrid's fear of being followed. She stared at her phone. It was 10:30.

"Why isn't she home?" she said to Rosie, who yawned and stretched on her bed in front of the fireplace.

Maggie rose from the couch and paced the small living room. Ingrid also had midterms with her German classes to prepare and review. Was it possible she caught a flight to Berlin? No, she would have told her.

Why didn't I keep in touch? Where the hell is she?

"Come on, Rosie. We're going for a walk." She grabbed the leash and collar and the two redheads stole out into the night. The streets were puddled with leftover rain from the last few days, and the air was thick with humidity.

Her ruminations on the photographs made the ten-block walk to Ingrid's apartment go quickly and she arrived before she realized it. Rosie headed directly up the front steps.

"You love Ingrid, don't you, girl?"

Maggie rang the doorbell. She knocked. She knocked harder. No answer. Maggie leaned over to look through the front bay window, but it was dark inside and curtains blocked the view. She rang the bell and knocked again. Damn. Maggie tried to guess where Ingrid could be. A bar, restaurant, café? She had no boyfriend right now, so probably not on a date. And, being a loner, she had few friends besides Maggie. Just a couple of colleagues and acquaintances.

Maggie led Rosie up the street to a neighborhood bar and restaurant. She peeked in but the place was nearly empty. She spun in a circle. *What now?* Just for the hell of it, she speed-dialed Ingrid again. No answer and, when she checked, no messages. What about the University library? It was closed by now. She looked down at Rosie who was tugging on her lead.

"What's up?"

Rosie was bent on tearing across the street so Maggie followed. The dog took off down a narrow alley, Maggie in tow. Finally they reached a dead end and Rosie sniffed and whined, sniffed the street again.

Maggie scoped out the alleyway--the backs of two-story brick buildings, trash cans, a dumpster overflowing with garbage--and started shivering despite the unusually mild temperature for March. She had begun to back out of the narrow path, pulling Rosie with her, when she turned to stare at the dumpster. On an impulse, Maggie let go of Rosie's lead. The dog barreled straight for the dumpster and started jumping up.

Oh God, no. Don't let it be, please. Maggie trudged to the dumpster, her eyes glued to the lid. She grabbed a nearby fruit crate waiting for the recycle bin and dragged it over. She stood on it and threw open the lid. She held her breath and looked in. It was dark, but streetlights shone enough light to see the interior of the dumpster. At first glance, she could see only trash.

"I must be nuts."

Rosie whuffed.

She leaned in and started moving garbage around. The stench made her eyes water but she kept at it. Nothing. Thank God.

Maggie dropped down and kicked the crate away. "Jeez, Rosie, what the heck did you drag me . . . Rosie?" She looked around for her dog and found her happily chewing on a leftover pork chop bone.

"Let's go home. You and I are watching too many *Criminal Minds*."

✦ ✦ ✦

The phone rang at 6:05 the next morning, Saturday. Maggie leaped out of bed and stumbled across the room in search of her cell.

"Hello? Ingrid?"

"Maggie?" came a male voice.

"Frank?"

"Yeah, it's me."

She blinked into the dim room, unspeaking, a large fist twisting in her belly. Frank Mead was a homicide detective for Washington Metro whom she'd worked with often.

"Were you expecting Ingrid?" he said.

"I was hoping. I hadn't heard from. . . Frank, why are you calling at six on a Saturday morning. Is it about Ingrid?"

"I'm afraid so." He stopped.

"Go on."

"She's dead, Maggie. She was shot to death at the National Gallery of Art just before closing time."

The fist tightened its grip inside her. "That can't be right," was all she could say.

"I'm on my way." He clicked off.

Maggie sat on the edge of her bed, the phone dead in her hand. Rosie crept toward her, ears back.

Twenty minutes later, Maggie had taken a quick shower and was trying with shaky fingers to button her blouse when the doorbell rang. She opened it to a fair-haired, short but well-built man in a blue button-down shirt and khaki sports jacket. He carried two venti Starbuck's coffees in his hands.

"Didn't think you wanted to bother brewing so I brought these." He moved to the kitchen and set the paper cups on the counter.

Maggie pushed her hair out of her face with a careless gesture and climbed onto a kitchen stool. He stood next to her at the counter.

"Hey, girl, come here," Mead called to Rosie in a soft voice. Rosie happily complied and wiggled between the two. Mead took Maggie's hand and rested it on Rosie's head.

Maggie petted her dog absently. "Are you sure it's Ingrid?"

He nodded.

"What happened?"

"The cleaning staff of the museum was going through each gallery and found what they thought was a pile of clothes. When they looked closer they found it was dead woman, bullet in her chest. Nothing seemed to be missing. Her bag with ID and money was right near her."

"How could someone kill her in such a public place?"

"Appears it was right at closing time so the security guard had made his last rounds. Museum went dark and no one was the wiser until early this morning when the cleaning crew came in."

Maggie stared out in space over his shoulder. "I knew I should have checked on her. I just knew something wasn't right when she didn't call back."

"Don't blame yourself, Maggie. You didn't kill her." He fixed his piercing blue eyes on her. "You okay?"

"She was my best friend, Frank. Since we were fourteen. No, I'm not okay."

"Want some time? I can come back later."

"What? And let the case cool? No way. I know the routine." She rubbed her forehead.

"You need answers and you need them now."

"Look, I know this is difficult." He started for the door. "I'll be back in little while."

"No. Don't you dare leave. I. . . I just need a few minutes, you know, to take this in." Her face burned red-hot, the blood prickling her cheeks like needles. Her vision blurred and fire rose into her throat. Her chest felt like it would burst. She clutched her head, breathing hard. Suddenly, she leaned down, picked up a vase and hurled it across the room. It smashed against the stone hearth and fractured into countless pieces of delicate china.

Rosie bailed out of the kitchen with a yowl.

Mead came up behind Maggie, touched her shoulder. She turned, eyes wide, mouth open, stunned by her own anger. Without warning, she fell against him and buried her head into his chest, crying silently.

Ten minutes later, Mead gazed into the dead fireplace, feeling an inexplicable sadness at the sight of the broken vase. He glanced at the closed door to the bedroom. Maggie had gone to wash her face, to compose herself. She had promised to be only a few minutes. Ten had gone by. He wanted to shout that the scene was getting colder by the minute, but bit his tongue. He had some sensitivity, right? He held his hands out in front of him and watched them tremble. Damn but he could still feel her in his arms. So vulnerable, so soft, defenseless, so like . . . Uh-uh, don't go there, asshole. He pulled out a package of Tums, ripped it open and chomped down a half-dozen.

His cell rang and he flipped it open, listened, barked instructions, stretched, sat, stood, sat again. Patience as thin as a communion wafer at St. Mike's, Mead strode to the bedroom door, knocked and peeked in. She was sitting on her bed.

"Maggie?"

"Come in."

He sat on a chair near her bed, bent forward, elbows on his knees.

"I'm sorry, Frank. I didn't mean to take it out on you." She turned red-rimmed eyes on him. "I can talk now."

He hesitated, said finally, "Was something out of the ordinary going on with Ingrid?"

She inhaled and told him about her last conversation with Ingrid, about her friend's suspicions that her grandfather, Klaus Rettke, was a Nazi.

Mead raised an eyebrow. "A Nazi? Where is he now?"

"Dead," Maggie said. "He died of a heart attack a month ago."

"What else did Ingrid tell you?"

"She was afraid that someone was stalking her." Maggie relayed the information about the photographs.

"I'd like to see those pictures."

She reached for her bag and pulled them out.

"This is a Van Gogh, isn't it?" he said.

"I think so."

"It says Vincent down at the bottom."

Maggie grabbed the photo. "Oh God, I didn't even see that. I could have helped her, Frank, maybe prevented this, if I had started looking into. . . why didn't I? So I had mid-terms and papers, so what? School could've waited, it . . ." she clipped off her words.

"Maggie, stop. You know it wouldn't have changed anything. Someone wanted her dead. We have to find out why."

"It's related to this painting, I'm sure."

"Maybe," he said. "Interesting that the photos are of a Van Gogh."

"Why interesting?"

"Ingrid was found under a portrait of Van Gogh at the National Gallery. Could she have been there to see the painting?"

Maggie shook her head. "I don't know. Maybe. But why? Unless she was trying to understand her grandfather better."

"What do you know about her grandfather?"

"According to Ingrid, he was an art dealer in Europe, bought and sold paintings. Went to auctions, helped clients bid on pieces. I guess he loved the National Gallery. He and Ingrid used to have lunch at *The Cascades* occasionally. You know the café at the Museum."

"What did Rettke do here in Washington?"

"Nothing as far as work. He was probably about eighty-five. He visited museums, libraries, read a lot, took photographs. He loved photography, Ingrid said." She stopped, looked down at her feet. "Actually, that's really all I know. I only met him a few times, and his accent was so strong, I could hardly understand him."

"We'll be going through Ingrid's apartment."

"Can I help? I mean maybe I can--"

"Sorry, Maggie, but this is still an official investigation. You can go in after we've searched."

Maggie chewed her lower lip.

"Where did her grandfather live?" Mead took out a notebook and pen.

"A condo somewhere near the National Cathedral, I think."

"We'll find it. I assume it's not been rented or sold yet," Mead said. "He's only been dead a month?"

She looked at him. "You don't suppose he was murdered too?"

"I'll check into cause of death." Mead picked up the photographs again. "What about the painting? Do you think you can find out more about it?"

"Yes, I'll talk to Rudolf. He has lots of contacts."

"Rudolf?"

"Rudolf Hofer. My ex-husband. He's a curator at the National Gallery."

Frank's eyes widened at the revelation. He'd worked with Maggie on several cases over the last four years. The department consulted with her when digital photography was needed. He never even knew she was married, but then he had never seen her wearing a wedding ring.

"Did Ingrid's grandfather have money, valuables, maybe artwork, jewelry, real estate?"

"Not that she told me. He was comfortable, I guess, but not wealthy."

"Insurance?"

"I don't know."

"We'll check it out." Mead moved to the French windows draped with silk curtains the color of café au lait and looked down at the street. That's when he noticed the papers on the night stand. He couldn't miss the bold words: *Decree of Divorce. It is therefore ordered, adjudged and decreed that plaintiff, Margaret Lee Thornhill be granted an absolute divorce from defendant, Rudolf Martin Hofer; that the parties be restored to all rights and privileges of a single and unmarried person . . .*

Maggie came up behind him, snatched the papers away. Then she glared at him with green-eyed daggers, as if he were to blame for the loss of her best friend *and* her husband. Shit, she was sexy.

"Sorry," he said. "I didn't know you were married until you mentioned your ex just now."

"We were married two years and separated for a year. I never changed my name."

"You don't have to explain."

She swiped at a rebellious tear sliding down her cheek.

Mead stuffed his hands in his chino pockets. "You're not going to throw anything across the room again, are you?"

She gave him a weak smile.

He responded in kind.

"Frank?"

"Yeah."

"I want to see the body."

"You'll have to make an identification."

"No, I mean now. I want to see the body at the museum, at the crime scene. Not at the morgue."

He narrowed his eyes.

"Is she still there?"

"You think that's a good idea?"

"Maybe, maybe not, but I have to. You understand?"

"Not exactly," he said.

She ran a hand through her mop of red hair. "I want to see her as I remember, not cold and white and naked on a slab. I know she's still dead, but, well, it will mean a lot to me if I can see her before they. . . they zip her into a black bag." She looked into his eyes. "That plastic bag is so. . . damn. . . final. I'm just not ready for that. I need to say goodbye first."

Mead stared at her without speaking. Then he flipped open his cell and barked a few orders.

Strange request, Mead thought. But then, Maggie was a strange and passionate woman.

Chapter 3

Inside the West Wing of the Smithsonian's National Gallery of Art, Maggie shadowed Mead to Gallery 84 on the main floor and the 19th Century French paintings. Straight through the Sculpture Hall, left, then right into a garden court and a final left into a swarm of cops, CSI's and a unit from the medical examiner's office.

She immediately zeroed in on the body at the far side of the room. It lay under a melancholy self-portrait of Vincent Van Gogh. She approached with trepidation. Mead's presence within arm's distance felt reassuring.

The first thing she recognized was her friend's coat, a tan raincoat with a hood. She bent over and nearly gasped at the blond hair. Her secret hope that perhaps the dead woman was *not* Ingrid was crushed. This nightmare was real.

"Can I turn her over?" she whispered.

"What? Yeah, no, let me do that." Mead leaned down and took Ingrid's arm and gently rolled her onto her back. After nearly twelve hours, the body evidenced signs of full rigor. The skin presented waxy, mottled with purple where gravity had attracted the blood. The lips were pale, the eyes, open, appeared flattened from the loss of fluid.

"Ingrid," was all Maggie could utter. She gazed at her for endless minutes. If only she could hug her, say one last goodbye, say she was sorry. Lying there, limbs bent, her dear friend looked like a cold, beautiful marionette whose strings had broken.

"Come on." Mead helped her to her feet and led her away from the body. He pulled out the roll of Tums again and popped three more.

Maggie watched but made no comment.

His eyes caught hers and he smiled. "Murder does that to me. Some kind of relationship between adrenaline and acid."

She winced.

"Did you notice anything unusual about her?" he said. "Clothes, hair, anything?"

"No. . . no. That was her coat, bag. And her lovely hair. The color was natural, would you believe. Any woman would kill for. . . oh God."

"Excuse me, Lieutenant?" Sergeant Ramón Delacruz, a slick-haired man, barely thirty, in a pale gray suit approached. Maggie knew him from cases she'd worked on as a digital photographer consultant. He nodded to her, leaned into Mead's ear for a minute. Mead responded with, "The gallery will be closed to the public today. Period, end of story."

Mead turned to Maggie and steered her to the other end of the gallery where she sank down onto a stone bench.

Her eyes followed the crime lab team as they resumed their work--an orchestrated dance around the body, choreographed to the tiniest movement. They lifted fingerprints, footprints, dust, fibers, anything that might provide a clue.

"The medical examiner, has he been--?" she asked.

"Ramón said he had an initial look and was waiting for you before removing the body."

"Thanks, Frank, for letting me see her."

"Sure."

Maggie turned away from the scene when two men rolled a gurney into the gallery.

"Let's look at those pictures again," he said.

She pulled them out of her bag.

"I agree with you about the black and white snap," Mead said. "My parents had lots of these in their albums. Definitely the 1940s. Plus that's Hermann Goering, no doubt about that."

"Klaus Rettke is on his left and a man named Alfred Rosenberg on his right. Another Nazi monster."

"Rosenberg? I know that name."

Maggie told him about the ERR.

"Those Nazis were organized, I'll give them that."

"The fourth man is a mystery but I'd say he doesn't want to be in the picture."

"Hmm," Mead said.

"Also something odd," she said. "You see these other frames, or edges of frames near the painting? It was taken in some kind of gallery. But no museum or gallery I know of displays works of art so close to each other. Although it's possible they did in the 40s." Another question for Rudolf.

"What about an auction house?" he said.

"Yes, maybe an auction house." Her words slowed. "Maybe Rettke took the photograph for one of the houses."

"Did the Nazis auction the art they looted?"

"I don't know. My guess is they mostly kept it, divided it up."

"Well, auction house or not, Rettke could have taken these, considering their age, right?" Mead asked.

"For sure."

Mead let out a long exhalation. "Which leads me to wonder, if the painting in the photographs is real, then where is it?"

"Ingrid didn't know."

"Who knew about it? Who saw those photos?"

"No one. At least that's what she said. "Only you, Maggie. I trust only you." Mead said nothing.

"And why was Ingrid here?" Maggie said. "Maybe she was meeting someone about the painting? Someone who had information."

"Or who wanted information. Did she have duplicates?" Mead asked.

"Yes. She'd made copies, kept those and gave the originals to me so I could work with them."

"Work with them?"

"She wanted me to try to authenticate the painting from the photos."

"Is that possible?"

"I don't know. Yet."

Mead rubbed a light stubble on his chin. "So maybe she brought them to the museum today to show them to an art dealer, private collector or auction house rep. Maybe she hoped they'd recognize the painting and --"

"If she had them with her, where are they?" Maggie said. "Did they find them in her bag?"

Mead stood without a word and walked toward the body. He and Delacruz exchanged a few words then he returned. "No photos."

"Maybe the killer took them?"

"Or she never brought them with her. Maybe they're still at her apartment," Mead said. "Did Ingrid keep an appointment book?"

"Online. Her calendar would be on her phone," she said.

"Yeah, well that's missing too."

Maggie fell back against the wall, suddenly weak.

"You okay?"

She shrugged a shoulder.

"Is it possible Ingrid found the painting?" he said.

Maggie paused, shook her head. "She would have told me. Maybe. To be honest, I don't know anymore. Maybe she did find it."

"Then where is it? Where would she keep it?"

"Do you think she brought it here?"

"Kinda hard to walk out of a museum, or into one, for that matter, carrying a framed painting."

"Maybe it wasn't in a frame. Maybe it was just a rolled up canvas."

He paused, looked back to the Van Gogh portrait at the far end of the gallery. "Could it be a genuine Van Gogh?"

"Would someone kill for a fake?" she asked.

"If he presumed it was real. So," he said. "We're back to the number one question. Who was Ingrid meeting here at the museum?"

Maggie saw the neon words in her mind. *Her killer.*

Chapter 4

It wasn't possible, but Maggie could swear she heard the zip of the body bag after her dearest friend was stowed into it. She watched as the techs lifted the black bundle and settled it onto the gurney. They rolled it away. Just like that. Ingrid was gone.

At that moment loud voices erupted from the outer hall. Mead's was one of them. She took a few steps toward the doorway and recognized the other. She pressed her back to the wall and squeezed her eyes shut. Then she drew in a deep breath, called upon all the reserves she had left and turned the corner.

The voices stopped in mid-anger.

"Maggie, is that you?" a tall, broad-shouldered man, gray sprinkled in his dark brown hair, asked in surprise. "What are you doing here? Do you realize what's happened? Ingrid's been murdered, right here in, in my museum, for God's sake. There, in that hall."

He spun around to the gallery then back. "*Mein Gott*, Maggie. How could this happen to me?" The man touched his forehead and wiped a drop of invisible sweat.

"To you?" she said, her voice husky.

"*Nein*, no, Maggie. I didn't mean. . . I am so sorry. This is terrible."

"Do you mind if I interrupt?" Mead said. "This is still a crime scene, sir, and we need to clear everyone out of here."

"Well, surely you don't mean me."

Maggie put a hand on Mead's arm. "Frank, this is Rudolf Hofer," Maggie said. "He's a curator for the National Gallery."

Mead grimaced and nodded. "Now--"

Hofer ignored the cop. "I'm so sorry, my dear." He straightened an already perfect tie then took her hands in his. "Poor Ingrid. You must be devastated." With barely a breath, he turned on Mead. "This is catastrophic. Do you realize we have a gala fundraiser for the President of the United States here tonight? In less than eight hours. The Executive Director will be here any moment. You've got to get your people out of here. The caterers will be arriving, the guests, dignitaries--" Hofer looked at his watch. "The President himself will be arriving in exactly nine hours. Good grief."

Maggie's face flamed.

"I'm sorry, Mr. Hofer," Mead said, voice stretched thin. "But murders take precedence over parties. Even parties with VIP's. We'll let you know when we're done. In the meantime, I would make sure the gala is confined to the other wing. This entire wing will be sealed off until further notice."

"You can't do that. Couldn't you just take your pictures, collect your evidence or whatever you do, and get the hell out?" He straightened his tie again. "I'm going to check with our attorney."

"You do that. In the meantime, I'm in charge."

Maggie would've bet Mead left out some swear words because of her.

"This. . . is. . . outrageous." Hofer sputtered and practically ran out of the room.

Mead shook his head.

"Now you know why he's my *ex*-husband."

Once Hofer had fled, Mead lowered himself wearily on the bench. Maggie joined him.

"Don't say it," she said.

"Say what?"

"What you're thinking about Rudolf. He. . . he wasn't always like that. At least I don't think he was. My recollections are so jumbled right now. Oh, I don't know, maybe he was exactly like that. I was just dumb and blind and--"

"Hey, you don't have to explain anything to me," he said, a hint of his dimples showing.

Maggie thought dimples on a homicide cop were counter-productive. "Are you married?"

"Not anymore."

"Divorced?" she asked.

"My wife died."

"Oh. I'm sorry." *Damn he'd told her that before. Why didn't she pay attention?*

"Me too."

They both turned to watch the crime team flitting around the gallery space.

"Want me get someone to drive you home?" he said. "I have to stay until they're finished."

"No, it's okay. I don't have the energy to move."

Delacruz rushed over. "Catering trucks're pulling up to the side doors as we speak." The sergeant stood with hand on hips.

"Oh Christ, what a mess," Maggie said. "Rudolf is going to be so pissed."

"Yeah, well, seems like he can handle piss," Mead said. To Delacruz, "How much longer will they be?" referring to the crime team.

"Hour, maybe more." Delacruz headed off.

"Say, I meant to ask," Mead said to Maggie. "Do you need to call anyone? Did Ingrid have family that should be notified?"

"No family in the States. A few distant cousins in Berlin." Her voice cracked and she waved a hand to preclude more conversation about Ingrid. She stood. "I'm going to look at the Van Goghs."

"Good idea. Maybe he can tell us what the hell's going on." Mead followed her to the nearest painting.

The two of them stood a dozen yards from the crime scene peering at a painting called *Bulb Fields*.

"Ahh," Maggie said. "This was one of his earlier works in The Hague, 1883. Soft, simple. Low horizon."

"Not his famous riotous lines and color," Mead said. "Of course maybe those were the results of his turbulent emotions later."

Maggie looked at him.

"He was mentally ill, even I know that. Maybe suffering from syphilis like his brother, Theo."

Maggie was impressed with Mead's familiarity with Van Gogh.

They moved to another painting. This one in more vivid greens and yellows, a white house in the far background.

"Interesting that he stuck the house at the top, almost like it's not there. Mostly wheat fields," Mead said.

"The house is actually the focal point, drawing your eye to the horizon. It was Vincent's point of view. And the one he wanted us to have."

"*Wheat field at Auvers with White House, oil on canvas, June, 1890,*" Mead read off the label.

"God, a month before he died."

"You mean killed himself, right?" Mead said.

"Actually, maybe not. There's some new evidence to suggest that some teenage boys who were constantly harassing him might have accidentally shot him," Maggie said, gazing at the painting.

"No kidding? Why were they harassing him?"

"Well, by this time he was pretty disturbed. He probably looked like a homeless man, smelled like one too. Plus he was aloof and unfriendly, argumentative, not a genial guy you'd want to hang out with."

"Incredible. Accidental, eh? Or murder, perhaps?" Mead said. "Now that's a case I'd like to re-open."

"Maybe you will if it ties in with Ingrid's murder. And if we can locate Vincent's missing painting." Maggie stopped, looked at him. "Frank, I need to examine these photographs. Digitally."

"What are you thinking?" he said.

"When Ingrid and I met last, three days ago, she practically begged me to find out if this painting was genuine. She thought her grandfather might have stolen it."

"If he was chummy with Goering and Rosenberg, he'd have to have some set of balls to steal a painting from them."

"On the other hand, if he was part of the ERR, he might have had a lot of practice confiscating paintings. It could've been very easy and very tempting. He actually may have stolen that Van Gogh. You don't just keep photographs of a painting hidden for sixty years for no reason."

"I agree, but proving that's not going to be easy."

"Photos are what I know, Frank. It can't hurt for me to analyze them, see if I can learn anything about the painting."

They watched the crime lab team packing up.

"Your ex is German, right?"

"Yes."

"I assume he speaks German," Mead said.

"He and Ingrid used to converse regularly."

"Do you speak German?"

"Barely passable. I got better at it when I was married to Rudolf."

"Sounds like I need to talk to your ex." Mead sighed. "Those pictures of the painting," he began. "They were incredibly vivid to have been taken in the forties. I didn't know color film was so advanced back then."

"It was quite remarkable," she said.

"Invented by Kodak?"

"German film, actually. They were ahead of their time."

"I know they were fanatics about recording everything," he said. "The film footage they shot is nothing short of stunning. But I've never seen anything in color."

"Color was used mostly in stills," she said.

"Still, sixty years old and they haven't faded."

"They used special dyes," she said, "which gave the pictures depth and warmth and durability you don't find even today."

"Everything's digital today. Any film left?"

"Some, not much."

They fell silent, each deep in thought.

"Where did Klaus Rettke live during the war?" Mead asked.

"Berlin was his home, but Ingrid said he was in Paris from '39 to '44."

"Paris, hmm?"

"Yeah, too bad we don't have a time machine," she said. Her eyes focused in the distance.

"You've got an idea?"

Her lips upturned at the corners. "Not for a time machine. But the answers may still be in Paris." Waiting for me to find them.

Chapter 5

Mead drove Maggie home an hour later in his new silver BMW. She kidded him about taxpayers picking up the cost for fancy police cars and he argued that it was his personal car. She laughed, but her respect for him upped another notch. Hmm. Appreciation for Van Gogh paintings and BMWs. What else would she learn about Frank Mead?

Maggie unlocked the door to her brownstone, stepped inside the turn-of- the-century vestibule and waited. She peeked through the glass window on the front door until Mead drove off then slipped outside and hailed a cab.

Mead would be furious but this was something she had to do. Her initial plan was to search Ingrid's flat, but on second thought, she decided Ingrid's *grandfather's* apartment would prove more fruitful. Maggie had a set of Ingrid's keys that her friend had given her for emergencies. She only hoped Rettke's key was on that ring. She'd already checked her gmail contacts for his address. If Mead found the address and showed up, she could argue that since she was Ingrid's Executor, and Ingrid was Executor for her grandfather, she was, ergo, Rettke's Executor. Right? Mead would have a field day with that one.

Ten minutes later she gripped the keys in her hand and scurried into the building. She entered the elevator and pressed Four. The elevator doors slid open and she stepped out into a Provençal landscape. The hallway was plushly carpeted in pile thick and verdant as grass. Rolling hills of sage and gold dotted by colorful stucco houses were painted on the walls. Perhaps this building made Klaus feel at home.

She turned left and trod slowly toward the apartment. At the door, Maggie fumbled with the keys, and, after three tries, found the correct one and turned the latch. She walked into the quiet hall and locked the door behind her. Her eyes took in the large living room, decorated in elegant antique European fashion: an eighteenth century secretary, veneered in ebony and tulipwood, ladder back armchairs with shell motifs, a satin-covered Louis XV settee. Tall windows draped with purple velvet on the far walls provided enough light so she didn't need to turn on any lamps.

Maggie hesitated. She wasn't sure if the police would arrive at any moment. They would be searching for clues to Ingrid's death. And Rettke's death. She wanted clues to their lives as well. She set her bag and keys down on a small table and headed straight for a desk under the windows. It was a splendid piece from the late eighteenth century, finished in rich cherry with mahogany inlays. Maggie pulled open the middle drawer: pens, writing paper, nothing more. She tried the side drawers and found bills, receipts, bank envelopes.

Next she pulled out one of the drawers and set it on the floor. She examined the framework of the desk to see if there were any hidden compartments.

Two hours later she had inspected the entire room and, to her frustration, found nothing. No photo albums, no letters, no diary. She collapsed on the couch and racked her brain for other possibilities. Mead was checking bank accounts, insurance companies and real estate holdings, but could Rettke have had a safe deposit box? She doubted it. Ingrid told her Klaus didn't trust banks. Where would he put valuables, then? Was there a security safe in the apartment?

Maggie scanned the room and noticed four pieces of art and a large mirror hanging on the living room walls. She approached each and peeked behind. No wall safe. She studied the paintings. Prints with numbers and the artist name at the bottom right. No Van Gogh here.

She made her way into the small bedroom and repeated her search. Nothing. She sank back into the couch in the living room, sure she was missing something. Her eyes drifted across the room and landed on the big screen television. For a moment it didn't register.

She bolted upright. Of course, Ingrid had told her that's where she found the photographs. Behind the big screen. Didn't seem like Klaus Rettke was a big screen kind of guy. She strode over to it. Panasonic, fifty-inch screen. Maggie ran her fingers over the front panel. It wasn't a flat panel but had depth to it--more of a projection system. She moved around to the back and studied it. How did Ingrid get into it? From her purse, she pulled out a metal nail file and began to pry the metal frame around the screen. It squealed in protest but popped off easily. That's how. The screen itself was held in place with small screws in the corners. Using the nail file again, she managed to twist them off.

Blood rushed in her ears as she grappled with the glass. It lifted off the box and into her hands. She set it gently on the floor as a musty smell wafted out. She turned her attention to the interior and sighed in disappointment. Empty. What did she expect? Ingrid had already been there.

Maggie leaned closer, felt around the inside walls. One seemed to bow out and when she pressed it, it gave. She pushed again and ran her fingers around the borders of the wall. A screw fell out. She slid a finger behind the wall and found it was loose. She pulled. The inside wall popped out with a snap. Maggie let out a cry of delight. A secret compartment. She moved closer and spied what appeared to be a book, leather-bound and dust-covered, smelling of another century.

Before she could reach in, footsteps sounded in the hallway, muted but purposeful on the carpeting. She held her breath, wishing them down the corridor. They seemed to recede. She exhaled.

Then a key turned in the front door lock.

Maggie jumped to her feet, arms wrapped around the book as much to keep her heart from leaping out of her chest as to protect it.

Rudolf Hofer stepped into the apartment.

"Maggie? I didn't expect to see you here. I mean--"

"What are you doing here, Rudolf?"

They faced each other in awkward silence.

"I thought you'd be busy supervising the gala," she said. "After all the fuss you made at the Gallery, I--"

"That's what I have staff for."

Staff. You mean minions. She bit her tongue to avoid the sharp response. Instead she said, "How did you get a key?"

"What do you mean? Klaus gave me a key, of course." Rudolf closed the door.

"I don't believe it. Why would he give you a key?"

He held a hand up as if to halt her anger.

"Were you that close with Ingrid's grandfather?" she asked.

"Please, Maggie," Rudolf said. "Yes, Klaus and I . . . we had gotten to be good friends. We spoke all the time in German and. . . you didn't know this, did you? Sit down, please. Let me explain." His eyes widened at the open-front television and then stopped to rest on the book she was holding.

"That belonged to Klaus?" he said. "Hidden in the big screen. Clever."

"Rudolf, you shouldn't be here."

He gestured to the couch. "Please."

Maggie lowered herself onto the arm of the couch while he pulled over a chair. She did not set the book down.

"Klaus and I had many similar interests. In art, particularly. We were lovers of Impressionists and Post-Impressionists. We talked often of the different artists and their styles, how to distinguish one from another." He stopped. "You don't believe me, do you?"

"I'm not sure what to believe. Even if you did become so chummy with Rettke, why would he give you a key to his apartment?"

Rudolf's face reddened.

"Why?"

"I asked him for it."

She stared at him.

"When things weren't going so well with us, you and me, Maggie, I, um, would come here for a night and--"

"You used this apartment for your liaisons? You brought women here?" The words came in staccato bursts. "Rettke allowed--?"

"Now, wait. Klaus knew nothing about that. Those were times when he traveled. He had no idea, I, no, he never would have allowed that."

She dropped her head, words lost. All these secrets . . . could she handle what she would find out about her ex or her best friend?

"Was Klaus Rettke a Nazi?" The words were out of her mouth so fast she couldn't call them back.

"What?" Rudolf, jaws twitching, clearly did not expect this non-sequitur.

"I asked you a question and I want the truth. Was he a Nazi?"

"No. Of course not. Absolutely not. Why would you say such a thing?" Rudolf said.

"Do you know what he did during the war?"

"He was an art dealer. You know that."

She turned away from him but never set the book down.

"What is that book you're holding? It belonged to Klaus, ja?" He stood.

She wanted to scream at him, throw something, order him out of the apartment, but she hesitated, realizing she needed his help. Hating it.

"Sit down, Rudolf. I want to ask you something."

He sat, folded his arms.

She studied his face and pondered how she could possibly have loved this man. Was it love? Perhaps she had just been enchanted by his European charm and the entrée he provided her into the art and museum world. *My God, am I so shallow?*

"Look, Maggie. I'm very sorry about Ingrid. Is there anything I can do? Are you taking care of the arrangements? For the funeral?" He paused. "You are her Executor, no?"

Several years ago Maggie and Ingrid had made a pact that if neither of them were married, all their belongings would be bequeathed to the other. Maggie never anticipated having to deal with this so early in her life.

"Yes," she said. "I am. But I can't make arrangements until the police release the body."

"How long will that be?"

"It's a homicide investigation." As if that were answer enough. "Rudolf, I'm trying to help the police find out who killed Ingrid."

"I didn't realize you were a detective."

She wanted to slap the smirk off his face. God, what a rollercoaster ride her emotions were on. "A few days before she died, Ingrid showed me photographs of a painting. It might be a Van Gogh."

"What? A Van Gogh? What photographs?"

"Let me finish," she said. "We don't know if the painting belonged to Rettke or if he was selling it to a collector or what. If we can locate the painting or at least authenticate it from the photos I--"

"Klaus had a Van Gogh, a genuine Van Gogh?"

She sat back. "I don't know if it's genuine."

"So all you have are pictures? Where are they? Let me see them."

"I don't have them here. They're at the lab." Her face burned with the lie. They were six feet away in her bag on the desk.

He folded his hands together and cracked his knuckles.

"You know I hate that sound."

"Sorry," he said.

"Look, Rudolf, I need an art expert. Someone who can authenticate the painting, someone with expertise in Post-Impressionism, preferably familiar with the works of Vincent Van Gogh."

"But you don't have the painting, right?"

"No, just the photographs," she said.

"Well, how are you going to authenticate it from photographs? I don't think that can be done."

"Maybe not, but I'd like to try."

"You may be the best digital analyst in town, in the country, even, but this? It's not possible."

"Is there a curator at the National Gallery who can help me?" she asked, ignoring his comment.

A furrow creased Rudolf's forehead. It indicated impatience. She'd seen it often in their two years of marriage. *Was it only two years? And now separated for one?*

"Yes, perhaps. I might know someone. Henri Benoit, *doctor* Henri Benoit, an art historian. He's curated several shows for us but also does work for Christie's. Let me talk to him and get back to you." Rudolf flared his fingers about to crack his knuckles again. He didn't. Instead, he reached over and took her hand in his. She pulled away.

"Maggie." He cleared his throat. "Maggie, why don't we get together sometime? Just for dinner or a drink perhaps? Especially now, you are alone, I mean, without your best friend--"

She drew back in surprise.

"I miss you," he whispered, "even a year later, *Liebschen.*"

Liebschen. He called her that when he wanted something. Goosebumps rippled over her skin. "I don't think that's a good idea," she managed to say.

"But why? What harm can it be to have dinner?"

Because you'll want to go to bed with me and I couldn't bear the thought.

"Look, don't answer now," he said. "Think about it. Please. There's so much to talk about, now with Ingrid gone, you will need someone to speak German to." He gently brushed her lips with his finger. Then he stood and grinned down at her. His eyes gleamed like silver marbles and the look sent slivers of ice down her back. She was instantly reminded of why she'd left him.

"You'd better go, Rudolf."

"Maggie, please, let me help you, um, in whatever you are trying to do. Is that Klaus' book? Is it written in German? French? Maybe it will tell you where the painting is." He stopped. "You know if you are Ingrid's beneficiary, that painting may belong to you."

Maggie jerked her shoulders back and looked up at him. Before she could open her mouth he said, "I can translate for you, both languages, you know. Let me help. I, too, want to find out who murdered Ingrid."

And you want to get your hands on that painting. She shook her head, which felt heavy on her shoulders. "Please go."

He gazed at her for a moment then headed for the door.

"Leave the key on the hall table."

His jaws clicked in anger. He slapped the small piece of metal on the marble top and threw open the door. Without a word, he was gone.

Chapter 6

Maggie arrived home well after midnight. Following her confrontation with Rudolf, she'd picked up Rosie and spent several hours at the university library, researching the Van Gogh painting. Now, her whole body tingled, overdosed on adrenaline and caffeine. Thoughts blew around in her head, none alighting long enough to focus on. Rudolf, his damned impudence . . . balls. . . his sexuality.

The painting, too, kept reappearing in her mind. And then there was Ingrid. Maggie couldn't believe she was gone. Her mind began to wander to their times together over the years--their disastrous blind double dates, their dreamy trip to Bermuda, their Christmas vacations up in Vermont with Maggie's Aunt Sara. Tears formed in her eyes. She let out a long sigh. *Don't think about that now. Find out what happened to her.* Maybe Klaus Rettke's diary would answer some of the myriad questions that had accumulated in the last few days.

Despite the hour she decided to work for a while in her home office, concentrate on something useful. She switched on her computer and clicked on the photographs she'd scanned and downloaded earlier. She located one image of the painting that showed something of its surroundings. She enlarged it on the screen and studied it.

The Van Gogh sat on some sort of shelf; next to it on the left was part of another painting. Maggie enlarged that section and enhanced it to its full sharpness. The pixels blurred at first, the subject's edges distorting. At another resolution, the lines sharpened. As the work came into focus, Maggie could make out the brush strokes of this second painting. Not as vigorous in texture and light as Van Gogh, but softer and longer in shades of peach and ecru. The shape of a head came into view and finally a profile. Delicate, snub-nosed. A little girl.

She magnified then softened the image. She felt it was meant to be soft. An Impressionist? She could find no signature but she knew it was not a Van Gogh.

A whimper caught her attention. Rosie stood by the French doors, prancing. They were always locked because her second story garden accessed a fire escape. Rare in a brownstone, Maggie's ancestral home boasted a small patio walled in by Eugenia hedges. A small patch of grass served Rosie well. Fire regulations required a fire escape for buildings over one story. This one led to the alleyway below. But it also invited intruders.

"Okay, okay," Maggie said. A glance at the clock on the mantel told her it was nearly two in the morning. She opened the patio doors and a sharp wind bit into her face.

Rosie went charging into the garden with a sound between a bark and a bay.

"Quit torturing the squirrels," Maggie called after her.

Rosie started a low growl from the back of her throat. The sound froze Maggie in place. The patio was in darkness, the moon obscured by a curtain of dense clouds. She reached over for the switch and flicked on the outside lights. Nothing happened. She tried again. Had the bulb burned out? The dog set up a howl loud enough to wake the entire street.

"Rosie." Maggie cried out, fear bubbling to the surface.

Rosie made for the bushes in the far corner. Maggie thought she saw them move, heard the rustling of the leaves. Then she saw a vague outline of a figure in the darkness, a large, bulky figure. Before she could move, the shadow vaulted over the hedges and down the fire escape.

Maggie's brain couldn't react fast enough to give her arms and legs marching orders. Rosie barked and snapped her out of her reverie. She bolted to the hedge.

"Hey, hey you, what do you want, what the hell are you doing? Get back here, God damn it. Stop you miserable coward." The words trailed off as the intruder vanished into the dark.

Doors and windows in the buildings on both sides opened. "Hello? What's going on? Should I call the police?" An old man's voice. Another called out, "Maggie? Is that you? Are you okay?" Vanessa, her neighbor and dog sitter.

"It's okay, we're okay," she shouted back.

"Maggie, I'll come right over," Vanessa said.

"No, no. I'm calling the cops right now. It was just a prowler, I mean a . . . a little . . . break-in." Smart. A *little* break-in? "Really, Vanessa, I'll call you tomorrow." The police would probably want to talk to neighbors anyway.

Maggie shooed Rosie inside, closed and locked the patio doors behind her. Then she fumbled in her purse for her cell. She'd call Mead even if he was Homicide. As she dialed, her eyes stayed on the glass doors. What was she thinking, screaming after that guy? What if he came back? She roamed the living room in search of a weapon. The fireplace poker was the best she could come up with. Better late than never, she guessed.

Mead didn't answer. Hell. She left a message. When would he get it? She was about to call the station when her phone rang. Mead.

"I'll be there in fifteen minutes, maybe ten," he said.

Maggie burrowed into the couch, caressing a pillow to her chest. Rosie lay down at her feet, sensing her distress. A bone-deep weariness hit her like a physical blow and she wedged into the leather's softness. This wasn't just an intruder. Not just an unrelated incident. This had something to do with Ingrid's murder. The photographs. The painting. Her blood seemed to stop moving through her body and her hands were ice.

She had started to translate Rettke's diary but her German was rusty. She even considered asking Rudolf for help, then decided she was up to the task herself if she just concentrated, and had her English-German dictionary at her side.

The bell rang and Mead was there, a crime scene technician in tow. Maggie showed them to the patio where the tech unpacked his kit and began his evidence collection.

"The patio light didn't work," she said, a stream of thoughts blurting out. "I don't know why, it just--"

"Maybe it was burned out?" Mead said. He reached up and, with gloves on, tested the bulb. "Just loose."

"Well, it wasn't loose yesterday. He, that, that creep -- he loosened it."

Mead just looked at her. "Okay." He turned to the tech. "Joe, check the bulb for prints." To Maggie, "Let's go inside."

He led her in and closed the door behind him. "So, tell me exactly what happened."

Maggie folded her arms. "I already did in my phone message."

"Details."

She rubbed her arms as if to warm them. "I was starting analysis on the painting. I mean the photograph. At the computer." She pointed to an alcove off the living room that served as her office and proceeded to repeat her story.

"You're sure it was a man you saw?"

"I didn't actually see him. Just a large shape. He climbed over the bushes and down the fire escape. I yelled at him to stop but, I don't know, it must have been a man. I woke up all the neighbors and they offered to call the police, but, you know, it's so easy to get in here, there just isn't--"

He put a hand on her arm.

"I'm babbling."

Mead walked to the door and examined the lock.

She couldn't shut up. "And why didn't he leave when I came home and turned all the lights on in here? If he wanted to steal something, he had plenty of opportunity. I just got home a little while ago." She stopped. "God, I wonder how long he was watching me." She shivered.

"Hey, how about some coffee? Not that you need anything to pump you up." Mead popped a Tums.

She clamped her mouth shut and headed for the kitchen. "Coffee will only make your stomach worse."

"Yeah, well, I gotta have some vices." Mead pulled up a stool and sat at the colorful tile counter that divided the kitchen from the dining room.

Maggie's mind raced, but her limbs hadn't caught up. She spilled coffee grounds on the counter, wiped them up, scattered them again. Mead said nothing.

She opened a cabinet and brought out two mugs. One slipped out of her hand and crashed on the hardwood floor.

"Easy does it," Mead said.

"No, it's okay."

"Let me help." He walked around the counter.

"I said no. I've got it." Her voice cracked like the mug. She turned and pulled out a dustpan to sweep up the pottery shards.

"You're just a little edgy, with good--" he started.

"What the hell do you expect? Some guy breaks into my place at two o'clock in the frigging morning, maybe was watching me through the window for hours." A growl from deep in her throat leaped out.

He didn't refute her idea.

She reached for a new mug, poured two cups then took a third to the garden for the tech. Mead stayed seated at the counter. When she came back she grabbed the dead flowers in the vase on the counter and dumped them in the trash.

"I was wondering when you were going to do that," he said.

She looked at him.

"They've been bugging me." He smiled.

She rolled her eyes.

"What about the photographs?" he said. "Did you learn anything about the painting?"

"You think it's connected, don't you? You think this incident is related to Ingrid's death?"

"Don't you?" he asked.

The air went out of her.

Mead said nothing. He wandered around her living room, mug in hand.

"Eclectic mix," he said, referring to her furnishings. "Pottery from where, Mexico? Candles, pillows--the Far East? Paintings, Tuscany, maybe?"

"Yeah. Whenever I travel, I pick up stuff. Never try to match it or--"

"I like it," he said. "Colorful. Warm." He turned to her.

For the first time she noticed how pale and red-eyed he looked.

"I woke you up, didn't I?" she said.

He smiled with a flash of those dimples. "Me, nah. Cops don't sleep. We're like sharks– we swim around with one eye open all the time."

Joe, the tech, interrupted.

"Thanks for the coffee." Joe set the mug on the counter. He checked his kit and headed to the door. "I'll be in touch, Lieutenant."

Mead nodded. "So back to the painting," he said to her.

She drew in a breath and brushed her thick hair behind her ears in vain. "Okay. First, look at this." She showed him a printout of the secondary painting in the photo. "I enhanced this other painting, even though only a small portion of it shows in the photograph. It looks like an Impressionist."

"Like Van Gogh?"

"Actually he was considered Post-Impressionist."

"Whatever. Go on."

"It means that this picture was not taken in a museum or gallery, but probably at an auction house where they were bidding off several works from the period. They're much too close together."

"We knew that already."

"I found out more about Van Gogh at the library," she said. "First, it seems Vincent did not always sign his name the same way in the same place. Sometimes he signed on the lower left, sometimes the lower right. Sometimes he underlined his name, sometimes he did not. Often he did not sign at all."

"What? It depended on his mood?"

She raised an eyebrow. "Mood or not, we won't be able to authenticate the painting from the artist's signature."

"Great."

"I did find the painting, however, in color. Let me get my notes." She pawed through her bag, came up with a pad. *Still Life: Vase with Oleanders* by Vincent Van Gogh, *Canvas 56 x 36*, in inches that's about 22 x14, signed in lower left: *Vincent, Arles, August, 1888.*

"Arles. Isn't that the Provence town where Van Gogh's asylum was?" he asked.

"How did you know that?"

"I saw *Lust for Life*, you know with Kirk Douglas?"

She smiled. "Me too. Now listen to this. The painting was originally part of a collection belonging to *Jean Dauberville* of Auvers, France. However, the present owner is unknown. The painting is said to have gone missing around 1944." She paused. "Or been stolen."

"Or confiscated."

She gazed out in mid-space. "Frank? Did you find out anything about Rettke's death?"

"Tomorrow morning or should I say this morning?" He looked at his watch. "I should know something. I'm having the autopsy files sent." Mead carried his mug to the patio doors and looked out.

"There was an autopsy?" Maggie said. "I'm surprised, after all, he was in his late eighties. I mean, unless there's a reason to suspect foul play, wouldn't it be deemed natural?"

"Apparently he had an accident."

"Oh, yes, I remember. Ingrid said he slipped and fell in the shower. She thought he'd had a heart attack either before or after."

"It was most probably an accident," he said, "maybe due to a heart attack. However, there was quite a bit of blood from a head wound so the M-E had to follow up."

Maggie watched him a minute. The wide shoulders beneath the old jacket, the straight back. For the first time, she realized he was attractive, in a kind of *laissez faire* way.

He turned to her and she felt her face flush. "So I'll check the file and see if they found anything suspicious."

She moved to join him at the door.

"You look whipped," he said. "Go to bed."

She nodded, not meeting his gaze. He unsettled her with his gentleness. She'd rather see him as the irascible jerk she used to think he was. It bugged her that it bugged her.

"You going to be okay here? Alone, I mean?" Mead said.

"Yeah, sure."

"I mean, I could stay, if you want."

"What?"

"Stay. Just until morning. . . on the couch, that is. If you're nervous being alone and all." His face colored pink. "I probably won't sleep now anyway."

"Uh, well, I think I'll be okay."

They looked at each other.

"After all, I've got Rosie," Maggie added.

They turned to the big dog asleep in front of the cold fireplace and, smiling, shook their heads.

✦ ✦ ✦

Five hours later, Maggie woke to the music of Johann Sebastian Bach. Her cell. She made a grab for it and knocked it off the night table.

"Shit."

"Good morning to you too." Frank Mead's voice sounded hoarse. He'd probably never gone to sleep, like he'd said.

Before she could form a coherent word he said, "Sorry to wake you but thought you should know. Klaus Rettke."

"Yeah?" Maggie struggled to sit up against her pillows.

"Autopsy confirms he died of a brain hemorrhage from his fall in the shower."

"Not a heart attack," she said.

"Nope. I'm looking at the details on the wound right now," he said. "Long, clean laceration, a few secondary bruises from the fall itself. No defensive wounds on his hands or arms. Could've hit his head on the shower handle. That simple."

"That simple?" she said then, "Or?"

"Or someone could've hit it for him."

Chapter 7

Maggie clicked off from Frank and sat in bed mulling over his last words. In a way it made sense if Rettke had been murdered too. Or was her imagination off on one of its tangents? That was the word Ingrid liked to use. Tangent.

"*Maggie, can't you ever stay focused? You're always going off on a tangent.*" Ingrid smiled when she said it, but still she said it. Maggie could never live up to Ingrid's very German, very orderly, concentration skills. And yet, in direct contradiction, Ingrid never bothered with details. That's why she's always late, Maggie thought. *Was* always late. God.

Rosie leaped up as Maggie threw the covers off.

"Spring break, Rosie. We've got two weeks off. Let's go find Ingrid's painting."

She showered, dressed, and fired up her Mac. Then she fed Rosie her breakfast kibbles, made some coffee and downed a blueberry muffin before the two went off for their morning walk. It was Saturday and the day had emerged sunny and dry. She loved this time of day and year, before the southern humidity set in. They gamboled down the steps of the brownstone. Rosie heeled by her side as Maggie had taught her and the two enjoyed a quiet stroll together.

Maggie's brownstone on Dumbarton Street in Georgetown was a work in progress. She'd inherited it from her family and it dated back to the 1850s. Her mind drifted to the mummified remains she'd found in the basement four years ago when she began to remodel. It still struck her dumb even today to think that her ancestor, famed Civil War photographer Joseph Thornhill, committed the most infamous murder since Judas and buried the body in her basement. All in self-defense. Reporters, television media, historians and academics of all walks had hounded her for months. She'd laid it all to rest, literally and figuratively, when she wrote her own account of what had happened. The article appeared in a hundred journals and gave her no small amount of celebrity. But it was over now and she was trying to resume a normal life.

Frank Mead had lived through that with her. Before Rudolf. That was when she began to look at him in a new way. Not as an ordinary dumbass cop, as she thought when they first met four years ago, but as an educated and intellectual equal. What a snob she had been. Snob enough to marry Rudolf for all the wrong reasons.

When she and Rosie returned home an hour later, it was barely nine a.m. Maggie checked her emails then went online. The Library of Congress was probably her best option for research, but first she'd try the Internet.

She typed in *ERR and Nazis*. Pages and pages appeared. Dozens. Hundreds. She clicked on one entry from the American Association of Museums. "The *Einsatzstab Reichsleiter Rosenberg*, known as the ERR was a task force charged with confiscating works of art from Jews and Freemasons and took orders directly from the Party."

An hour later her fingers rested on the keyboard, weary of their journey back in time to one of the most horrendous periods in history. Poor Ingrid. To spend her last days believing her grandfather was a Nazi. Her eyes traveled down the web page but was interrupted by the doorbell.

Rosie didn't bark, which meant she knew who was on the other side of the door.

Maggie peered through the peephole and saw Frank Mead, hands on his hips, wearing a gray jogging suit, staring back at her, a wry smile on his face. She opened it.

"Hey," he said. "I was running in the neighborhood and I, um, wanted to check in."

"I didn't know you ran."

"I didn't know you were married," he said. "There's a lot you don't know about me." He grinned.

"Come in."

They looked at each other for a moment. She stepped back from the door.

"Coffee?"

"Never say no." He followed her into the kitchen where she poured a cup for him and a third for herself.

"I've been researching the ERR. Tons of information." She stood and moved to her desk and computer. "Take a look."

Mead sat in her chair, eyes on the monitor and fell silent for a while.

When he was finished reading the screen, she said, "If you keep going you'll learn that Hermann Goering started to use the ERR for his own ends early in the fall of 1940."

"I knew he was an art aficionado. Collected works for his country home, Carinhall."

She picked up a piece of paper. "The ERR dominated art confiscation in France, where many pieces were catalogued and stored at the Jeu de Paume Museum in Paris."

Mead sipped his coffee. "Jeu de Paume. There was someone there, worked there, if I recall, who protected some of the art from the Nazis. A woman."

Maggie raised an eyebrow.

"Yeah, I'm kind of a history buff," he said. "World War Two is a particular interest of mine."

"I thought the Civil War was."

"That too, but you've got that war sewn up." He grinned. "I told you there's a lot about me you don't know."

Her face went hot at the notion she would like to know more. She turned back to the computer and the web site she was logged onto. "You're right about the woman. Her name was Rose Valland. Listen." She read: 'If it weren't for an unlikely spy, Rose Valland, curator at the Louvre and later the Jeu de Paume, many artifacts might have vanished into the Reich forever. Madame Valland was one of the few French citizens permitted to continue working at the museum during the German Occupation. She managed to stay abreast of its operations and gather spectacular information. In fact, Rose Valland was able to copy the Nazi confiscation inventories and photo archives and keep track of the destinations to which confiscated works were being shipped."

"Rose Valland. Of course. In fact, there was an old Burt Lancaster movie, *The Train*--it was all about the stolen art being shipped out of Paris and about Rose Valland. Brave lady. She copied the inventories under the very noses of the Nazis."

"Copied the inventories?" Maggie asked. "I wonder. Did she copy them by hand? Or did she photograph them?"

"No idea."

Maggie skimmed several pages. "Wait, here it is. The Nazis took photos of everything they stole and Rose would take the negatives home at night and a friend would make prints of them. After the War the French were able to provide the Allies with information on where the objects were hidden. Thanks to her."

"Interesting. Rose Valland may not have been a photographer but she used photography to save the world's art. I could see you doing that."

"Me? Don't be ridiculous." For a split second Maggie felt a spark of vanity. Was she like Rose? Trying to find and save a lost piece of art, a lost piece of history? Nonsense. She walked to the patio doors, opened them and Rosie bounded out to the garden.

Mead came up behind her.

"Think about it," he said. "Rose Valland defied the Nazis and saved hundreds of pieces of valuable artwork. You're hot on the trail of one that was lost. I'd say you two would probably be good friends today."

She smiled despite herself and studied his face. A nice face.

"And both of you are pretty daring. I mean Rose had Nazis after her, you–" Mead stopped.

"Go on. Say it. I've got a killer in the wings," Maggie said. "Don't think I'm not aware of that."

"Yeah, well," he said and changed the subject. "Rose spoke better French than you."

"Hey, who needs language? What do they say about pictures and words?"

He set his cup down and headed toward the door.

"Frank," she called.

He turned.

"No, never mind. I'll see you later."

The door clicked shut behind him

Maggie turned back to the garden, pangs of guilt invading every pore of her body. Why didn't she own up about the diary she stole, yes stole, from Rettke's apartment? The more time went by without confessing, the more trouble she'd be in. She promised herself to hand it over soon. Very soon. After she read it.

She hurried into the bedroom and retrieved the diary. Curling her feet under her, she settled onto the couch, lamp bright over her shoulder, German dictionary at her side, dog on the floor in front of her. She began to translate the old man's words, slowly, painfully, until his handwriting became decipherable and the German language became more familiar. . . like the days she spoke it to Rudolf and Ingrid.

✦ ✦ ✦

Paris, France, Winter, 1941

Klaus Rettke sweated beneath his uniform as he stepped out of the Mercedes Benz Cabriolet staff car and strode down the *Avenue du Bois*. The wool was warm, true, but the real reason for his perspiration was angst. Rosenberg was suspicious of his movements. He had to prove his loyalty and what better way than to make an example of a Jew.

Several soft-top cargo trucks screeched to a stop up the street in front of *Le Jeune Galerie d'Art*. Four workmen dressed in dark green coats with red swastika armbands leaped down from the trucks and waited, eyes on Rettke.

When he reached the gallery, Rettke turned to the men. "*Hierbleiben!*"

While they waited, he entered through the front glass doors. A bell sang out and within a moment a young woman, merely a girl, but well dressed and coiffed, came to greet him. She stopped before she reached him, looked out the front doors and the smile faded from her lips.

"*Bon Jour, Mademoiselle*," Rettke said. "I'm looking for the owner of this establishment. *Monsieur* Steiner, Josef Steiner."

"Er, *le Directeur* is not here right now." Her tight face and unsteady gaze gave away the lie.

Rettke raised his chin and looked down at her. "What is your name?"

Her eyes rounded but she took a deep breath. "Collette Rousseau."

"You work here?"

"I am assistant to *le Directeur*."

"Quite young to be an assistant, no?" He didn't wait for an answer. "Do you know why I am here?"

At that moment, two men walked out from a back room and into the gallery. The older man, dark hair shot with gray and eyes that held a look of perpetual sadness, as if he carried the world on his shoulders, spoke in a hushed voice. "You? What are you doing here?"

The younger man, from facial similarities, was obviously the son. He turned to his father and opened his mouth but when Josef raised a hand, he kept silent.

Rettke said, "Ah, *Monsieur* Steiner. And this is your son, I assume? Jakob?"

"Never mind my son. Why are you here? You are never to come here."

"I am never to come here? And who are you to tell me where I may or may not go?"

"Father, who is this man? How do you know him?"

"Go in the back. I will deal with this," Josef said.

Rettke turned to Jakob. "Do you know who I am?"

"You are a Nazi and that is all I need to know." Jakob Steiner puffed out his chest. Collette tried to pull him by the arm.

"Father, what is happening?"

Rettke clicked his heels together and all motion stopped. "I will tell your son, then, why I am here." He moved to stand in front of a Renoir painting of two girls at a piano.

"No, please, I will--" Josef froze as Rettke's gaze lit upon him.

Rettke turned to Jakob. "My name is Klaus Wilhelm Rettke. I am a member of the *Einsatzstab Reichsleiter Rosenberg*. Do you know what the ERR is?"

"Yes, of course I know--you are monsters, stealing valuable art from the citizens of Paris, from the people of the world."

Rettke's jaw worked in anger. Then, abruptly, he burst out in laughter. He walked slowly toward the Steiners, now standing side by side. In a calm voice he said, "I am surprised your father did not tell you about us."

"Leave him out of this." Josef jumped in. "He does not need to know of such things. He is too young and--"

"What things?" Jakob shouted the words. "What things do I not need to know?"

Josef's face reddened and his breathing became heavy.

"Tsk, tsk, tsk," Rettke admonished, which angered the younger Steiner more.

Collette took hold of Jakob's arm, "S'il vous plait, Monsieur Jakob. Your father is not well. Do not agitate him."

Josef bulled his way past her. "Herr Rettke, I have dispensation here. Look, these papers, you yourself authorized protection of my shop. How, why are you saying this?"

Rettke stood stock still in rigid military form. The door to the gallery had opened and Alfred Rosenberg entered. The head of the ERR smiled at him as he approached. His eyes gazed around the room taking in the contemporary art and his thin lips curled in a sneer. He stood watching Rettke.

"Herr Rettke, do not let me interrupt you, please." Rosenberg waved a gloved hand. "Go on."

Rettke licked his upper lip. "Ah, I see you do not understand, Herr Steiner. Let me explain. No one, no one and nothing is protected unless I say so."

"But you did say so, you said--"

Rettke held up a hand. He could feel Rosenberg's cold eyes on his back. "I must inform you here and now that this place of business no longer has such dispensation."

Jakob's voice rose an octave. "I don't understand. Father, what is this protection? What does he mean?"

"You don't understand?" Rettke's anger erupted and he slammed his fist on the nearest object. A small statue of a nude female toppled off a stand and shattered.

"No, no, my God, the Degas. Oh, God." Josef Steiner knelt to pick up the pieces.

"Get up, Jew. Now." Rettke's words were spoken softly yet with menace. "Get me your inventory list," he said to Collette.

Josef Steiner dropped his arms to his side and tears welled in his eyes. "Why did you have to destroy her? Such beautiful art."

"Beautiful art?" Rettke said. "You call this *entartete kunst* beautiful? It is a disgrace to the great masters, to our *Fuhrer*. To me." He stomped through the gallery and yanked a painting off the wall. Another Degas. *Madame Camus at the Piano.*

Josef followed, fluttering his hands as if to catch the next falling object.

"You call this art? This is decadent; it defiles the word art. And it will be gone."

"No, please, you mustn't, please--" Josef tried but it came out a bare squeak. He clutched his chest.

"Father," Jakob dogged his heels.

Rettke went to the front door and called the men in.

"Take it all and check the back, storage rooms, cellar, everywhere. I want nothing left behind."

Rettke caught Rosenberg's grin as he watched from the sidelines.

Josef Steiner stumbled over to the first workman. "No, no, you cannot do this to me."

The workmen did not bother to reply, just shoved Steiner out of the way.

"Stop it. Don't do that," the young Steiner cried out. He ran to his father, who had visibly paled and clutched at his throat. "Sit down, father, sit here."

Before Jakob could move his father to a seat, Josef began heaving and gasping for breath. "Ahhh, the pain." He collapsed to the floor.

"Father, is it your heart?" Jakob turned to Rettke.

"He needs help. Please, a doctor. Collette, call a doctor."

She hurried to a desk and lifted the receiver of the phone.

"Put that down." Rettke said this quietly as he stood reading the inventory list. He could feel Rosenberg's eyes hot on his neck as his own heart skittered against his ribcage.

Collette froze, hand on the phone. All the while, soldiers went about their business removing every object of art from walls and pedestals. Their heavy black boots resounded on the wood floor, creating vibrations that shook the little shop. Paintings jumped on their fasteners, statues shook on their pedestals. She dropped the phone when she saw Jakob raise his fist and start shouting.

"You monsters, my father is--"

Collette rushed to him, pulled at his arm. "Jakob, please, you must help your father. *Maintenant, si'l vous plait.*"

Jakob blinked. He kneeled by his father who said, "Son, I am so sorry. I did what I thought was right, what I thought would save us from this. . . but. . . they. . . they cannot be trusted."

"We will be back to collect the stored inventory in the morning," Rettke said. "Be sure it is ready."

With that he turned and strode toward the door. When he reached for the knob he turned back to see the father grasp the son by the collar and whisper in his ear.

"Family secrets?" Rettke laughed as he slammed the door behind him.

Jakob sobbed as Josef Steiner died in his arms. Now he reflected in stunned silence on his father's final words. At least he had cheated Rettke out of that. All his grief and anger came crashing down on him and he continued to kneel and hold his father's hand, paralyzed by confusion and fear. When he realized the Gallery had become quiet, he rocked back on his knees and pushed himself to his feet. The place was in ruins. Art not confiscated had been destroyed or defaced.

Thank God, father, you cannot see this. It is good you are dead.

Tears streamed down his cheeks.

He looked down at Josef and once more contemplated his father's last words. Drying his eyes with the heels of his hands, Jakob Steiner straightened his back and filled his lungs with resolve. His father had duped the Nazis. And he, the son, would continue that deception.

Rettke held the collar of his overcoat tight around his neck with one hand to keep out the frigid wind. With the other hand, he pressed the coarse wool close to his body to keep his package from falling. The coat was a worn civilian wool in navy blue and his hat was a size too small for his head. They would do. He could not risk wearing his uniform on this undertaking. He kept his head down and cursed the cold.

Finally, he reached his destination: 34 *Rue Malar*, a narrow cobbled street in the *Rue Cler* District. The house was situated adjacent to a tiny *pension* and at that moment guests were coming through the door. Rettke did a quick turnabout and walked across the street to gaze in the window of the *Patisserie* at the *pain* and *éclairs* so elegantly arranged on trays. When the couple had gone, he turned back to Number 34 and pushed open the front door.

Inside the tiny dark vestibule he breathed in the smell of boiled cabbage and felt the warmth of the interior seep into his muscles. He climbed the steps and knocked on the door at the top.

It was opened by a thin, pinched-face man in his early forties, with thinning gray-brown hair and a small mustache that formed an upside down V over his mouth.

"Ah, Herr Rettke, I presume?"

"You are Van Meegeren?"

"Hans Van Meegeren at your service." The man ushered him in and closed and locked the door behind him.

Rettke noticed a drink of amber liquid in his hand.

"Would you like a whiskey?" Van Meegeren offered.

"No. I would like to get to business."

"Yes, yes. May I take your coat?" Van Meegeren set his glass down and helped Rettke off with his coat.

Rettke kept one hand always on the prize package he had conveyed. When Van Meegeren saw the rolled up canvas, his eyes brightened, the dull whiskey veil lifted.

"That is it? The painting?"

Rettke looked around the apartment for a place to set it down.

"This way to my studio," Van Meegeren said.

Rettke followed the artist into a well-lit room. Skylights in the ceiling as well as large windows on the rear courtyard provided splendid natural light and in the center of the floor was a large wooden worktable.

"This is where I do my sketching," Van Meegeren said.

Rettke glanced around again, taking in several easels, perhaps a hundred colorful paint jars, dozens of paintbrushes, and bottles of all sorts of tinctures and concoctions. Canvasses of varying sizes stood around the room and Rettke recognized Vermeer, Rembrandt, and DaVinci.

Unrolling the precious painting he'd brought, he was angry that his hands trembled and his mouth dried. Why should he be so nervous? But this was natural, no? How far could he trust Van Meegeren? Where did his sympathies lie? Was he political or just mercenary? Too late to ask these questions now. He needed the best and Van Meegeren was the best.

Van Meegeren helped him flatten the canvas with weights in the four corners. The two men stared in fascination at the painting: the deep lapis lazuli background behind a maize-colored table. On the table sat a simple lopsided vase filled with oleanders of brick red. And, in the lower left corner, as if written by a child, was the simple name, Vincent.

Minutes went by and neither spoke.

The artist broke the silence by retrieving a magnifying glass from a nearby table. He bent to study the work under the glass as Rettke studied him.

"Well," Rettke said. "Can you do it?"

It seemed a long time before Van Meegeren answered and Rettke's patience was at low ebb. He clenched his jaw to keep from repeating the question.

Finally Van Meegeren set down the magnifier and ambled over to his whiskey glass. He turned to Rettke. "You know that I generally do not copy paintings that already exist."

"What do you mean?"

"I copy the style, paint a wholly new picture to look like a Master."

Rettke waved his hand. "I don't care what you *generally* do. Can you duplicate this painting so no one will be able to tell it is not genuine? That is all I care about and will pay you good money for the job. Very good money."

"The money we talked about on the phone?"

"*Ja, ja*, naturally."

Van Meegeren's eyes gleamed. "As I said, this is not the way in which I work." He shrugged his shoulders and waited.

"What are you saying? That you will not fulfill our bargain?" Panic began to rise in Rettke's throat. There was no turning back now. "What do you want?"

"Well, after giving it careful consideration, evaluating the risk, the additional work, time, the materials needed to--"

"What do you want?"

"I'm afraid it's going to cost a little more than we agreed upon."

It was already going to cost the price of castle on the Rhine. "How much more?" Rettke said, teeth clamped in his jaw.

Van Meegeren made a show of lighting a pipe, blowing smoke upward into the skylight and suffusing the air with a fruity smell. He named a new price. Exorbitant, outrageous.

Rettke clenched his fists and glared at Van Meegeren. What choice did he have?

"Can you do it?" Rettke said finally.

Van Meegeren nodded. "Of course. That is why you are here, no?"

"Will you do it?"

"Ah, yes." He moved toward the rolled up canvas and gazed down at the painting. "Yes, I will do it." He blew another puff of smoke toward Rettke. "And, Herr Rettke, I promise you this. No one, no one. . . will ever know it is not an authentic Van Gogh."

Chapter 8

The clock on the mantel chimed twice. Maggie set the journal down with a reluctant sigh. Frustration seeped through her body. Rettke had provided some insight into his activities but not much. Why would he? After all, he was not writing this to be deciphered sixty years later by his granddaughter or her friend. Still a few names stood out. Steiner. Van Meegeren. Both significant. But how did they fit into Ingrid's murder?

The diary would have to wait. She had a three o'clock appointment. After changing her clothes and flagging a cab, she walked the last two blocks to the Smithsonian Mall. At the entrance to the National Gallery of Art, she spotted him immediately. He stood on the front steps of the contemporary East Building. Dark hair reached nearly to his shoulders and danced around his face in the wind. The tan trench coat he wore blew open, revealing a black turtleneck and khaki slacks. He was Dr. Henri Benoit, curator of nineteenth century art and the expert Rudolf had recommended.

Their eyes met as she walked up the steps. He smiled and Maggie wondered if he modeled for *Esquire* magazine on the side.

"*Bonjour.* Miz Thornhill?"

"Maggie, please." She held out her hand and he took it.

"*Je suis* Henri."

She expected him to bring her hand to his lips so she pulled it away, perhaps too abruptly. "Shall we go in?"

He took her arm and they walked side by side up the wide concrete steps to the sharply-angled sterile East Wing. Maggie felt his hand on her elbow and wondered at the difference between American and French men.

"This is my favorite building of the museum," Henri said as they reached the doors. "Do you like it as well?"

"Actually, I prefer the original West Wing."

"Ah, a traditionalist."

They arrived at the Cascades Café and Maggie suddenly questioned whether meeting here, where Ingrid and her grandfather had often lunched, was such a good idea. For a moment she was jolted by the reminder that they were both dead.

Henri pulled out a chair for her then sat in the closest seat rather than on the opposite side.

"Thanks for meeting me," she said once they ordered. Despite the busyness of the café and museum store nearby, an indoor waterfall provided a calming backdrop to their conversation.

"I'm very happy to help. First, I would like to say how sorry I am for your loss. Your good friend, *non?* I heard about this terrible thing in the papers. They did not say the name, of course, but Rudolf, he--"

"Yes, he told you about her."

"Ah, *oui.* It is okay?"

"Yes, of course. That's really why I wanted to talk to you." She dismissed a twinge of anger at Rudolf. She always seemed angry at Rudolf these days. Ridiculous. Of course he would have told Benoit.

A waitress delivered their orders of espresso and mocha and gave Maggie a minute to collect her thoughts.

"He mentioned, then, that Ingrid had photographs of a painting. Possibly a Van Gogh."

"He did and I am most anxious to see them," Henri said.

"Well, it may not be a genuine Van Gogh." Maggie pulled an envelope out of her bag.

Henri took the prints, ignored his drink and leaned forward to study them.

She stirred her drink, spooning the whipped cream into her mouth. His eyes were indigo like a sky before dark. She studied his features: A rather large nose and square chin accented by a deep cleft. Irritatingly attractive. And European. Why was she always attracted to European men? She slid her chair back a few inches.

He stared at the photos for several minutes, shuffling one behind the other.

"Would this help?" She reached into her bag again and handed him her magnifying loupe.

"*Oui, merci.*"

Minutes went by.

She tapped her fingers on the table.

"Where did Ingrid get these?"

"From her grandfather."

"And do you know where this painting might be?"

"No."

Henri rubbed the shadow of a dark beard on his cheek.

Maggie wondered whether he had shaved that morning.

He put the photographs down and looked at her.

"Could it be a Van Gogh?"

Henri exhaled, didn't respond right away. He picked up the photographs again, examined each one, first with the loupe and then without. Each photo, with, without.

Finally he said, "*C'est possible* but from photographs it is difficult to tell. I suspect it could be a lost Van Gogh, a painting most likely confiscated during World War Two and never recovered by the original owners." He paused. "You see in this photo these other paintings?"

"Yes. At first, I thought it might have been shot at an auction house," she said. "But now I think it was taken at the Jeu du Paume. The Room of Martyrs."

He nodded.

She relayed the information she had researched at the library. When she got to the ERR, Henri dropped his eyes.

"Ah, *Oui*. The Germans were most meticulous about cataloguing their works. There are a considerable number of paintings still missing from the Occupation." He leaned over and touched her arm. "Maggie, if this is a genuine Van Gogh, *Je serai très extatique.*" His eyes sparked silvery lights.

"Is there a way to verify the painting's authenticity from the photos?" she asked.

"It is so, er, complicated. The question is really *what* is authentic?"

She waited while he drank his espresso and waved to the waiter. He leaned back in his chair, crossing one long leg over the other.

"You see, to declare a work authentic there must be certain evidence. First you must consider *who* claims it is authentic," he said. "Is this person a scholar whom the world believes can confirm such an imprimatur on a work of art? Someone from this museum or the Met, *peut-être?*"

"But even those experts have to base their opinion on something. What criteria do they use?"

"That too is a problem," he said. "In France, the government often establishes the heirs of a recently deceased artist as the legal authenticators of the art. However, there has been much controversy. The descendants have too much of a personal stake in the outcome." He ran his fingers through his hair, tousling it in a casual way.

Maggie found herself staring.

"Then you have the auction houses that provide their own experts based on their own standards," Henri went on. "The first objective they must meet is to minimize research costs and to present works that will not be subject to litigation."

Maggie blew out a breath. "What do *you* look for?"

"Beside a beautiful woman with brains, you mean?"

She felt a rush of blood to her face.

Henri continued as if he didn't notice. "Well, I start with what is called a *stylistic* analysis, which I shall explain in a minute. Next I use whatever tools of science I have at my disposal depending upon where I am in the world. This would be of interest to you, *non?* You are a digital photographer?"

She smiled.

"Finally, but perhaps, most important and most difficult to accomplish, is provenance. Verifiable provenance."

"Provenance. The written history of the work," she said.

He shook his head. "*Encore.* Not so simple. A definitive provenance that dates back to the artist's hand is extremely rare. Most works that arrive on the art market have changed hands many, many times. Plus records are often lost or destroyed over the years. Particularly in wars or situations of political unrest." He moved his chair closer. "In fact, there is a case in the papers right now where a number of well-known paintings had been clearly labeled by the leading prewar collector in Amsterdam, Jacques Goudstikker, yet still the paintings are in dispute."

She frowned.

"So," he continued. "Establishing provenance is far from a simple matter."

"Tell me about stylistic analysis."

"That is where photographs can be somewhat useful. A stylistic or aesthetic assessment can be done by someone very familiar with a good number of the known *oeuvre* of the artist or time period. You are familiar with Van Gogh's work?"

"Only from visiting art museums," she said.

A chirping sound interrupted and Henri reached for his cell phone. "*Oui, c'nest pas--*" A few more sentences in French.

"I'm sorry, Maggie, but I must go. A silly but necessary emergency. May I take these photographs with me to examine later? I will get them back to you tomorrow, if that is all right."

She reached into her bag and pulled out a business card. Then she wrote her home number on the back. "You can keep them, they're copies. Call me anytime."

"Do you think all this has something to do with, I mean--" He hesitated.

"Ingrid's murder? Yes," she said. "I do."

"You said her grandfather had these? Who was her grandfather?" Benoit asked.

"Didn't Rudolf tell you?"

He shook his head.

"Klaus Rettke," she said.

Henri's eyes widened.

Before she could say more, his cell phone rang again and he snatched it off his belt. He spoke in French for several minutes, leaving her to contemplate the obvious. *He knows of Rettke. And he knows Rettke was Ingrid's grandfather. Rudolf must have told him. Why is he surprised?*

When his call was complete, Henri, said, "I'm so sorry, but it seems my emergency is even more urgent. The staff is in an upheaval about shipping a Renoir." He smiled. "We will meet again soon and talk more about your ideas, I promise."

"Of course, but I just wanted to ask--"

Henri, already standing, threw a twenty-dollar bill on the table. "Later, then. *Au revoir.*"

Her frown deepened as she watched his retreating form.

Of course he would know about Rettke and the ERR. Maggie had so many questions for him. Damn his emergency. What now? Back to the diary. She ran down the steps of the museum and out to the street. She decided on the Metro instead of a cab and began to walk, thoughts focused on Klaus Rettke and the Nazis. Twenty minutes later, she waited for the train on the platform of the Smithsonian Station.

She was distracted for a moment by a group of tourists walking by and pointing up. She looked. Above her were arched ceilings with cutaways for lights. It was a beautiful subway station, if subway stations could ever be beautiful. Posters of Toulouse-Lautrec, Picasso, Klee, Miro adorned the walls. Small vitrines held replicas of the heads of King Tutankhamen and Queen Nefertiti. She stared at a miniature of an Egyptian coffin and her mind flashed to her friend, alive and smiling. *I'll find the painting for you, Ingrid. I promise.*

The lights on the platform began to blink. People shuffled closer to the edge and closer to Maggie. She lowered her bag to the floor, its weight straining her shoulder. A train whistle blew in on sound waves into the station. The metroliner was less than a minute away and she could see a pinprick of light off to the left.

She noticed a man, all in black, standing close on her right side. Something about him was odd. He was large in girth, swarthy, his face not memorable. He didn't look at her, just stood with his hands in his pockets. That was it. His raincoat was wrong, all wrong. Too large for him, too bulky. Big enough to stow a weapon without being noticed.

Maggie stepped backward through the throng, ignoring the grumblings of the waiting passengers. She felt herself being herded forward by the crowd. She resisted, finally gaining space between herself and the train just as it pulled into the station. The squeal of metal on metal as the brakes engaged.

The train doors opened. She looked around to see if the man was still there. Had he gotten onto the train? Did she imagine him?

She was alone on the platform now as the train doors slid closed and the train rolled lazily out of the station. Her chest palpitations began to subside. She reached out to retrieve her bag. That was when she realized what had really happened. How stupid, how utterly brainless. In her panic to get away from that man and from the edge of the platform she missed the real crime. Her bag was gone.

Chapter 9

Frank Mead stretched his size nines under a gray metal desk and rested his hands in his lap. He was distracted listening to her, *trying to* listen to her, spill forth about the incident in the train station.

She reminded him of his late wife. The hair, the fire in her eyes, the...

"Frank, did you hear anything I said? What are you going to do about it?" Maggie said, leaning over his desk.

He swiveled in his chair. "What would you like me to do about it?"

She threw up her hands.

"All right, calm down. Look, Maggie, this happens every day in this city. Hundreds of bags get snatched." He pushed back his chair then walked to the corner of his desk and half sat on it. An uncomfortable worm had crept into his chest. This was no ordinary purse snatching. He knew it and he knew she knew it.

"Sit down," he said.

She didn't.

"Tell me what he looked like."

"Tall, at least six feet. Dark, very dark skin, not black, Arab maybe. Kind of, of shiny."

"Shiny?"

She shrugged her shoulders. "Well, oily black hair and sweaty skin, eyes black and, and shiny. I don't know how else to--"

"Could he have been the guy who broke into your place? The one who could've killed you if you had chased him down the fire escape?"

She stared at him. "He also wore a raincoat, but it was too big on him."

"Sure, to seize and hide. I can check the description against known purse snatchers but frankly--"

"I know. It's hopeless."

She collapsed into a chair across from him.

"One thing I know for sure," she said. "This wasn't just a random purse-snatching. It's too much of a coincidence. Ingrid's murder, the break-in at my house, now this."

Mead agreed but felt reluctant to say so. She was already on the edge. He waited until the fire went out. Finally, she expelled a long breath and sank back into the chair like a wilted lily.

"The guy was standing right next to me, maybe the same guy who killed Ingrid. And, I think he--" She hesitated. "I think he would have pushed me onto the tracks if I hadn't backed away from the edge." She looked up at him.

"I'm listening."

She rubbed her forehead with her fingers. "I don't know what to think. But there was something about the guy, something sinister." Her voice trailed off.

"Sure there was. Did you expect a clean-cut college boy? Listen, Maggie. How do you think these perps do it? Purse snatching, I mean. Swing down from a *subway vine* and lift it off your shoulder? These creeps bide their time, watch their prey and pick the one that's easiest to heist. They make you nervous." He paused. "Where was your bag?"

"I had set it down on the platform, near my right foot." She shook her head. "I thought I picked it up when I tried to get away from him, but obviously not. Brainless."

He stood and crossed the room, hands on hips. "Were the photographs in the bag?"

She folded her arms and crossed her legs as if to defend herself from some accusation he might launch.

Any more body twists and she'd be a pretzel, he mused.

"No the photographs weren't in the bag." She looked at him, the connection dawning. "But how on earth would he have known about the photos, let alone where they were?"

He shrugged. "Most likely he was after cash or credit cards. Who have you told about the pictures?"

"What?" She sat forward. "This is my fault?"

"Cool it, Maggie." He held up a hand. "I'm on your side, remember? I just want to know who knows about these photographs. Everyone, anyone. Even your dog."

"Yeah. Sorry." She told him about Henri. "I gave him copies. The original photos are with your crime lab. And the only others are the digitized ones on my computer." She rose slowly. "Well, this isn't getting me anywhere." She reached down for her bag then remembered. "I loved that silly bag. Bought it in Florence, and--oh God, my keys, my wallet--"

Mead thought she was going to cry and took a step towards her.

She turned for the door.

He felt at a loss. He followed her to the glass-paneled door of his office. Lopsided blinds barely contained the sights and sounds of the Metro Police Station beyond.

Should he tell her to be careful, be observant, watch her back? Instead all he said was, "Need a ride?" Dumbass thing to say.

"No."

"Do you have a way to get into your house?" he said.

"I've got an extra key with my neighbor." Her voice was barely audible. "At least my cell was in my pocket or that would've been gone too."

"You'd better change the locks on your doors," he added. Really fuckin' dumb. That ought to make her feel safe.

Maggie left without a backwards glance.

Mead was about to chase after her, tell her he'd keep an eye on her, make sure she was safe. Right. He stopped in his tracks at the frozen tableau in the outer office: nine cops, male and female watched her exit.

Mead watched too, feeling totally out of control. His eyes followed her as she walked through the long squad room, her straight back, auburn hair looped in a thick braid, loose tendrils falling about her neck.

He swallowed hard, marking the sway of her hips as she finally turned the corner.

Jesus, I wish I still smoked.

The silence got his attention. All eyes were on him.

"Don't you assholes have anything to do, for Chrissakes?"

He dove into his office and slammed the door behind him.

That night, after chasing down a locksmith, reporting all her stolen credit cards and replacing her driver's license with a temp, Maggie was emotionally drained. Even so, her restless energy wouldn't let her relax. She decided not to wait for Henri but to learn about authenticating paintings on her own.

In her office, wearing jeans and a Hoyas sweatshirt, she searched the Internet and found dozens of web sites regarding the subject of art authentication. Web sites on the science of, on math and art, Holocaust assets, art forgeries. Forgeries. This caught her attention. She read for an hour.

Finally, she stretched and circled her living room, ideas forming a tornado in her mind, second by second funneling into a theory. The doorbell rang and the twister spun away. She looked at the clock on the mantel. Nine-thirty. Who could that be?

A knock followed the bell. Rosie barked.

"Maggie, it's Frank. You there?"

She opened the door.

Mead leaned one arm on the door jamb. His tie was gone, the collar of his blue shirt loosened.

She looked at him.

"Can I come in?" he said.

Maggie stepped aside. "I was having a glass of wine. Want one?"

"I'd rather a beer."

"Sorry."

"I guess this isn't my lucky day. Wine'll do."

He followed her into the kitchen and she filled a glass for him and topped off hers.

"What are you doing here, Frank?" she said.

"I wanted to tell you that I don't think the incident today was random. I think something is going on here with those pictures. I don't know what, yet, but it ties into Ingrid and her grandfather. And whatever it is is a threat to someone." He set the wine glass down. "Listen, Maggie, let me have someone else work on those photographs. You're too close to this, too personal, and frankly, I'm--"

"I know, I hear you. I think you're right. But, for just that reason: my personal stake in this, I have to keep going."

Mead worked his jaw.

"I said it before. I'm not getting off this case. I have the photographs and I'm going to figure out what they have to do with Ingrid's death. With you or without you."

He rubbed his unshaved chin. "Damn you're stubborn."

"Yeah, that's what I hear." She tried a smile.

"Christ," he said, barely under his breath.

She handed him his wine glass. "I've been doing some research on the paintings. Do you want to hear what I've come up with?"

She saw by his raised eyebrows that he was hooked. "Sit down and listen."

He hoisted himself onto the counter stool.

She picked up papers from a desk buried in stacks of books, journals and papers and read: "Contrary to popular belief, the detection of forgery is a different process than the authentication of works of art. Science is generally very good at producing evidence of falsification but often is equally poor at proving authenticity." She stopped. "Naturally, it's all quite complicated."

"Naturally."

She continued. "There could be an authentic work done by the artist alone, or by his studio of assistants in the same style, or by a school of people influenced by the artist." She looked up. "And, there's a difference between a copy and forgery. A copy is a work done after a known artist, but a forgery is a purposeful attempt to mislead the viewer as to the identity of the artist."

"So what you're telling me," he said, "is the Van Gogh in the photos could be authentic, could've been done by a school of Van Gogh artists, could be a copy or could be a forgery. Great. That narrows it down."

Rosie let out a soft whuff. Mead petted her head and she nuzzled against his leg.

"There's a lot about technology and art on the Net too." She took her wine to her computer and sat down. She clacked away at the keyboard, searching, until she found the article on the science of art. "Chemical analyses, ultraviolet fluorescence, x-ray and infrared reflectography. Ink and canvas could tell a good story too."

He nodded, still at the kitchen counter.

"Problem is, all of these techniques require the painting itself, not a photo of the painting," she said. "How could we use the *photographs* to determine whether it's a Van Gogh?"

Both of them jumped as thunder boomed outside and the patio lit up with a streak of lightning. Maggie shivered, more from remembering her intruder than from the storm.

"Maybe I'm nuts," she said. "Maybe science simply won't solve this one."

"You mean the mystery of the painting or Ingrid's murder?"

Her eyes sparked. "Wait a minute. What if I could compare the painting in the photograph with a photograph of a known Van Gogh--say one at the National Gallery of Art? Side by side, on the computer, Rettke's painting could be whittled down to their tiniest bit, byte, actually, until a comparison could be made. I could analyze the brush strokes, the textures, the density--" She stopped. "Of course, of course. The color."

"What?"

"The color can tell us a lot. Van Gogh used lots of different blues. Prussion blue, cobalt blue, lapis lazuli and others." She pointed a finger at him. "If I could demonstrate that multispectral images--"

"What? Can you speak English, please?"

"Images that are in the infrared spectral region. They can tell us--"

"You have an infrared camera?"

"The lab has a camera fitted with band pass filters. That should do it."

Mead shook his head. "Whatever."

"With multispectral imaging, I can map the color of a known Van Gogh and compare it to the painting in the photograph. If we're lucky, well, the answer may be in the blues."

Mead looked at her.

"Maybe not," she went on. "It could be many Post-Impressionists used the same blues, or even artists trying to copy Van Gogh."

"Still," Mead said, "putting all these scientific comparisons together could at the very least rule out authenticity."

"The more I research it, Frank, the more I think there's a chance, a good chance that using a photograph could work. I'd have to develop the program myself, of course."

"Of course." Mead cracked a grin.

"And why not?" she said. "There are a number of scientists working on similar theories. Some are in Holland. The Dutch are famous for their art conservation. And there's a mathematician working at the Met to authenticate the old masters like Rembrandt. I could call and talk to them--"

She spun around the room like a top, arms waving, fingers pointing.

"Well, if anyone can do it, you can."

She didn't hear. "Tomorrow. Tomorrow, I will take pictures at the Gallery. There's a famous Van Gogh--um, you know that." She let some air out and collapsed in a chair facing the kitchen counter and Mead. "God, listen to me."

"You are a bit wound up." He stood. "Maggie, please. I want you to watch your back. Keep your eyes opened wherever you go. Wherever you are. Do you get my drift?"

She nodded.

"Seriously, do you really know what I'm saying here? This isn't a game, a woman is dead."

"Yes. I know, Frank. I know."

He shook his head. "Well, you better get some sleep. You've got a busy day tomorrow. Me too."

Once again, she considered telling him about Rettke's diary and the entries she'd worked out so far. For some reason unclear to her, she couldn't, didn't want to tell Mead. Not yet. Maggie chewed her lip. Was it possible Ingrid was aware of her grandfather's activities during the war? At the very least she would have had some suspicion. And, if in fact she did know about Rettke, and never told her, what did that say about their 'close' friendship?

"Go to bed, Maggie." Mead interrupted her thoughts. "We'll talk tomorrow."

She almost shouted his name to call him back. Tell him about the diary. The longer she waited, the harder it would be. But she stopped herself and he was gone.

Chapter 10

The next morning, Maggie arrived with her camera equipment at the National Gallery of Art. She headed straight for the permanent exhibition hall, where the self-portrait of Vincent Van Gogh hung.

She stopped short of the exhibition hall, anxious about entering. The crime scene tape was gone and all evidence of the violence that had taken place had vanished as well. The museum was busy and she reflected on how many people were there because of the sensational headlines: "Woman Murdered at National Gallery." But since it was a rainy Saturday, maybe Ingrid's death had nothing to do with the crowds. Students sat cross-legged on the old pine plank floor sketching the famous paintings on the walls and elderly couples stood up close to read the text next to each work of art.

Maggie proceeded across the room toward the painting in question. *Self Portrait, September,1888, Oil on Canvas*. Ingrid had stood here only a few days before. Maggie tiptoed closer to the painting, leaned in to study it. She could understand her friend's attraction to the work. She found herself drawn to the artist's face: Van Gogh's soulful eyes, his pinched nose, the hollowed cheeks, which tapered to a pointed chin, discernible even beneath the red beard. A tortured soul, moody, temperamental, probably classified today as bipolar.

Maggie had considered taking pictures after museum hours but she would have had to contact Rudolf. No, this was best. She clipped her police consultant badge onto her jacket collar, set up her tripod and affixed the digital camera to it.

"Hey, Miss, you're not allowed . . . oh, it's you, Miz Thornhill. Sorry, y'all go right ahead," the security guard said with a nod.

"Thanks, Donny." Maggie felt a slight twinge of embarrassment. Donny knew her ex-husband, of course. Did he know that she and Rudolf were no longer man and wife?

She made the final adjustments to her equipment and took a dozen photographs of the Van Gogh portrait. After reviewing the images in her viewfinder she felt satisfied with the shots. As she disengaged the camera from the tripod, she sensed someone behind her.

Please don't be Rudolf.

It was not her former husband. It was a stranger. A man in his mid-fifties, short, perhaps five foot five, but stocky and bald, his pate spotted with patches of discolored skin. He wore a coat of navy blue cashmere.

"It is beautiful, yes?" he said.

"What?"

"The Van Gogh." He tipped his head toward the portrait. His brown eyes were small and deep set but intense like an eel's.

"Oh, yes, it is. Very beautiful." She turned to resume her work but the man didn't move away.

"Excuse me, Miss, you're a friend of Klaus Rettke's granddaughter, are you not?"

Her skin tingled as it did whenever her radar upped a notch.

"Who are you? How do you know me?"

The man offered a sad smile. "I knew your friend. . . and her grandfather. I'm sorry about her death. Please, let me introduce myself. My name is Aaron Beckman. My father, Samuel, he was a collector, you see. He collected paintings, many fine paintings, Impressionists in particular."

Maggie tried to distinguish his European accent. German? She noticed then that Beckman had one hand in the pocket of his dark blue coat and one on his umbrella, which he used as a cane.

He caught Maggie watching and pulled the hidden hand out.

She stepped back.

"Please, do not be afraid of me. There is nothing in my pocket. But I see why you are worried, after all, your friend–" His voice trailed off.

"How did you know Ingrid?"

"Actually, it was Rettke I was, er, somewhat familiar with. Let me explain. My father purchased a painting in 1945, just after the war. I believe the man who sold the painting to him got it from Rettke. The painting was a Vincent Van Gogh. Genuine. It had passed through many hands and my father was--" Beckman took his time before speaking. "My father was terribly happy to have found it. He would have paid anything for the painting. As it was, he paid a good deal. Three million dollars. At that time, a lot of money." He paused to gather his thoughts.

Maggie watched him through narrowed eyes.

Beckman picked up his story. "My father passed away recently. I inherited the painting, and I, unlike my father, am not an art aficionado. To me, a painting is money." Beckman lowered his voice. "As it happens, I have a particular need of money right now, so, I attempted to sell it. Of course, the painting, any work of art, has to be authenticated properly, papers are not enough, the experts say. So, you can imagine my shock when--" His eyes moistened. "When I'm told by Christie's Auction House that the Van Gogh is a fake. A fake. How can that be, I say to myself? I do not understand. My father paid millions. For a fake? Not possible. He was a very precise, very careful man.

"So I traveled to Amsterdam to visit the heirs of the man who sold the painting to my father. The family of Hans Van Meegeren. You know the name?"

She knew the name from Rettke's diary but she didn't offer that information. Beckman seemed not to notice her silence.

"He was a master art forger, *the* master art forger of the time, perhaps for all time," Beckman said. "But that is another story. The family had no idea what I was talking about. And I believed them. For many reasons too complicated to explain. But they had one bit of information that was most valuable. They said the original painting came from Rettke and that somehow Rettke had duped Van Meegeren into believing he had a genuine Van Gogh."

"I don't understand."

"Rettke wanted Van Meegeren to make a copy but the Van Gogh he brought the forger was already a copy. It must have been."

Maggie stared at him.

Beckman, whose eyes had been fixed on the self-portrait as he spoke, now turned to Maggie.

"Rettke switched the painting, somehow, after the deal was struck, when neither Van Meegeren nor my father had any reason to verify it again. He switched it with a copy. I don't know how, but he did, surely as we are standing here." His eyes squinted at her. "Your friend's grandfather duped my father. And he cheated me of my rightful inheritance."

"Now just a minute, Mr. Beckman, I--"

"You, Miss, please, you must have some information from your friend, papers she kept, her grandfather's papers, the provenance of the paintings he sold, records he kept. . . something. You were the only one close to her." He stopped, caught his breath. "You know where the real painting is, don't you?"

Alarms went off in her head, setting her skin prickling. Who was this man? Could he have killed Ingrid? She started to reach for her cell phone, but he grabbed her arm.

"Take your hand off me." Maggie looked around for Donny but the guard must have started his rounds.

"Forgive me, Miss. I mean you no harm. But I must have the real painting," Beckman said. The words were spoken softly, which added to their menace. "You see, I, need it. I need it badly, please."

Maggie stepped backward. Beckman's voice had stretched to the snapping point.

"Mr. Beckman," she tried to soothe him, keep him from doing something he'd regret. "Perhaps we could sit down somewhere and talk about this in a reasonable manner?"

Suddenly, Beckman's eyes widened. He was no longer looking at her but at something across the room. He wiped beads of sweat off his upper lip. Just as suddenly, he dropped his head. When he lifted it, fear had replaced the anger in his eyes.

Maggie spun around and scanned the room. She saw only the same museum visitors. She blinked and looked again for who might have frightened Beckman.

When she turned back, she caught a glimpse of a dark blue coat retreating through the doorway.

✦ ✦ ✦

Outside on the street, the sun made a brief appearance, then vanished behind grim dark clouds. Maggie decided to avoid the Metro this time and not just because of the weather. She could finally admit it to herself. She was afraid.

Where was Aaron Beckman? She scanned the street in all directions. He had disappeared. But his words remained imprinted on her mind. If what Beckman said was true, then Klaus Rettke had switched a real Van Gogh for a fake and sold it as genuine. This conformed with Rettke's diary: he had confiscated the painting from Josef Steiner then brought it to Hans Van Meegeren to be copied. If that were true, how did Van Meegeren sell the painting to Samuel Beckman? Did he steal it from Rettke, pull a switch? Frustrated, she hailed a cab for home. But she couldn't turn her mind off. As she bounced over potholes in the backseat of the taxi, her brain ticked off the possibilities.

Aaron Beckman. Samuel Beckman, the father, was dead. Did the son kill Ingrid? If Aaron wanted the painting, why would he kill the only person who might know where it was? But Ingrid didn't know, did she? Ach. Her head hurt. She stared out the window at the Federal buildings. Mead needed to know about Beckman. The man filled in a substantial piece of the puzzle. And he seemed desperate, which made him dangerous. She pulled out her phone. Dead.

"Driver," she called out. "I've changed my mind. Can you take me to the Metro Police Station?"

✦ ✦ ✦

All eyes were on her as she adjusted her camera equipment on her shoulders and strode into Mead's office. She stopped to return their stares and they all scurried about, grins on their faces.

"What the hell? Am I some sort of joke around here?" She dropped her bags and stood, hands on hips, daring Mead to say the wrong thing.

He walked behind her and closed the door, but not before he gave his colleagues outside his own scathing look.

"You paranoid? Sit down."

She did and in ten minutes blurted out the incident with Aaron Beckman. Mead wrote while she talked.

"Have you ever seen him before?

"No."

"Heard the name, anything, from Ingrid, maybe?"

"No." She chewed her lower lip to keep from blurting out news about the diary. She had more to read first.

He threw down the pen and let out a long low whistle. "I'll see what I can find out about the Beckmans. What do you know about this Van Meegeren?"

"He was a Dutch painter who became disenchanted with the art world. I guess the critics referred to him as a technician as opposed to an artist, which he took offense to."

"Hmm, so would I," Mead said.

"So Van Meegeren set out to prove to the art critics that he could not only copy the style of the Dutch masters but paint a work so beautiful it would rival the masters."

"So he copied a Rembrandt?"

"Vermeer, actually, not Rembrandt. And not exactly copied because he painted in the *style* of the painter, rather than copy a painting already in existence," Maggie said. "He was actually pretty clever. Van Meegeren would purchase an authentic 17th century canvas and mix his own paints from raw materials, just as Vermeer would have done." She smiled. "Then he came up with a way to make the painting look old. He used phenol formaldehyde to cause the paints to harden after application. Finally he would bake it to really make sure the pigments cracked."

"Jeez. That made it look old?"

"He'd fill in the cracks with black India ink, washing it over the surface. I guess it worked. Van Meegeren's paintings are worth a hell of a lot of money, even today."

"Shit. Maybe I can try forging a can of Campbell's Tomato Soup," Mead said. "Sounds easy."

Maggie noticed how tired he looked. His jacket was draped over a chair, his tie askew, pale gray shirtsleeves rolled up.

"What's up with you?" she said.

"What do you mean?"

"You look beat."

He rubbed his eyes. "Not sleeping too good."

She picked up a photograph on his desk, one she hadn't noticed before. Mead and a pretty red-headed woman. "Your wife?"

He nodded, got up and poured two mugs of coffee. He handed her one, expecting her to drink it black, which happened to be the way she liked it.

"Where was it taken?" she asked.

"Maui, Six years ago."

"What's her name?" She paused. "Sorry, it's none of my business."

"Jean Constance O'Reilly. Jeannie."

Maggie studied the photograph. Mead was a bit thinner in body, thicker in hair. His smile was wide, the dimples out for all the world to see. He seemed happy, tan, relaxed. The woman, well, she looked happy too.

"She wasn't a cop, was she?"

He shook his head. "School teacher. Taught special kids, you know, mentally and physically challenged." He reached over to take the photograph. "And then she was gone. Two years after this picture." He put the photo in a drawer.

Mead didn't say how she died, but Maggie vaguely recalled stories about a cop in New York whose wife took an overdose. At the time there were stories in the newspapers about the plight of cops' wives, the high number of cop suicides, wrecked families. Yeah, she remembered. Hell, that would have been 2000, just when Mead came to D.C. He didn't waste any time running away from it. Maggie said nothing, picked up another photo.

"That's Amanda, my daughter. She's in New York with my mother. Likes the Big Apple."

A knock on the door saved them both from the awkwardness. Ramón Delacruz, dressed in a brown silk suit and brightly colored tie stepped in.

"Yo, 'scuse me, Frank. Hey, Miz Thornhill." Delacruz flashed a set of straight white teeth. Movie star teeth.

"Hello Sergeant," she said.

"I got the film you wanted from the archives at the Holocaust Museum. Naturally it's

sixteen milimeter crapola. Want me to set it up?"

"What's this?" she said.

"Ramón's been doing some research on the Nazi confiscation of art. Found some footage at the Holocaust Museum archives. Might be useless or might be of interest. At any rate, it could give us some general background. Maybe even about the ERR."

"Okay if I stay?" she asked.

"Sure. Might not be pretty, especially if *Herr* Klaus Rettke is in it."

"I'm good." Her lungs moved into double time and belied the coolness in her words.

Chapter 11

Mead guided Maggie to the second floor of the Metro Police building and into a small conference room. The room boasted a beat-up table and chairs, a metal cart with a TV and DVD player and a white screen hanging crookedly from a roller on the wall.

"Ah," Maggie said. "High tech."

"Only the best for Metro PD," Mead said.

Delacruz, besides being the squad's Lothario, was also the techie for the division. His technical prowess, however, was severely limited when he tackled a pre-historic 16mm film projector situated on a small handcart. Now he was gingerly threading a reel of film onto the sprockets of the ancient machine. "Holy Mama, no wonder they don't use these friggin' things no more."

Mead plopped himself into a chair next to Maggie and eyed the brown-edged film. "Film looks sixty years old."

"I didn't think there were any sixteen milimeter projectors around anymore," Maggie said.

"Hey, this is Washington, where history is an art form," Mead said.

"History, my ass, oops, 'scuse me, my eye. I hope to hell the projector don't chew up the film," Delacruz mumbled. "There." He stood and adjusted the lens. "So, what's the main feature?" Delacruz pulled over a chair, swung it around so the back was facing him and sat, legs apart.

"Bestseller from World War Two," Mead said. "We're going to find out more about art and the Nazis."

"There's got to be something about the ERR in it," Maggie said.

"What's the ERR?" Delacruz asked.

"An agency set up to confiscate art from undesirables," Maggie said.

"Undesirables? You mean like the Jews?"

"Pretty much," she said.

"Did the Nazis take the footage?" Delacruz asked.

"I believe so," Mead said.

"How are we going to understand it? You speak German, Frank?"

"Supposed to be narrated in English." Mead didn't offer Maggie's translation abilities.

Delacruz flipped the lights off and switched the projector on.

Mead's eyes blinked and squinted at the herky-jerky black and white footage. The story was narrated in reasonably comprehensible English by a German filmmaker. He glanced sideways at Maggie and wondered whether Rettke might actually be in the film.

"It is autumn in Paris, September of nineteen forty-one," the narrator began. The camera panned across gardens and historic buildings.

"An ordinary day in the French capital, leaves turning red and gold, a slight chill to the air, the Seine River flowing behind me as it has done for centuries. But this is no ordinary day here in the city of art and culture. It is a day of new beginnings. For Paris has become a central part of the Third Reich."

German foot soldiers followed tanks and jeeps up the Champs Elysée. Paris citizens posed woodenly on either side, eyes wide, dumbstruck, fists clenched in anger. This was their city, taken from them overnight. Paris under German Occupation.

The narrator resumed. "The *Einsatzstab Reichsleiter Rosenberg*, also known as the ERR--"

"Ahh," Delacruz murmured.

"--is directly under the supervision of Party leader, *Reichsminister* Alfred Rosenberg."

The camera panned *Le Musée du Louvre*, a stunning series of 12th century buildings in U-shape configuration, its old stone, now a faded buff color, the film pre-dating the famous glass pyramid of today's entryway.

"Herr Rosenberg has been placed in this most important position by *Reichsmarschall* Hermann Goering, head of the Luftwaffe. Herr Goering, an ardent art lover, collector, and benefactor is personally interested in the cultural artifacts of Europe."

"I bet he is," Maggie said.

The camera swept over rooms crowded with paintings, sculptures, and other artifacts.

"What a cache," Mead said. "I wonder how much of it wound up in Goering's hands."

"Indeed, under Goering's reign," the correspondent continued as if in response, "the ERR amassed a large number of art works from the most well-known Jewish collections."

The film suddenly began flapping on the dingy screen and the projector spit and came to a halt.

"Fuck," Delacruz said and hopped up. "Oops, sorry."

Mead caught Maggie suppressing a grin at Delacruz' attempts at gentility. His mind, though, was on Rettke. Who was he? The premiere confiscator of the ERR? A Nazi ideologue? Could he have been some kind of spy infiltrating the agency? Not likely. Maybe he was just an innocent German caught in the throes of the Reich madness. Perhaps the Party needed his talents and he was too fearful to say no.

"Here we go." Delacruz interrupted Mead's thoughts.

The projector whirred into noisy action and black and white figures jounced their way across the screen, the narrator's voice picking up the pieces of his story.

The film went on for ten more minutes and Mead thrummed his fingers on the arms of the chair. Nothing more of help. Finally the camera settled on a group of four men, three wearing German uniforms of a style Mead had never seen before. Government officials? Slowly, the photographer zeroed in on the faces close up. One by one, each countenance came into view.

Maggie sat up suddenly. "Whoa, whoa, back up. Can you back it up?"

Delacruz whistled. "Oh sure. No problem. Fuck." He played with the machine and rewound the film back a few frames. Then he switched it on again.

"There," Maggie said.

"What? There what?" Delacruz said.

"The second guy from the left. Can you freeze the frame?"

"You shittin' me or what? This is sixteen milimeter. You think it's easy to go backwards, for Chrissakes?"

"Awright, awright, shut it down," Mead said. "Try to find that spot again, with those four guys."

Delacruz played with the projector. Flicked it on, flicked it off.

They watched the film for about thirty seconds.

"There, right there," Maggie spoke now, on the edge of her chair.

The sergeant clicked off the machine and the room went dark.

She turned to Mead. "Are you thinking what I'm thinking?"

"What are you thinking?"

"Those are the same four men in Ingrid's photograph. I need to get that clip."

"Good luck," Delacruz muttered.

Maggie walked to the projector. Mead followed.

"Video editing's not my forté," she said, hands on her hips, staring at the machine. "This equipment is as state-of-the-art as my long-dead grandmother's Victrola."

"Hey, I remember Victrolas," Delacruz said. "My great aunt--"

Mead shot him a look and the sergeant clammed up.

Maggie played with the knobs on the antiquated analog machine and moved the film through frame by frame. "I'm afraid the old film will tear at the worst possible spot."

Mead leaned over her shoulder.

"Damn it, Frank. Go sit down and let me do this." Maggie said, her voice an octave above normal.

Mead grimaced and stuck his hands into his pockets. "Tense, are we?"

"Sorry."

After a minute he said, "Jeez, aren't you a digital expert?"

"This isn't digital, it's film, for heaven's sake."

Mead whistled and sat down. He kept crossing and re-crossing his legs.

Ten minutes went by. "Hey, what's this?" she said.

Mead was at her side before she finished the sentence.

"What? What?"

"This is it. This clip looks just like one of Ingrid's photos--the one where the painting in question is lined up next to other paintings. As if in a museum or at an auction house." Maggie moved from one frame to the next on the video editing system, then back again. Pressing a button on the console in front of her, she turned on the audio.

"--as we can see here at the Room of Martyrs at the Jeu de Paume in Paris," the narrator said.

"My God," she said, switching off the audio track.

"What?" Delacruz said.

"It shows us where the photographs were taken." She wheeled around to face Mead. "This means Rettke most likely took the photo of the Van Gogh there. Maybe that was his job--to take photos of the stolen works of art, all the ones brought to Paris."

"You think he was a photographer?" Mead said. "Hmm. Maybe it was his job to record all the confiscated works, keep track of their destinations, even their provenance. At least it gives us a starting point."

"Someone want to fill me in?" Delacruz said.

"If the painting in the photographs was confiscated during World War Two, there might be records of it, maybe through the Holocaust Museum or the Wiesenthal Agency," Maggie said.

"So we can track down its whereabouts," Mead said. "Now what about the four Nazis in the film?"

"Right." She returned to searching frame by frame until her neck must've ached from the awkward position.

"Don't give up," he said. "It's there."

"Got it."

Mead jumped up and rushed over. "Where?"

She held a hand up to keep him away and slid the film off the reels. Then she laid the section of film down on the table. With a manicure scissors from her bag she cut out the frame in question.

"Hey, what the hell are you doing? Don't--" Mead started.

"Not to worry, I can splice it back into the film." She turned to him and grinned, holding the tiny celluloid square by the edge. "Now, I've got a photo negative to work with."

"And you want me to tell Archives what?" Delacruz asked.

"Nothing," Mead said. "Hold onto the film until Maggie's finished fixing it." He turned to her, scowling.

She smiled.

Mead drove her back to the University Lab and they hustled into the building. He punched the elevator button over and over.

"It won't get here any faster," she said.

They reached her office on the fourth floor and he followed on her heels. "So, how long will this take?"

She looked at him with a frown. "An hour, more or less."

"Which, more or less?" His cell phone beeped. "Mead. Yeah?" he shouted into it. "I'm not yelling. What?"

Maggie set her computer up then went off to scan the film. When she returned, he was clipping his phone to his belt.

"Gotta go," he said. "Call me when you have something to look at."

She didn't respond as he left. Her eyes were already on the computer screen.

"You're welcome," he muttered.

When Mead had gone, Maggie stared at the closed door. What the hell was wrong with her? He was only trying to help and she was being a bitch. Face it, she told herself. This was her self-defense mechanism. She knew Mead was interested. Hell, she was interested. Bad move to get involved now. With a deep sigh, she turned back to the computer.

It took less time than she'd anticipated. In an hour, Maggie had a grainy blow-up of the four men in the German propaganda film. She examined and re-examined the second man from the left. That was Rettke, she was sure. The other men were Goering and Rosenberg. And that fourth man was definitely the mysterious one that looked scared to death. These were the same four men as in Ingrid's picture.

She gazed at them in the grainy photograph and wondered about the unknown man. He'd be in his eighties today, like Rettke. Could he be Ingrid's killer?

Chapter 12

Later that day at the Faculty Lounge at Georgetown University, Maggie spotted Henri from afar and threaded her way through faculty and student servers, dozens of tables and chairs, and a salad bar to reach him. He stood and smiled and she was once again struck by those eyes, ink-blue like new denim.

They ordered sandwiches and coffee and, impatient for answers, Maggie launched right in.

"Henri, before we talk about the painting, tell me what you know about Klaus Rettke."

Henri looked at her with an unhappy expression, brows furrowed and eyes narrowed.

She continued. "Look, Rettke is dead and so is his granddaughter, my best friend. I want to know why someone killed her."

"Klaus Rettke was a member of the ERR. You know who they were?"

Maggie nodded.

"Indeed, he was the primary man who confiscated works of art in Paris. He photographed them, catalogued them and shipped them to specified locations all over the Reich."

Maggie said nothing for several long minutes. She turned the possibilities over in her mind. Finally, when she realized Henri was staring at her, she said. "Is there any chance he was a member of the underground or a personal savior of the art? Could he have been trying to save the art?" It sounded ridiculous even to herself.

"Ahh, a personal savior? You mean like Rose Valland?"

"Like Rose, yes."

"*Mais non, Cherie.* I wish I could say that was so, but *non.*" He stopped and stared into his cup. "To say Madame Valland and Klaus Rettke in the same breath is almost sacrilegious."

Maggie concentrated on her coffee. "You make it sound like Rose Valland was a saint."

"In a way she was. Because of her, many pieces of art have been recovered and returned to the world." He touched her hand. "Maggie, please understand my clumsiness here. You are trying to help find out who killed your friend. But it is too late, both for her and for Klaus Rettke. He was a monster and that is the truth."

"Let's talk about the painting then."

"Of course." His shoulders straightened and he seemed eager to move on. "Now, the painting."

"Is it a Van Gogh?"

"There is no way I can be absolutely sure from a photograph. If you asked me to testify in court as such, I would have to say *I don't know.*"

"But you believe it is a Van Gogh?"

He ran his finger along the edge of his cup. "I believe it *may* be a genuine Van Gogh, one which has been missing since World War Two."

"Confiscated?"

"Very possibly. What do you know about the painting?" he asked.

"From my research," she said, " I know that it's called several things depending upon which source you use: *Vase With Oleanders* or *Flower Vase on Yellow Background.* And that it seems to have disappeared in the nineteen forties."

He finished his coffee and took a bite of his ham and cheese croissant. "Do you know much about the spoils of war?" he asked.

"A little, thanks to Rudolf. I know that the Nazis seized a great many works of art and cultural artifacts during the War. And, recently, I've been reading stories about museums attempting to verify the provenance of pieces in their collections to ensure they aren't among the stolen ones. Also," she went on, "there are a number of Holocaust survivors and their descendants who are suing today for the rightful return of their property."

"*Oui*. Even more than sixty years later, lost and stolen objects continue to appear on the art market and in private museum and state collections. Incredibly valuable pieces." His eyes shone. "Recently, in fact, they discovered gold treasures excavated by Schliemann at Troy. And old master drawings from the Franz Koenigs collection." He paused. "Questions of ownership, however, are unresolved. They're constantly the subject of court battles. It's a huge black market business as well."

Maggie stretched a strand of long, wavy hair around her finger, a childhood habit she couldn't shake.

Henri went on. "There are a number of unscrupulous collectors who will go to any length, including breaking the law, to have the works they desire." Henri lapsed into silence. "It is sad. So much beauty lost to the world."

"If this painting is a real Van Gogh, how much would it be worth today?"

He shrugged. "Who knows? Fifty million euros, er, perhaps sixty-five million dollars or more." He leaned forward and Maggie caught a wisp of his after-shave.

"That much?" she managed despite the distraction.

"In 1998 Christie's sold a self-portrait of Van Gogh, painted in the asylum in which he resided at *St. Remy*, for an astounding seventy-one million dollars."

She opened her mouth then closed it.

"The point is the painting would be priceless from an art and history perspective. Tell me, Maggie, do you have any idea where it might be? Did Rettke leave your friend any clues?"

She shook her head. "I wish he did. It might solve her murder." At that moment, her eye caught a face sitting several tables away, newspaper rolled in his hands. The face was familiar. A dark skinned man, Middle Eastern, black hair and eyes. Like the man who stole her bag in the train station. An electric jolt ran through her. Was it him? She stared but the man kept reading the paper. She couldn't be sure.

Henri brought her back to their conversation. "What I wouldn't give to see this painting in the museum. Such a coup." He leaned back in his chair. "Maggie? Are you all right?"

"Yes, yes, of course. Where were we? If the painting in the photograph is not an authentic Van Gogh, if it's a forgery, how would we know?" she asked.

"It would be very difficult to determine, especially if it's a good forgery. A photograph has far too little information to be able to perform a true appraisal." Henri shook his head. "There would be no reliable way to authenticate."

They fell silent and sipped the last of their coffee. Maggie's eyes traveled to the dark man, but he was still into his paper.

She looked at Henri and felt safe in his company. Maybe not safe like with Frank Mead but

. . . now where did that come from? Her mind was difficult to control these days, thoughts meandering up weird, unexpected paths.

With a deep exhalation she said, "I've been thinking about how to resolve this dilemma. I've come up with an idea." She took a breath. "You're familiar with how science is used in the authentication process. Infrared reflectography, spectral imaging--"

"Oui."

"Anyway, I've been thinking of another way to use science, digital photography actually, to do something similar."

"Go on," Henri said.

"I propose to digitally compare a known Van Gogh with the painting in question."

He frowned.

"Stay with me," she said. "I take a photograph of a Van Gogh at the museum. I then design a program that will read the characteristics of the painting and match them with Rettke's painting." She began to get into the technicalities then stopped when she noticed his eyes narrow.

"I realize that digital photography is your field," he said, "but I don't see how comparing *photographs* of paintings can be accurate, or useful, for that matter. They're still photographs."

She flashed a quick smile, not giving him a chance to argue.

"Hear me out. We have two pictures, one a known Van Gogh, one Rettke's painting. Visualize them side by side on the computer. There are thousands of details in these electronic images, more than you can imagine. If I could match elements of the one painting with the second--"

"You mean like fingerprints?"

"Yes, in a way. I'll need your help as an art expert. If I could measure them side by side against each other, what would I be looking for in terms of comparison?"

His eyebrows came together.

"Forget the fact that we're looking at photographs," Maggie said, excitement raising goose bumps on her skin. "Think in terms of working with the actual paintings. What would I be looking for in comparing two paintings?"

"Well, so many things," he began. "Brushstrokes--the length, type, pressure, thickness. Textures--thin, fine, coarse, impasto--"

"Impasto?"

"It means highly textured, thick with brush marks."

Maggie nodded. "What else?"

"Tone. Very important is the tone of a painting--such as chiaroscuro, which, literally, means light and dark. Contrasts in tone are very distinctive between painters. Then there is glaze. Is it transparent or translucent?" He paused for a breath. "Underdrawing or underpainting--did the artist block in the drawing first and begin adding colors to the basics, then there's--"

"Okay, stop. I get the idea," Maggie said. "But this is good news. It means that we can at least narrow down the field. If Rettke's Van Gogh doesn't match the one in the Gallery based on those criteria then it's, well, eliminated as authentic, isn't it?"

"Perhaps, but it is tricky. There were master forgers who could reproduce some of the artist's techniques, down to the glaze and tone and texture."

"Yes, I understand. But I'm not talking about a good forgery. A *bad* forgery would stick out like a. . . a ten-year old's finger-painting in a field of Rembrandts, right?"

He smiled. "*Écoutez*, Maggie. I don't want to discourage you. Go ahead and design a program. It's definitely worth a try. I'll help you if I can."

She pushed her coffee cup under the pot the waitress brought by. Once again she turned to the table where the dark man sat. He was gone. Her heart dropped its cadence a beat. She turned to Henri and asked, "Do you know an art expert named Emil Kahn?"

Henri seemed to blanche. Or was that her imagination?

"Emil is quite famous, does consulting for the auction houses, museums, and the National Gallery from time to time. Why?"

"Lieutenant Mead, the homicide cop that's investigating Ingrid's murder, suggested bringing him in as police expert. I guess he's worked with him before. Perhaps you and I can meet with Dr. Kahn and pool our information."

"Ah, *oui*. Emil would be an excellent choice, indeed."

The sudden flatness in his eyes and the rigid line of his mouth, however, told her he thought otherwise.

Chapter 13

The next morning, Maggie arrived at the National Gallery of Art and descended the stairs to the lower level and Henri's office. There she would meet Dr. Emil Kahn. *The* Emil Kahn. Internet research had produced pages of information on the art expert who "knew Van Gogh like the fingers of his hands." Kahn had been in the art field more than fifty years and all the well-known auction houses as well as wealthy collectors paid him highly for his services. She worried, however, that he was not someone who relied on science and technology for his expert opinion.

The blood surged through her body, her heart high on adrenaline. She wished Mead was joining them. . . at least she'd have one proponent for her theories. But he had to be in court on another case. Still there was Henri, although he had proven a reluctant disciple. Today, she'd have to present her argument to both art dilettantes.

Henri's windowless office was splashed with the vivid colors of a poster of a Cezanne exhibition. A small conference table rested in the corner and an elderly man was seated in a dark leather chair beside it. A cane leaned against the wall.

Henri stood by his desk talking on the phone. He waved her in and gestured to the other man.

"Dr. Kahn?" she said. "Please, don't get up. I'm happy to meet you. Maggie Thornhill." She took off her raincoat, brushed a few strands of hair back and sat down.

"Miss Thornhill--"

"Maggie, please."

"Maggie. First, please let me offer my condolences about your friend. Henri briefed me."

"Thank you," she said.

"So," he began. "I, too, am pleased that we meet. I have heard a great deal about you."

"Yes?" She speculated on his accent. French? He wore a navy blazer and button-down white shirt, more Ivy League than continental.

"Ah, you want me to pin the blame on Henri. Well, my dear, your name is synonymous with digital photography in this town."

She smiled, recognizing Kahn as a charmer. "Well thank you, but I hardly think that's the case."

"Henri did brief me on this situation. In fact, he shared with me your friend's photographs." He looked at Henri, who set the phone down at that instant.

"So sorry. I promise no more interruptions." Henri took Maggie's hand and squeezed it gently. Then he pulled out a chair. "*Alors*, shall we begin?"

Kahn turned to Maggie. "Now what's this about a software program to prove a painting's authenticity?"

"Well, *proving* authenticity is a bit optimistic. Remember, this is a photo, not the painting. However, I believe I can design a program to recognize patterns that can determine a painting's attribution; for instance, patterns in color contrast, brush strokes, impasto--" She shot Henri a smile to show she remembered his art lesson. Then she began to explain the technical features, how wavelet decomposition can break down a digital image for purposes of analysis.

Kahn twisted in his chair and drummed his fingers on the table.

She went on. "Technology is changing the face of art conservation. X-ray machines scan paintings for cracks, much the way they look under the skin for broken bones. The way needles are used in biopsies, in the art world they can pull paint chips from paintings for examination under a microscope. Infrared cameras and x-rays can look beneath a painted surface to see if another painting is hidden behind it. Pigment identification is employed to determine the date of the paints used." Maggie stopped, pushed her chair back. "Please stop me if you know all this."

Kahn nodded once. "Hmm. In fact, I believe so-called artificial intelligence has been used before to identify drawings of Delacroix."

"True," Henri said. "If I recall correctly they analyzed the length, thickness, and curvature of the lines. . . something about black and white pixels and ratio between them in a Delacroix versus another artist."

"Ah, so," Kahn said. "But unfortunately, the process is not always accurate. They could not use the results."

Now his accent sounded German and it reminded her of Ingrid. . . and Ingrid's grandfather. Her hands went cold. Maggie studied him more closely. Long thin face, prominent nose, slightly reddish complexion, topped by a head of thick silvery white hair.

Henri mumbled something about coffee to fill the awkward silence.

Neither of his guests responded.

Maggie addressed Kahn. "I'm not proposing that this method will be the DNA of art authentication, but I think the results could lend support to the evidence either for or against a painting being genuine."

Henri nodded, apparently more excited about the prospects than he had been the day before. Kahn, however, looked unconvinced, his brows drawn together in a v-shape. He looked at her with gray eyes just short of icy.

"All right, then. Tell me," Kahn said. "How exactly would you analyze these photographs in your quest for authenticity?"

She looked from Kahn to Henri, then back, took a breath and began. "First, I'd have to compress the photo in order to break it down into simpler parts, wavelets. These decomposed wavelets would give us the more basic subbands of the image."

"Subbands? Please," Kahn said. "I can send an e-mail but otherwise computers and I do not get on so well." His smile looked pained.

"Think of a musical tone--made up of a low fundamental frequency with higher frequency overtones. A photograph's lower subbands show the broad strokes of the painting, while the higher subbands display more intricate detail.

"It's similar to how they work in computer animation. Animators who create movies like *Finding Nemo* use such layering to devise the characters." Maggie stopped, realized she was losing him. Kahn didn't seem like a *Finding Nemo* kind of guy.

"Look, once we're down to the *subband* level of the image, we can do a statistical analysis," she said, " let's say, of the distance between the eyes on a face, or the orientation of vertical or horizontal lines. Wavelet decomposition is superb at analyzing textures. A smooth surface in a painting, like a calm lake, would show up in the lower frequency subbands while white water waves in the same painting would produce more activity in the higher frequency subbands."

"Makes sense, Emil," Henri said. He reached over for a pitcher of water on his desk and poured three glasses.

Maggie recognized that Henri was nervous, as if it was his responsibility for her and Emil to get along. She continued, "Why couldn't those subbands tell us a master from a forger? It's purely mathematical."

Kahn folded his hands in his lap. He took his time gathering his thoughts. "I am an old man, Maggie, and therefore, an old-fashioned man. I appreciate the possibilities that science has to offer art. However, as a professional in the art world, right now I would have to say that the final decision about who painted a certain painting has got to be based on *human* opinion."

"Opinion?" She was about to say more when she noticed the tiny smile at the corners of his mouth. "All right," she went on, "if you want to discount science, at least consider provenance. Where does that fit in?"

He cleared his throat. "It is rare to find a painting with a fully documented history. And for those documents to prove authenticity they must be very specifically formatted, in chronological order, with clearly stated relationships between owners and methods of transactions, and the list goes on. However--" He stopped and looked at her with eyes like ball bearings.

"Go on."

"There are some things you simply know intuitively when you are a student of a particular artist. For example, Vincent Van Gogh. I have studied his work for fifty years. I can look at a painting and tell you, ninety-nine percent of the time, what year he painted it in and where he was. I can tell you that he started to use blue-yellow opponency in 1887 and red-green later on, or that he used opponent color to highlight portraits of humans at a certain time in his life. How do I know this? Because I know his work, I know the man, the artist--in here." He thumped his chest.

"That is all well and good, Emil," Henri said. "But you have not studied all eight hundred and fifty-four of his paintings, nor has anyone living today. Many paintings are still missing since World War Two. That is the point." Henri pointed at Maggie. "Her software program could add to the repertoire of technology used to determine attribution. It can only help."

Kahn took his cane and rapped it on the carpeted floor. To Maggie he said, "How would your computer program account for the fact that artists sometimes change their style, perhaps in one painting, perhaps in one period of time? Spontaneous change. Brushstrokes entirely different than previously presented--smooth, soft lines, rather than vigorous, energetic slashes. An attempt to imitate another artist, maybe?"

Maggie knew she was losing the battle.

"Or," Kahn continued. "What about *schools* of an artist? Perhaps a student of Van Gogh tried to imitate the master and succeeded. Could you tell the difference?"

"Probably not," she admitted. "But aside from those exceptions why not?"

"There would be many more exceptions, I guarantee," Kahn said, a smile breaking through the gaunt face.

"In Van Gogh's case, he had no school of artists under him," Henri said. "So that should not be an issue."

"Don't be sure," Kahn said. "There were many young artists in Provence who could easily have copied the style, despite the fact that Van Gogh wasn't successful in his own lifetime." Kahn smiled at her again.

She felt patronized. "I appreciate all your advice, Dr. Kahn, and I understand your concerns."

"Do you?"

"What you're saying is that art experts like to rely on established traditions rather than innovative technology that might put their neck on the line." She watched the frown on Kahn's face deepen. "It would be extremely embarrassing for the Metropolitan Museum of Art or Sothebys to learn that their expensive purchases of art objects turn out to be fakes." She paused. "And, in this society, we'd have an epidemic of lawsuits."

Out of the corner of her eye, she could see Henri suppressing a smile.

"All right, my dear," Kahn said. "I see I cannot convince you otherwise. Would you still like my help on Van Gogh paintings?"

Would she? Maggie nodded but felt uneasy. After Kahn's vehement opposition a few moments ago, she didn't believe he could really be committed to help. She reached for her water as a distraction. When she looked up, Kahn was smiling at her. The smile never reached his eyes.

An hour later in his colonial home, one that was the same age as he, Emil Kahn lit a cigarette and tossed the match in the fireplace. Despite his daily regimen of exercise, his knees popped as he sat down in his favorite lounge chair and lifted his legs onto the matching footstool.

Getting old stinks. Eighty-four. How did that happen? When did it happen?

More and more now he would think back on his life. Memories seemed almost more important than the present. But the future? That was important, urgent, even. For his family relied on him.

His wife, Serena, still lovely despite the thickening waist and gray-turning-to-white hair, came into the room. "Emil, Tanya and Morey called, but you were in your office so I didn't interrupt. They said, 'Tell Grandpa,' hi, dude.'"

She laughed.

He loved her laugh. "What is this *dude* stuff? No respect for age."

"Ach, kids. Do you want your pills now?" Serena asked as she straightened out the couch pillows.

"I'll take them later."

As he watched her, that dreaded feeling returned. How could he keep her safe? And the kids? Protect his family. That's every man's right.

Fear lay like a coiled snake in his gut, always ready to squirm. The past was always in the way, always. He would never be rid of it. And now, this woman, this Margaret, Maggie, Thornhill. He had to offer his help, his expertise. No choice. How else could he keep an eye on her?

He sank into his swivel chair and let his head rest in his hands on the desk. Why? Why him? He was a good man, wasn't he? What did God think? Did God care more about a man's deeds or his intentions? Stop it. Stop it.

The words boomed in his head.

There is no choice and you will do what you have to do. Besides, it is far too late now.

Kahn stubbed out his cigarette in an ashtray near the chair and pushed himself up. He rolled his shoulders back and stretched his arms then proceeded to his office at the back of the house. He closed and locked the door. Serena knew not to bother him unless it was an emergency and even then she would call him on the intercom.

Right now he had a job to do. He stood over his desk staring down at the innocuous white envelope. He picked it up and held it in his hands, felt the smoothness, the crispness of the paper, now starting to show signs of wear. Then he opened it for the tenth time and slid out the contents. It was a color photograph of a Van Gogh painting and it looked up at him from the cherry wood surface of the desk.

He stared at it, as if to prevent it from disappearing. An old pendulum clock on the wall ticked away the minutes. His eyes lost focus and his mind drifted back in time. He could see the real painting so clearly: oil on canvas 56cm X 36cm, painted in Arles, France, August, 1888 by Vincent Van Gogh, signed Vincent in the lower left corner, whereabouts unknown, possibly stolen in 1944. *Still Life: Vase With Oleanders.* Perspective slightly off, colors not as bright as his other works, this painting had a uniqueness to it. It was darker than many of his still lifes, somehow matching the artist and his moods. But ethereal rather than earthy. Indeed, he thought, the painting touched the very core of his soul.

Ahh, Vincent, the world remembers you for color and light, for wheat fields and starry nights, for sunflowers and dramatic self-portraits. But this painting is truly you. The dark, deep tones, like your earlier potato farmers, reach within and draw out one's hidden emotions.

A phone rang somewhere in the house but Kahn paid it no mind. He picked up the photograph again and ran his fingers over the surface.

"I'm sorry, Vincent. So sorry."

Chapter 14

At eight o'clock on the night of her meeting with Kahn and Henri, Maggie re-read Klaus Rettke's diary entries. A mixture of anger and sadness welled up inside her. For Ingrid's sake, she wanted badly to believe her friend's grandfather wasn't a Nazi, to find some justification for his actions during the war. But there was little doubt. At least according to Henri.

Still, one thought kept nagging at her. Perhaps Rettke wanted, in fact, to save the paintings from the Nazis, not destroy them. Despite being intimidated by Alfred Rosenberg, perhaps he had stolen many works of art, not just one, and had them safely conveyed out of the country. Or at the very least, kept them catalogued and tracked so he could find them after the war. Like Rose Valland.

But that begged another question. If Rettke did save the paintings, was it for altruistic reasons . . . to return them to their rightful owners? Or for personal gain?

Maggie ran her fingers over the worn leather wishing that the words beneath the cover were different. The doorbell interrupted her reveries. She opened it to Frank Mead.

"Hey, thanks for coming," she said. "It's kind of late, but I wanted to bounce some ideas off you."

"I'm here to serve."

She smiled. "I just happen to have a beer for your trouble. Interested?"

"Oh yeah. I'm off duty."

She retrieved a Beck's from the refrigerator.

"Beck's, eh? That works." He yanked on his tie to loosen it and sat on the couch. Rosie ambled over and he ran his fingers through her fur.

"Tell me about your meeting with Emil Kahn," Mead said.

Maggie relayed her conversation with Emil and Henri.

"Sounds like Dr. Kahn's a bit of a *prima donna*. What's this Henri like?"

"Uh, besides gorgeous?"

Mead looked at her with a frown. "Watch out, he's French."

"What does that mean?"

"They're notorious charmers. Unlike good old American guys like me. Down to earth. Whatever I say is precisely what I mean."

"Are you putting me on?"

He smiled. "Okay, forget it. Now what ideas do you want to bounce off me?"

She hesitated a moment, knowing Mead was going to blow his stack when he heard about the diary.

All he said was, "You found what?" In a very soft voice.

She felt her mouth go dry. "Let me finish, Frank, before you go ballistic on me." She watched him squeeze his eyes shut and open them to pale blue marbles.

Maggie explained how she chanced upon Rettke's hiding place in the big screen TV. Then she went into the bedroom, brought out the diary and handed it to Mead.

He opened it gently, aware of the age and brittleness of its pages. He shook his head from side to side. "Maggie, I don't know what to say."

"I had to see what Rettke wrote first, for myself, for Ingrid, before I showed it to you."

"Oh, you were going to show it to me? Nice. When?"

"After I translated it. What good is it to you in German?"

"Don't you get it?"

Maggie knew he was trying to hang on to his patience.

"You can't be the translator. It's called conflict of interest, Maggie."

"I'm sorry, I just--"

He dropped his head into his hands. "Jesus, Jesus."

"Look, Frank." She touched his arm. "Let me finish the translation and you can have it. Get your own German interpreters. Whatever. But I, I have to know who Rettke was. I have to. For Ingrid."

"You already know who he was."

She picked up the diary. "Yes, I think I do."

"Listen to me, Maggie. Everything isn't about you. My job, my reputation, is on the line here. Do you realize how much trouble I could get in if someone found out you had evidence that wasn't turned over? I mean, what the hell are you thinking?"

She put her hand on his arm. "I'm really sorry, Frank. I'll take full responsibility. I'll bring it down to Metro and hand it over to the Commissioner himself if you want. Just, please give me another day."

He leaned back, squeezed his eyes closed a minute. "I'll give you 'til tomorrow noon to make a copy of it. Then I want this diary in police custody. Or you will be."

"Deal," she said.

Both of them stared at Rosie.

"What did you learn so far?" he asked.

Her eyes gleamed as she related the first two chapters of Rettke's journal. "I've put together an outline of the key facts. Interested?"

He threw up a hand and nodded, apparently too weary from berating her to do more. Her heart did a tiny flip as she looked into his eyes. He felt betrayed. By her.

She grabbed her notepad and ignored the tightness in her chest. "It starts in 1941 and I've made some notes."

"Go on."

"Here are the players he mentioned. First there's Josef Steiner, a Jewish art dealer who owned a gallery in Paris. Josef claimed to have protection for his gallery works, protection that was provided . . . then rescinded by Klaus Rettke. Question: Was Steiner a Nazi collaborator? Did he work with the ERR to save his galleries and art?

"Next there's Jakob Steiner, the son, maybe eighteen years old. He seemed innocent of his father's relationship with the Nazis. Or was he?

"Third is Collette Rousseau, a young girl who worked at the Gallery. She tried to aid the elder Steiner when he showed signs of a heart attack. Steiner died, by the way, after his confrontation with Rettke. So how much did Collette know about their relationship?

"And fourth, there's Alfred Rosenberg, the head of the ERR and from all I've read, a Nazi fanatic completely loyal to Hitler. What was Rettke's relationship with him? Were they friends, colleagues or the opposite?" She took a long, slow breath. "He's the second uniform in the black and white snapshot."

"I remember," Mead said.

"From the diary I had a feeling that Rettke feared Rosenberg. But then, if he stole a painting, why wouldn't he?"

Mead listened then said, "Maybe Steiner is the fourth man in the picture. The reluctant conspirator."

Maggie looked at him.

"Go on," he said.

"Next entry. Enter Hans Van Meegeren, infamous master forger. When Aaron Beckman approached me at the museum he said his father purchased the painting from Van Meegeren who somehow got it from Rettke." She went on, breathless. "From the diary, Rettke commissioned Van Meegeren to copy a painting he'd stolen from the Nazis. Now the guesswork: Did Rettke return the original and sell the fake? Is it possible he not only stole art *for* the Reich but *from* the Reich? And, made a profit from it." She looked down at the diary. "God, Ingrid's grandfather must have been mad. If this is true, maybe there are other paintings, other works of art that he copied and sold."

"What about Rose Valland?" Mead asked. "Rose must have known Rettke. They were both at the Jeu du Paume during the same time period. If the curator kept a secret log of the confiscated works, perhaps she knew of his deceit. Perhaps she was familiar with the Van Gogh he had forged."

Maggie stopped, pen in the middle of a word. "Track down Rose's writings." She scribbled. "If Rettke had a fake Van Gogh, where is it? Did he sell it?"

"We're checking his bank accounts but coming up with zilch," he said. "Big question--is it a real Van Gogh in the photographs or a Van Meegeren fake?"

"I know it's crazy but I don't think Rettke sold the real painting. I think he kept it." She mused a moment. "The painting was definitely motivation for murder. So where the hell could it be?"

At that moment, Mead's cell phone bleeped out a weak chirp. He listened, said "yeah" twice. Then he turned to her, subdued. "Aaron Beckman's dead."

"What?" Maggie said, picturing the creepy little man who stalked her in the museum. "What do you mean, dead?"

"Dead as in bullet to the heart."

She could feel her face drain of blood.

"Let's go to the hospital morgue," Mead said, "and see if this is the same guy from the museum."

After confirming the man in the morgue as the one she knew as Aaron Beckman, Maggie and Mead took the elevator to the third floor and a small conference room in the hospital where Sergeant Delacruz sat in front of a tiny elderly woman. The sergeant sat on a straight back chair and the woman seemed to almost disappear in a well-worn sofa.

Despite her frail appearance, Mrs. Samuel Beckman, mother of the deceased Aaron, was anything but. She fought her eighty-something years with a feisty attitude, designer outfit and makeup. Lots of it. Her silver hair shone in a coiffed bowl and her pancaked skin stretched tight over fragile cheekbones.

Maggie wondered how many collagen and Botox injections and cosmetic surgeries she'd endured and why would any woman put herself through that? Then Maggie recalled gazing at the new lines on her own face in the mirror that very morning.

Mead introduced everyone.

"So, you are the one," she said to Maggie. "It was your friend's grandfather who was responsible for this tragedy, this, horror that I have to live through again." Mrs. Beckman struggled to rise.

Mead touched her shoulder gently and urged her back into the cushions. "Just a minute, Miz Beckman. Please, sit, sit. I know you're upset, but we need your help on this. Okay?" He waited for her curt nod. "How did you know about Rettke's relationship with Miz Thornhill?"

"What? Oh, your Sergeant here told me."

Mead turned a heated glare on Delacruz, who leaped to his feet and said, "Why don't I get some coffee and soft drinks for everyone?" He was out the door before his boss could sputter.

Mead inhaled and turned to Mrs. Beckman. "Now, Miz Beckman, tell us your story."

"Again? I already talked to--"

"I understand, but it helps if several of us have the facts directly from you. Please."

Mrs. Beckman cleared her throat and clasped her thousand-dollar Gucci signature purse with iridescent pink nails. "All right, all right." She sighed the sigh of all the world's guilt.

"My husband, Samuel, God bless him, he's been dead twenty years, you know. . . well, Samuel bought a painting, an original Vincent Van Gogh, for three million dollars after the war. That was a lot of money in those days, you know. He bought it from a reputable art dealer who claims to have gotten it from that swine, Rettke." She shook a gnarled finger at Maggie.

"Go on now," Mead said.

"Samuel bought that painting in good faith and see, look at the fix I'm in. Poor Aaron, oh, dear God."

"Excuse me, Mrs. Beckman," Maggie said. "Did your husband have the painting authenticated?"

"He did, by a so-called expert that Rettke brought in. Expert. Rettke's expert. In a pig's eye."

"What about provenance? Were there any papers with it?" Maggie asked.

"I don't know. Probably. But I can't find them. Who knows, provenance, shmovenance. Anyway, my son, Aaron, my only son, you know, and now he's dead, he counted on that painting being real, he-- " No tears fell from her crinkled hazel eyes. She looked from Mead to Maggie and as if to justify her last statement said, "Well, he needed money, bad business deals and such, so I gave him the painting and what, what do you think? He finds out it is a fake, and not even a good fake, mind you."

"A good fake?" Mead asked.

Mrs. Beckman went on. "There's good, there's bad. Some forgers were better than others and now those forgeries are even worth money."

"Really?" Mead said.

"Oh, yes. Hans Van Meegeren was a master forger," the old woman said. "His copies are worth a great deal--certainly not what the original artist's work is, but a lot. Unfortunately, Van Meegeren was not the forger in this case. We checked with experts on that possibility too."

Maggie was puzzled now. *Not* a Van Meegeren?

Mrs. Beckman sighed again. "Somewhere, someone has the real Van Gogh."

And somewhere, someone has the real Van Meegeren, Maggie thought.

Mrs. Beckman continued, "Klaus Rettke knows, he knows." She shook a fist in the air and her feet left the floor.

"Klaus Rettke knew, Miz Beckman," Mead said. "He's dead, remember?"

"Good, I'm glad. My son is dead, *he* should be dead."

Maggie bit her lower lip as Mead put a hand on her arm.

Ramón Delacruz came in with a tray on which coffee cups and soda cans teetered. He set it down on a small card table. "Help yourself. What'd I miss?"

"Later," Mead said, his meaning clear. He reached on his desk for a file folder. He pulled out Maggie's enlargement of Rettke's photo. "Is this the painting, Miz Beckman?"

The old woman glanced at it and waved her hand in dismissal. "Of course, it's the painting. Don't tell me you don't even--"

"We have to confirm every detail," Mead said, his increased frustration demonstrated by his posture: stiff and all angles. He stood. "Well, Miz Beckman, you've been a great help. I may have some more questions for you later, if that's okay."

"Lieutenant," she said as he helped her up from the couch. "You will, um, I mean--?"

"Of course, Ma'am, we'll do our best to find Aaron's killer," he said.

She shook her head and not a hair moved. "Oh yeah, yeah, but what I was going to say was . . . you will find the painting, won't you?"

Chapter 15

Four Nazis. Or were there only three? Maggie sat at her desk at home and stared at the four men in the Nazi film clip. The same men as in Ingrid's photo. She had identified three of them. The fourth man, however, was unknown. He was taller than the others with dark, curly hair, prominent nose, sad eyes and no smile. In fact, she noted again how miserably unhappy he looked. Who was he? Maggie couldn't help but think he was the key to two murders. Perhaps a facial recognition program could identify him.

She switched on her scanner and printer and refilled her coffee cup for the third time. As she sipped, her mind drifted to the two art experts whose help she would need. Henri Benoit. She could visualize him so clearly—the five o'clock shadow on his face any time of day, the intense dark eyes, the narrow waist, wide shoulders--and wondered when was the last time she'd been in bed with a gorgeous man. Or any man, for that matter?

She only hoped she could count on Henri when she started working on her new art authentication program, ARTEC, she'd named it, which was already outlined in her mind.

Emil Kahn. Something told her not to trust him. But perhaps that was her pride talking. Kahn had made it clear that he didn't believe she could pull this off, that technology could not verify what an expert knew instinctively.

She scanned in the black and white image at a high resolution then exploded the fourth man's face so it filled the screen. He could then be matched with a series of known Nazis in a WWII database established by the Allies in 1947. A tingle began to rise on Maggie's arms as she anticipated the results. She split the screen and, with the fourth man's image on the left, began her comparative analysis between him and a stream of images of Nazis on the right.

She hit Enter and the program whirred into life. Images flashed by too quickly to recognize but if and when a match was found, the computer would signal her.

Her computer was high speed, still the huge amount of data took a while to process. In the meantime, she swung over to another computer on her U-shaped desk to get on the Internet.

In the Google search box, she typed in ERR and Nazi Germany. Even though she knew the essence of the Nazi organization, she hungered for more information. Streams of data poured out as if she'd hit the jackpot at Harrah's. Maggie scrolled through the documents but found nothing she didn't already know. Until she chanced upon this:

"*Fuhrer Decree*

Jews, Freemasons and the other ideological opponents of National Socialism allied to them are the instigators of the current war against the Reich. The organized intellectual struggle against these forces is a vitally necessary war task.

I have therefore instructed Reichsleiter Rosenberg to carry out this task in cooperation with the Head of the Armed Forces High Command. His Operational Staff for the occupied territories has the right to examine libraries, archives, lodges and other ideological and cultural institutions of all kinds to have them confiscated for the ideological purposes of the Nazi Party and the subsequent scientific research work of the 'Hohe Schule.' Maggie stopped. What's this? She immediately swiveled over to her other computer and checked. Aloud she read:

"In January 1940 Hitler informed all offices of the Party and State that Alfred Rosenberg, the Party's ideologue, should be assisted in assembling a library for the planned new educational and research institute of the Party, the *Hohe Schule*, to be located at the Chiemsee in Bavaria. The library would contain 500, 000 volumes and there would be a multi-purpose auditorium accommodating an audience of 3,000 people. Preparations for the Hohe Schule also included other branches within the Reich, such as a 'Centre for

Research on the Jewish Question' in Frankfurt." The Jewish Question. She turned back to the other document:

"*Cultural property, which is in the hands of or belongs to the Jews, or is ownerless, or for which no clearly identifiable origin can be established, is subject to the same regulations.*

The necessary measures within the eastern territories under German administration will be taken by Reichsleiter Rosenberg in his capacity as Reich Minister for the occupied eastern territories.

Adolf Hitler, Fuhrer HQ, 1 March, 1942"

The hair on her neck rose. This document was actually signed by Hitler. She punched the keyboard and clicked on two more sites. Photos of Alfred Rosenberg and Hermann Goering popped up. A bell alerted her to the main computer. She turned back to her digital analysis. The image was complete. No known match to the fourth man. Did that mean he wasn't a Nazi?

Her cell rang. She recognized the number.

"Hey, Frank."

"Aaron Beckman and Ingrid Rettke were killed with the same gun."

"Are you surprised?" she asked.

"The gun was a Walther PP.32 caliber automatic pistol."

"German?"

"Dating back to the thirties."

"Jeez, I guess it still works."

"Sure, if someone took care of it," he said. "Looks like someone did."

"What about ammunition? Wouldn't it be hard to get?"

"Nope."

Maggie exhaled. Then she filled him in on her computer work that day.

"So, still no idea who the fourth man is?" he said. "Maybe we're making too much of him. He's probably nobody."

❖ ❖ ❖

The next morning, Maggie stood outside on the steps of the police station. She'd gone to see Mead to return the diary as promised but he was out. She didn't leave it with his sergeant.

No one but Frank can put his hands on this.

Uniformed officers hurried by and the high-pitched whine of car sirens screamed in the distance. She pulled her jacket tighter to ward off a chilly gray start to the day. Better get back home. Work on the ARTEC program was in the preliminary stages and she had a long way to go before it could be tested on the Van Gogh image.

She took off down the street and hailed a cab on the corner. A light rain had started falling and she'd forgotten her umbrella. As the taxi pulled away from the curb, Maggie's thoughts drifted to Frank Mead. Through an old police friend she'd confirmed that Mead's wife had, indeed, committed suicide four years ago. He had really loved her, the friend said. But, like cops will do, he was married to her and the job. Hard to make it work with two wives.

God, how awful. To know that your love wasn't enough to save someone. Maggie wondered what that kind of love would be like. Nothing like her marriage to Rudolf, she was sure. Their love had been empty and shallow. Rudolf had never taken the time to really get to know her. But then did she really try to know him? What would it be like to feel the kind of love Mead felt for his wife? And to lose it. She shivered and not from the cold.

The cab turned the corner and pulled up in front of her brownstone. She paid the driver and alighted but did not go home. Instead, she climbed the eight steps of the house adjacent to hers and knocked on a brightly painted red front door.

For Maggie's peace of mind, she'd left Rosie with her neighbor, Vanessa Drammissi, after the break-in. She didn't know what she'd do if someone hurt Rosie. Yes, she did. She'd kill him with her bare hands.

"Vanessa, it's me." She heard a bark and the door opened to a blond spiky-haired woman in her early twenties.

"Hi Maggie. Hey, Rosie, it's Mom."

"You're a doll for watching her this morning, Van," Maggie said." To Rosie, "Hey girl." She kissed the dog on the snout.

"How's business?" Maggie asked.

"Ah, you know, some good, some bad. Cut a real cute guy's hair yesterday, though." Vanessa grinned through deep scarlet lipstick.

"Oh yeah?"

"Yeah, but I think he was married, you know?"

Maggie sighed. "I know." Rosie nudged her. "Thanks again, Van. I'll return the favor, I promise."

"S'okay. Me and Rosie, we're good pals."

Maggie picked up the dog's leash and led her out. The entry door had barely closed behind her when she spotted a dark sedan parked in front. Maggie slowed her step as she walked by and tried to get a view inside. But the windows were glazed a silvery black and she could see nothing. The engine was running, a soft purring sound that Mercedes made.

The decision hit her before she realized it. Don't go home.

With Rosie at her side, she made a U-turn and sprinted back up Vanessa's stairs, pulling out her cell phone on the way.

She pressed on the doorbell. "Vanessa, I forgot something." When her neighbor didn't answer, she pounded the door more aggressively. Out of the corner of her eye, she caught the front passenger door of the car opening. Vanessa suddenly appeared.

"Hey, what's--"

Maggie pushed her way in, tugging on Rosie's lead.

"--up?" Vanessa's eyes looked like egg whites with blue irises painted on them.

Maggie didn't answer but went straight to the front window and looked out. She panned the street then squeezed her eyes in relief. The Mercedes was gone, the street empty.

✦ ✦ ✦

Thirty minutes later, Mead arrived at Vanessa's. He walked Maggie and Rosie next door to her apartment. They didn't speak.

When they were inside her apartment Maggie burst out, "Frank, what the hell is going on? I know that car was following me, what if something happened to her, to Rosie? I'd go nuts."

"I know, I know," Mead said. "That's why I brought you something. For Rosie, actually."

Maggie took off her raincoat and threw it on the couch. He did the same, both ignoring the vintage wrought iron coat rack near the door. He pulled something out of his pocket.

"What's that?" she said.

"A jacket. For Rosie." He unfolded a blue piece of fabric with a logo from Canine Companions. "Got special permission for her to wear it for protection. Hers and yours."

"You're kidding?" Maggie said.

"Nah, that way you can take her everywhere, cabs, trains, restaurants, the works."

"That's wonderful, really, wonderful. Frank, oh, wow, I could kiss you."

"So, what's stopping you?" He grinned for the first time in days.

"Maybe I will." She leaned over and lightly touched his cheek with her lips.

"That's a kiss? Must be losing my touch."

She turned to her dog, cutting off any more discussion. "Look, Rosie, what Uncle Frank brought."

"Uncle Frank?" He pretended to ignore the comment and walked further into the living room. "So how's about some coffee?"

"Good idea." She hurried into the kitchen. "Caffeine. Just what I need for my nerves."

Mead headed for the couch, Rosie following closely at his heels. "I don't suppose you happened to get a plate number on the car?"

"No, by the time I realized--"

"Yeah, right. Describe it again."

"Mercedes, big. And black. New or fairly new." She handed him a mug and their fingers touched. Maggie pulled her hand back and sat down.

"Frank." She paused. "Thank you for that gift. It really means a lot, you know, having her with me all the time, especially after everything that's--" She stopped.

Rosie nudged Mead's hand. He patted her head and she laid it on his knee.

Maggie watched him pet Rosie. It seemed to relax him. "You know, petting a dog lowers your blood pressure."

"That's been proven scientifically?"

She smiled.

They lapsed into silence.

"Maggie," he said. "Two people have been killed. If the killer is trying to get his hands on that painting and he thinks you have it, or could get it, you could be next."

"But I don't have it and I think the killer knows that." She said this more to convince herself.

"How do you figure that?"

"Look, if a seventy million dollar painting, stolen during World War Two, came to light, there would be no way to keep it secret. It would be splashed all over the news. I mean, even Rudolf wouldn't be able to resist the publicity." She met his eyes. "I'm sure the killer is biding his time, waiting for me to find it. Scaring me, deliberately maybe, so I'll do something dumb and when I find it, which I will, he'll close in."

Mead seemed at a loss for words. "If you're wrong, there's a huge price to pay."

She nodded.

"What about the diary? Did you read any more?"

"Not yet. I tried to drop it off at your office this morning but you were out and I didn't want to leave it with--"

"Well, give it to me now."

She headed to the bedroom, returned with the diary.

He ran a hand through his fine blond hair. "Okay, what next? I have a feeling you're not telling me something," he said.

"I've been thinking about everything we know so far and something is bugging me."

"What?"

"Let's go back to the diary for a minute. Rettke takes the original painting to Hans Van Meegeren for copying. He gets the copy, takes it back to the Jeu du Paume, and keeps the original for himself. So what did Van Meegeren have to sell?"

Mead frowned. "You're right. Both paintings were accounted for."

"Unless--"

Mead waited.

"Unless Van Meegeren painted a *second* copy," Maggie said.

"Why?"

"Because he already recognized its value."

Mead said nothing for a moment. "Then there'd be *two* Van Meegerens and one real Van Gogh. We know Beckman didn't have the real one *or* a Van Meegeren, so, where does that leave us?"

"Back to square one." She threw up her hands. "How did Beckman get a copy that *wasn't* a Van Meegeren?"

Mead stood, hands in his pocket as if ready to leave. "What about your ARTEC program? Any progress?"

"Some, but there are so many parameters to consider, both from an art and technology standpoint. It makes me tired." Wisps of hair tumbled down her neck as she leaned back. She started to pin them up.

"Leave it, it's pretty like that." His cheeks flushed. "I'd better get going. A homicide cop's work is never done."

He walked to the door, grabbed his wrinkled raincoat. "You going be okay? Locks got deadbolts now? French doors too?"

"They've all been changed after the intruder and the purse snatching." She clasped her elbows with her hands, suddenly cold.

Mead reached down by his ankle and pulled out a small automatic. "Here. I want you to have this. Just in case, probably never need it. Still, keep it near."

He held it out but she didn't take it.

"Know how to use a gun?"

"Sort of," she said. "My dad and growing up in Vermont and all, well. No, I don't want it, Frank. Please, I'll be all right."

"Maggie, your best friend and now another man is dead. And you've had a break-in. Don't want Rosie in danger, do you?" He rubbed a hand on his chin.

She said nothing.

"The way I see it, you've got two choices. Either *I* can spend the night here or this gun can. Which will it be?"

Chapter 16

I t was close to nine the next morning when Maggie readied her office at the university's Electronic Photography Lab. She'd decided this was the best place for the meeting and now had all the equipment humming. Her head buzzed from lack of sleep and there was a hot wire in her blood. The two men who could change the course of her ARTEC investigation would be arriving in a few minutes.

She organized her notes and reviewed the numerous scientific techniques that were used for authenticating paintings. None of them were foolproof. All required the sanction of a human connoisseur, one respected in the field. More important, all required the actual painting. In fact, no painting had ever been certified by using photographs only. This could be the first.

A lot depended on these two art experts. Emil Kahn had been skeptical, almost hostile to her ideas. He would be hard to convince. Henri Benoit seemed supportive of her theories, but she couldn't be sure. Just contemplating the Frenchman, his dark hair, piercing eyes and crooked smile made her tingle. Maybe he just wanted to get in her pants. Or was that wishful thinking on her part?

She'd barely settled into her office and organized her notes, when Henri, in khakis and a tan sport jacket, strode through the door. Behind him, walking at a slower pace, was Emil. He wore a 1970's suit of a dull, dark gray, which might have been expensive in its time. Maggie wondered if it was coincidence that the two men turned up at the same time.

"Good morning, Gentlemen."

"Maggie," Emil Kahn said with a slight bow.

"*Bonjour*, Maggie," Henri said. "*Ça va?*"

"I'm fine, thanks." She realized she must look like a witch with dark saucers under her eyes and hair big and wild. She was concerned, however, about the way Kahn looked. Since their last meeting just a few days ago, he seemed to have aged. His cheeks had sunken deeper, exacerbating his already long, boney face.

"*Bon*," Henri said. "We are most anxious to see the work you have done, aren't we, Emil?"

"Ah, yes, yes," Emil said.

Maggie glanced at Henri's intense stare, turned quickly and walked away.

"Please, follow me." She led them to a counter tilted like a drafting table. The top was covered with felt and the height was meant for standing rather than sitting. She switched on an overhead bank of lights, which shone bright daylight onto the surface.

"Here are magnifying loupes for each of you. Please lay the photocopies out while I explain." She handed out stacks of paper. "Sample 'A' shows a close up of Van Gogh's brushstrokes in a photograph I took of his portrait at the National Gallery. In 'B' you see the brushstrokes in Rettke's photo of the *Vase With Oleanders*. By the way, both paintings are nearly the same size, so the brushstrokes could be compared without re-sizing the photos." She handed out more copies. "Again, in copy 'A', the known Van Gogh, in 'B', Rettke's painting."

By the time she was finished, each expert had twelve blowups of the known artist's work and twelve of Klaus Rettke's painting.

"Please. Take your time." She moved back to her desk and let them study the copies uninterrupted.

The men talked occasionally to each other, pointing out sections here and there, but for the most part, each did his own analysis.

While she waited, she curled her feet beneath her on the desk chair. She opened the folder of the digital images of the four Nazis from the film. Ingrid's grandfather, Hermann Goering, and Alfred Rosenberg. Still no clue as to the last man's identity.

She kicked her shoes off and padded to the flatbed machine, trying not to disturb Emil and Henri. She scanned the film frame again. Back at the computer she clicked on the image of the unknown Nazi and began to enhance. Some minutes went by as she worked with the face.

"What is that picture?" Kahn stole up behind her. "Where did you get it?"

She jumped. "Emil, you scared me."

"I'm sorry, my dear. I was just curious about what you were doing. Where did you get that photograph?"

She turned to face him and his expression unnerved her. Kahn's pupils seemed to fill the irises, painting his eyes solid black on white. His lips were tight and thin.

"Do you know these men?" she asked.

Henri had approached and, like Kahn, stared at the screen.

"Emil?" Henri said.

"I, er, of course recognize Hermann Goering, but no, I do not know the others," Kahn said.

"Who are they, Maggie?" Henri asked. "Wait a minute, wait, I know that man." He leaned into the screen and pointed. "That's Alfred Rosenberg, yes, the head of the ERR. I have seen his face before."

"And the other two men?" Kahn had regained his composure.

"One is Klaus Rettke," she said. "I don't know who the fourth man is." Maggie clicked off the screen and rolled her chair around. She looked directly at Kahn. "Do you?"

The old man shook his head. "But what does it matter? It was a long, long time ago."

"Well, I suggest we get back to work, *non?*" Henri said.

"Yes, let's," Maggie said. She headed for a small table with four chairs. The two men retrieved their photocopies and sat down next to her.

Maggie spoke first. "What do you think? Is this Vincent Van Gogh's brushstrokes?"

"Benoit and I both agree. There is no way to determine authenticity from a photograph," Kahn pronounced. "Not brushstrokes, color palette, signature, nor any other facet we look for in authenticating a work of art. A photograph, in a sense, is too one-dimensional. I, we, need the depth of the real painting in front of us."

She looked to Henri for confirmation. "You agree? The photograph can't tell us anything? Not even to eliminate the artist?"

"Maggie, *c'est trés difficile* with just a photograph. Like Emil says, it is too, er, flat to access details accurately." He threw up his hands. "I'm afraid I must agree with Emil."

"If it were a forgery, we would likewise have a similar problem," Kahn continued, suddenly coming to life. "One must have the actual painting to validate the artist. There is simply not enough information in a photograph."

"Hold on," Maggie said, a thought striking her. "If you had the real painting and it was a forgery, say by Hans Van Meegeren, you would be able to confirm that?"

She caught Kahn swallowing hard, the Adam's apple in his neck struggling for space.

"How do you know Hans Van Meegeren?" Henri asked.

She hesitated five seconds before telling the lie. "Rudolf told me about him."

"Ah, Hofer." Henri turned to Kahn. "Rudolf Hofer is her ex-husband."

Kahn raised an eyebrow. He cleared his throat, but his voice came out raspy. "Van Meegeren did not paint copies, my dear. He replicated the style of an artist in his own work, that is to say, he created an altogether new painting that would appear to be a Degas, a Pissaro or . . ."

"Or a Van Gogh," she finished. Kahn's 'my dears' were setting her teeth on edge. "Let's think about this a minute." She focused her eyes on the old man's. "Suppose Van Meegeren needed money," she said. "After all, it was the war, hard times, rationing. Perhaps he could not even make enough money to purchase his painting supplies or his family had no meat on the table." She slowed. "Let's say someone approached him with this project: to copy Van Gogh's *Vase With Oleanders*. Suppose he was told he would be highly paid and, to make it more of a challenge, he would have only a week to paint it. Might he consider altering his normal practice of forgery?" she asked. "People do all sorts of things for money, for greed, for creature comforts. Might Van Meegeren have painted a copy under these circumstances? This copy, in fact?"

Kahn paled, sweat beading on his upper lip. Maggie fell silent, her arguments falling away as she half-expected him to suffer a heart attack.

"You make a good argument for this." Henri broke the silence. "Van Meegeren was not a wealthy man, at least, not at this time in the war. Perhaps he did as you say."

"Is there any way to rule out Van Meegeren?" she asked.

Kahn shook his head. "Whether or not your premise regarding Van Meegeren is true or even likely, we are faced with the same situation as with the Van Gogh," Kahn said. "Yes, we can compare a known Van Meegeren with this painting of Rettke's. But a photograph is not enough. We need, no, we *must* have the painting."

Frustrated, Maggie agreed.

"Well, if you would like advice, my dear, do not waste your time on this, this little project," Kahn said. "Certainly if you locate the painting, if Rettke did, indeed, have the genuine article, well, then I can help you, but not with merely a picture." He looked at his watch. "Now I must run along. I'm sorry I have not been able to help you." Kahn looked relieved, not sorry.

She merely nodded.

Both men rose. Henri said to Kahn, "Go on, Emil, I'll catch up."

When the older man passed through the door, Henri turned to Maggie. "I would like to work with you on this, Maggie."

"I don't understand, you just said--"

"*Oui*, I know what I said. I didn't want to contradict the old man. Frankly, I think the photograph can tell us a great deal. I would like to help you."

"Henri, I, well, I don't know what to say. Of course, I would appreciate your help."

"What are the next steps?"

"Well, refining my program, comparing more photographs, analyzing other data besides brushstrokes, and--"

He took her hand and her words came to a stop. "I believe in you and I'll be there when you need me." He kissed her hand. "Whenever you need me." He smiled and his eyes lit up.

Before she could blink, he was out the door. His kiss lingered on her hand.

✦ ✦ ✦

Later that day, Maggie met Frank Mead at the penthouse on the 20th floor of an elegant high rise four blocks from the National Zoo. The home of Mrs. Samuel Beckman.

"This ought to be a blast," Mead said.

"Ah, do I detect a note of sarcasm?" She felt relieved that Mead didn't look forward to this interview either. "Remember, I met the old--"

The door opened at that moment and a maid in a starched black dress ushered them in. The grand hall would have set an Italian marble quarry up for life. Columns of ivory marble supported a majestic fourteen-foot ceiling. An immense table of decorative iron with a two-ton slab of marble atop graced the center of the room. On it was an artificial flower arrangement that would dwarf Maggie's whole living room, if she could even get it in the door.

"Cozy," Mead pronounced as the maid went off to find Mrs. Samuel Beckman.

Mrs. Beckman burst through a set of grand double doors, dressed in a pantsuit of bright turquoise and flowing neckerchiefs. Her looks and attitude defied her advanced years.

"Lieutenant Mead," Mrs. Beckman said. "I expect this is important. I must be leaving in a few minutes."

"We won't take much of your time," Mead began. "You remember Miz Thornhill?"

"Yes, yes, of course. I'm old, Lieutenant, not senile. How could I forget the friend of that miserable Nazi's granddaughter?"

Maggie clamped her teeth into a semblance of a smile.

"Come on, let's get on with it, then." Mrs. Beckman led the way to another splendid room, this one decorated in the richest of mahogany, teak and other exotic woods.

"She probably bought a whole rain forest to outfit this room," Maggie whispered.

"Sit, sit," Mrs. Beckman said, lowering herself onto a velvet settee.

17th century French, Maggie guessed. She took a seat on a small brocaded chair as Mead leaned into an upright, uncomfortable looking antique Louis the something.

The old lady squirmed on the sofa and made a begrudging attempt to be polite. "Oh, all right, I can spare a few minutes. But only a few. Coffee or tea, a drink? What?"

Mead opened his mouth when Maggie said, "Please, don't go to any trouble."

Mrs. Beckman pursed her lips and looked at Maggie through narrow, heavily eye-shadowed lids. "All right then, I won't." She turned to Mead. "Now, have you found the painting? Or my son's killer? Why are you here?"

The tension in Maggie's jaw tightened.

"No, it's still early in the case," Mead said with infinite patience. "I need to ask you some questions."

"You mean some *more* questions. I don't know what else I can tell you."

Maggie watched Mead adjust himself in the chair.

"What happened when your son decided to sell the painting?" Mead asked. "What exactly did he do, who did he talk to?"

Mrs. Beckman folded her hands in her lap and snorted. "Well, Aaron took the painting, the so-called Van Gogh, first to the Met." She turned to Maggie, "That's the Metropolitan Museum of Art to you."

Mead dropped his chin to his chest to hide a smile.

"Hmph. He had a lot of contacts in the museum world," the old woman went on. "And the auction world, for that matter. Anyhow, they kept it for a few days, then told him it wasn't a genuine Van Gogh. They said it wasn't even a Van Meegeren. Now ain't that a kick in the teeth? So," Mrs. Beckman continued, "Aaron decided to get in contact with the Van Meegeren family in Europe. You remember. . . it was Hans Van Meegeren himself who sold the painting to Samuel, my husband, right? Van Meegeren claims to have gotten the painting from that dirty Nazi bum, Rettke. Who knows? Anyhow, some of their descendants live in Paris and are still in the art business." She paused, as if to draw out her memories.

"Go on," Mead said. "The Van Meegerens?"

"Well, they, the sons, I mean, they told Aaron that no way would their father have sold anything but his own work or a genuine work. No way." She shook her head. "They said their father *did* sell the painting to my Samuel, sold it as the genuine. And if Hans Van Meegeren said it was the real thing, then it was the real thing. Or so the sons claim. Hmph. Thing is, Aaron believed them."

"So, Van Meegeren did sell the original to your husband, who later willed it to your son," Maggie said.

"Yes. Frankly, I find it very funny."

"What's that?" Mead asked.

"That a forger could be an honest man. What do they say, honor among thieves?" She boosted herself off the couch with both hands. "I have to go."

Maggie and Mead jumped to their feet.

"Just one or two more questions, please, Miz Beckman. We'll walk out with you," Mead said. "What did Aaron do then, knowing he had a forgery?"

She shrugged. "Ach, he was thoroughly confounded. I mean if this was supposed to be the real deal, how come it was a fake? Aaron, he, well, he didn't know what to do."

"Mrs. Beckman," Maggie said. "What about insurance? Was the painting insured? Wouldn't your son have filed a claim?"

"God only knows if it was insured. That's another problem. I can't find the paperwork on it. Neither can Aaron's wife. Nowhere. No provenance, no sales receipt, no insurance. So, you see, I'm screwed. Royally." The old woman clucked and shook her head. "What a bum deal. I can't even collect a dime for the painting."

"Maybe it wasn't insured because it wasn't authentic?" Maggie suggested and glanced at Mead.

"Don't be ridiculous, young lady. Didn't you hear anything I just said? If my husband said it was genuine then it was genuine. He would have told me if it was a scam or something."

The old lady started for the door. Maggie and Mead rushed to keep up.

"Where is the painting now?" Maggie asked.

Suddenly the maid was there, helping Mrs. Beckman on with her coat. She turned back to them, buttoning the top button. "I put the damn thing in a closet, can't even look at it." Her face contorted into a painful frown.

"I understand," Mead said. "But I'd like to have it for the investigation, if you don't mind."

The old lady looked at him, snorted again. "Oh for . . . I'll get it for you and why the hell you didn't ask for it before, I don't--" Her voice trailed off with her as she disappeared down a hallway.

Maggie looked at Mead, who said, "The painting's evidence. But what on earth will we do with it?"

"Get it authenticated ourselves," she said. "Actually, I'm dying to see it, in the flesh, er, pigment, so to speak. Fake or not."

The old lady returned, pressing the painting to her chest with both arms. She thrust it into Mead's outstretched hands.

"Here, take the damn thing, it's brought nothing but misery." To Maggie's surprise, tears filled Mrs. Beckman's eyes.

Mead held the painting up for Maggie, who covered her mouth with one hand as she stared, no, gaped at it.

God, Rettke's painting. Her pulse raced. She lifted a finger to touch it.

Mead pulled it back. "We'll keep this safe and return it to you as soon as we can, Miz Beckman."

Maggie's gaze followed the Van Gogh as Mead tucked it under his arm. She wanted to examine it closely, photograph it, analyze it. Her mind spun with the possibilities.

"Thank you for your time," Mead said. "We'll see ourselves out."

Maggie felt him jostle her elbow. She pulled herself out of her trance as he pushed her to the door.

Just as Mead turned the knob, Mrs. Beckman called out, "Check on that insurance, will you, Lieutenant? The insurance."

Outside on the street, Maggie waited while Mead unlocked the trunk of his car and placed the painting in. Then he took off his jacket and, she noted, not for the first time, the wide shoulders, muscular arms. His cell phone rang and gave her a chance to study him furtively. She found herself comparing him to Henri. Mead, a street-wise homicide cop with a penchant for history. Henri, a museum professional with a Ph.D. in art history. Still, this cop was college educated, not exactly blue-collar. Hell, she'd married an art professional already and look where that wound up.

Maggie felt an odd sexual stirring in her body, pleasantly familiar even after a long period of chasteness. The feeling surprised her. Did she feel the same way in Henri's presence? She caught Mead looking at her, a tiny smirk on his mouth. Instinctively Maggie turned away. Damn it, but he could read her mind.

"Now what?" she said, feeling the heat in her face.

Mead leaned on his car and folded his arms. "If the painting in my trunk is not a real Van Gogh, and not a Van Meegeren forgery, then it's a copy by another artist. So now we have two copies and an original. Which one did Ingrid's grandfather have or think he had? Not the unknown artist's copy since Beckman had that."

"And was killed for it," Maggie said. "So, let's confirm that the painting in your car, Beckman's painting, was done by someone other than Van Meegeren. Maybe an art expert will recognize the forger."

Mead gave a low whistle. "This whole thing makes me tired. I'll get it to the NGA for authentication. Probably your Frenchman, what's his name, Benoit or--?"

"He's not my Frenchman, Frank."

"--or Emil Kahn will do the work." He paused. "This insurance thing bugs me. The old lady couldn't find an insurance policy on the painting, but that doesn't mean there wasn't one."

"Right."

"Who insures expensive paintings?"

"Lloyd's of London, for one," she said. "They probably did back in the forties too. Other than that I have no idea."

"Well, I don't know what you're going to do next, but I'm going to follow up on the insurance angle." He stopped. "What's that funny look on your face?"

Maggie settled her eyes on his. "I think it's time for a trip," she said.

"A trip? Yeah? To where?"

"To the place where the answers may lie." She smiled wistfully but did not say the words aloud: I've always wanted to see Paris in the spring.

Chapter 17

Mead pushed around the stack of papers on his deck, lifted his face to the ceiling and squeezed his eyes shut.

"You look like shit, boss," Delacruz said, poking his head in the doorway. Somehow even at midnight, the sergeant looked like he just walked out of the tailor shop. "Go home, Frank. Give it a rest."

"What are you, my mother?"

"Fuck you, too." Delacruz left.

Mead leaned back in his swivel chair. He was exhausted but he'd never sleep so he got up and made for the coffee machine. He poured a cup of day-old swill, tasted it, shook his head and thought back to Maggie's phone call. She was leaving for Europe in a few days. Paris. Just the name of that city took him back in time to the trip he and Jeannie had taken there a year before she died. He shoved the memories to the back of his mind.

Worse yet. Maggie was going with Henri Benoit. Mead dragged the name out to three syllables. Hen-er-ee. What does she know about that pretty boy? Just because her ex recommended him. Hofer. Another European. That one, German. What did Maggie see in these guys? What was wrong with a home-grown American male? What, like you, asshole? he chided himself.

But there was a tiny pinprick of light ahead. Maggie had asked him over for breakfast the next day, hell, in less than nine hours. She had a favor to ask. Maybe she wanted him to do a background on the Frenchman. Not a bad idea, he thought. Even if she doesn't ask. Yeah, fuck you, Hen-er-ee.

Still the fact that she needed him, Mead, for something, was, well, something. He looked at his watch. 12:25 a.m. His neck cramped and he rocked his head from side to side to stretch it out. Then he turned off the light, grabbed his jacket and headed for the door. He stopped, hand on the knob. The thought of going home to an empty apartment just didn't appeal to him right now. He did an about-face, pulled the office blinds closed and kicked off his shoes. Then he lay down on the small Salvation Army couch he'd coveted, negotiated a price and bought from a yard sale years ago, and draped his jacket around his shoulders. Here he could rest.

At six-thirty, Mead was startled awake by noise in the outer offices. The police station was waking up too. He could hear phones ringing, chairs scraping the floor and wisecracks splitting the air. Ahh. The smell of fresh-brewed coffee drifted in. For a minute, he lay there and blinked into the dimness of his office. His mouth tasted like dirt. He swung his legs around and sat up. His jacket landed on the floor. He stepped over it and stretched the kinks out of his body.

Should go home and catch a shower and put on some clean clothes.

He looked at his watch. Still plenty of time before he saw Maggie. He sighed and rubbed his stubbled chin.

Surprisingly, the lumpy couch was pretty comfortable despite a few creaky springs here and there. He spotted the old chalkboard across the room, the one he'd been scribbling on last night. Trying to piece together all the clues of this screwy case.

Mead ambled out to the men's room. He washed his face in cold water and wiped the drops with his sleeve. He caught his reflection in the mirror. His eyes looked red from the inside out and his cheeks were puffy. He returned to his office and tried to decide what to do next.

A knock on the door and Jo Ellen, the dispatcher, poked her head in.

"Thought you were in here," she said, a smile breaking out on her beautiful, mocha face.

"Is that coffee?" Mead said.

"Sure is." She handed him a steaming mug. "Fresh too, not like that crap there in your pot."

"Hey, it was fresh when I made it."

"Yeah? And when was that? Year of the flood?" She sashayed in, tight skirt outlining her ample girth and grabbed the pot. "I'll brew you some more." She rolled her eyes. "What the hell is growin' in here anyways?"

"Hmm, you make good java." His attention was on the chalkboard and last night's scribbles.

"Later, Lieutenant." Jo Ellen closed the door behind her.

Mead stared at the board. In yellow chalk on the dark gray slate he had written:

Gun--WORLD WAR II-—whose--stolen

Beckman had fake painting--not Van Meegeren

Rettke paid Van Meegeren to make copy

Van Meegeren made 2 copies

Other forgery--by whom--when--how did Beckman get it

Insurance -— paintings insured--what company

Mead underlined the last question twice. Then he sat down and stared at the chalkboard until the words began to blur. Finally, he set the empty mug down, grabbed his jacket off the floor and headed home for a shower. In an hour, he would find out about the favor Maggie wanted. Whatever it was, the answer was definitely, emphatically, and absolutely, NO.

At ten minutes to nine, Mead pressed the bell on Maggie's door. When she opened it, he guessed she'd been up a while. Jesse Cook was playing on the stereo, the smell of coffee was strong, and a pile of muffins were sitting on a plate on the kitchen counter.

Rosie greeted him with a wagging tail.

"Hey, little lady. How's life treating you?" He rubbed her head.

Maggie smiled. "She's a great dog, don't you think? I mean retrievers are real dogs, not phoo-phoo dogs, like poodles, if you know what I mean."

"I know what you mean."

"Have you ever had a dog, Frank?"

He looked at her. "Yeah, I had a few growing up."

"Really? What kind?"

"Poodles."

She didn't acknowledge the response. "Give me your jacket and sit at the counter. Help yourself to a muffin or two, they're blueberry and apple raisin, and there's fresh coffee, strong French roast. Um, so what kind of dogs did you have?"

"Sounds like you've already had a few cups."

"What? What do you mean?"

"I mean you're talking a mile a minute."

"Oh," she said, taking a huge breath. "Yeah, I guess. I'm nervous."

"Nervous? Why? I make you nervous all of a sudden?"

"Only because, I mean, when I--" She stopped, looked down into her mug. "I want to ask a favor, Frank."

"Spit it out, Maggie. What?"

"Can you watch Rosie when I go to Paris? I'm scared to leave her at the vet or a boarding place and Vanessa is out of town. I'd feel so much better if you could, I mean she wouldn't be any trouble, she's such a good girl and--"

"Whoa, whoa and whoa. Are you nuts? Me? Watch your dog? Don't you have any friends, a cousin, an uncle twice removed, someone?"

"There is no one, Frank, not since Ingrid was killed. Like I said, Vanessa next door usually does but she's--" Maggie shut up abruptly and curled her lips in a grimace. "Frank?"

"What about Rudolf?"

"He's a cat person."

"Right. Jesus, Maggie, I'm a cop. You know what that means, I'm hardly home, she'd be better off at--"

"No, listen, I figured it out. She can go with you in the car, she loves riding and you can leave her, she can stay for a long time by her--"

"Great. Take her to the crime scenes and maybe she can sniff out the perps. Now why didn't I think of that?" He slapped his forehead.

Maggie blinked.

Mead stared at her.

She turned away. "I'll be right back." She ran from the room, Rosie at her heels.

Mead sat at the counter, counting the ways he was pissed. First, at Maggie. How could she ask him something so totally friggin' nuts? Second, at himself for his response.

Real sensitive. The least you could've done was say it gently or something.

He grabbed a muffin and stuffed a bite in his mouth, washed it down with coffee.

Maggie came back and sat across from him.

"I'm sorry, Frank, it was a really stupid idea."

She'd been crying. Face puffy, eyes red.

Rosie nudged his hand and he petted her without thinking. Terrific. I'm being worked over by two gorgeous redheads. I'm fucked for sure.

"Have another muffin," Maggie said.

He looked into her eyes and took another bite.

"Listen, I didn't mean to be a jerk about this, but be real. How could I take care of her, when I'm on a--?"

"Remember Joey Sabado? He was a homicide lieutenant in the 23rd and he always had his Jack Russell with him."

Mead bit his lip. "Yeah, well that Jack was a detective, solved a couple of cases." He looked up at her and finally smiled, begrudgingly.

She smiled back. "No, you're right. You can't handle a dog right now."

"What do you mean handle? I can handle a dog fine. Do I need the aggravation is the real question. Does she belong in a cop car all day, that's the real question. Jesus."

Maggie nodded, took a sip of coffee. "Right, forget it."

Silence except for Rosie's tail thumping the hardwood floor as she looked up at him.

"So tell me," Mead said. "How did you get this dog to finesse me like this?" Rosie stared up at him.

"Oh, she just knows what she wants."

Mead dropped his head and shook it from side to side. "Okay, all right. I know when I'm beat. I'll take her . . . try her out for a few days. But, and I mean this, if she gets in the way, I'm taking her to the kennel. Give me their number. In fact, right now."

Maggie reached in a drawer and handed him a card.

"And, if that dog doesn't solve this goddamn case by the time you're back, you're toast."

Maggie's smile broadened.

"Holy shit, I can't believe I'm doing this."

"Oh God, Frank, thank you, thank you. You don't know how much this means to me." Her eyes brimmed.

"Yeah, well, what are cops for? To serve and protect." He turned to Rosie. "Maybe I can train you for the K-9 Squad."

"And you can carry the dog food and bowl with you," Maggie said. "In case you don't go home, you can feed her anywhere. I have a water container too."

"Hmm, and walk her anywhere, too."

"Well, yeah."

Rosie's head rested on Mead's knee and she looked up at him with sad amber eyes.

"Boy, she's good, isn't she?" Mead said.

"She really likes you."

"Yeah, right." He let out a long slow sigh. "How long will you be gone?"

"Five days."

Great. Hen-er-ee gets five days with Maggie. I get five days with . . . He looked down at Rosie.

"Frank?" she said.

He looked at her.

"I can't thank you enough."

"When should I come get her?" he said.

"I'm leaving the morning after tomorrow real early, so tomorrow night would be best.

"I'll call before I come by. And listen, we should stay in touch when you're in Paris. I've got Delacruz tracking down the insurance angle and you might be able to follow up there."

"Of course. I'll be renting a European cell. I'll call you with the number."

"Right. See you later." He turned to Rosie. "You too." He was out the door.

On the street he walked the block to his car, mind spinning. I must be out of my fucking, cotton-pickin' mind. Dog sitting. What the hell next? Well, never mind, she'll wind up in the kennel for sure.

He climbed into his car and sat there, wishing for the thousandth time that he still smoked. For a brief moment, he thought of the guys in the department and how this would make great joke fodder for years. He didn't care about that right now. Instead, questions came popping into his mind.

Why me? Why did Maggie pick me for this job? Are we best friends or what? Doesn't she have any friends? What the hell is she thinking? That I'm a sucker? Yeah, that's it.

Mead slapped the steering wheel. "Jackass."

Still, a part of him liked the idea that she'd asked him to take care of the most important thing in her life. Made him feel kinda warm. Maybe she asked you because she trusts you. Yeah.

He sucked in a deep breath and blew it out slowly. He visualized Maggie's face before him, the Eiffel Tower in the background. And Hen-er-ee at her side. Shit.

✦ ✦ ✦

When Mead returned to his office, Delacruz was sitting in his chair, feet propped up on Mead's desk. He was clipping his already manicured nails. When he saw his boss, he quickly lowered his legs and slid the nail trimmer in his pocket.

"Don't you have your own desk to use as a spa?" Mead said and popped a couple of Tums.

Delacruz jumped up. "Got some info for you." He picked up a yellow pad from the desk.

Mead went around the desk and sank into his chair.

"Insurance on the paintings back then. Not an easy thing to track. In fact, I wasn't able to trace it specifically to that Van Gogh. Talked to some Brit at Lloyds of London who said the best thing is to contact the Wiesenthal Center."

Mead nodded.

"You know them?"

"Simon Wiesenthal was a famous Nazi hunter. He kept tabs on all the Nazis after the war. Started his own agency over the years. They'd probably know something about Holocaust assets."

"Yeah, well, only problem, their main office is in Los Angeles," Delacruz said.

"Yeah? Ever hear of a telephone?"

"I tried. They won't give out info over the phone. I figured it would be better if--"

"Don't they have an office in New York?"

"They do, but a smaller one. The only other big one is in Paris, of all places." He smiled. "Paris, France, not Texas, by the way."

Mead snorted.

"Want me to go to LA?" Delacruz offered with a grin.

"As a matter of fact, no. Maggie Thornhill's leaving for Paris in a day. She can do the legwork."

"Aww, Frank, no L.A? Movie stars, sunshine, blond surfer girls?"

"Aww, Ramón, too bad." He paused and broke out in a wide grin. "But I may be able to fix you up with a beautiful redhead I know."

Chapter 18

Paris, France, Today

Maggie stepped off the jet way of the Air France 777 into Terminal 2 at Charles de Gaulle Airport and inhaled the sooty air. Ahh, Paris. She followed Henri as he threaded his way through noisy crowds toward the exit, glad they had no additional baggage to their carry-ons.

Henri turned and said, "Terminal 3 is still closed after it collapsed in May. Killed several people." He pointed to barricades. "The architects, structural engineers and construction company are still fighting over blame. Sad."

Sad? Not exactly the word she'd use. A shudder went through her as she spied several mounds of broken glass and chunks of plaster.

"This way to the rental car," he said.

"I thought cabs and the Metro were the best way to get around Paris," she yelled from several yards behind.

"Not for me. I like to drive here." He grinned. "It brings out my competitive instincts."

Swell.

Thirty minutes later, after much haggling and gesticulating in fast-paced French, they were seated in a Peugeot 607, a French sedan you rarely saw in the States.

"What was all that about?" she asked.

"The French aren't happy until they have the last word." He looked at her as he started the engine. "That includes me." He shifted into gear and shot backwards out of the space then raced toward the exit.

Maggie gripped the seat.

Soon, however, her attention was caught by her surroundings. A smile nudged at her mouth and for a few moments she ignored the reason she was there. She gazed at the centuries-old architecture: pale blond brick and stone, Mansard roofs peculiar to France, and rusty wrought iron balconies, pink and red geraniums spilling through the rails. On the narrow, crooked streets, old women, kerchiefed in bright colors, hobbled with their shopping bags while young men and women in the short, tight skirts and high-fashion boots, hustled between them, never slowing a pace.

Paris was astonishingly noisy. Vehicles honked and chugged and bleated, people shouted, laughed and chattered. And streets were jammed with hoards of pedestrians on the uneven, narrow cobblestones. Cars double- and triple-parked, their drivers hopping out to run into *un tabac* to buy smokes with no thought to drivers stuck behind them. No one seemed to mind.

Maggie loved it immediately.

"Does everyone here smoke?" She felt foolish as soon as the words were out.

Henri laughed. "As a matter of fact, yes."

By the time they reached the city, she wished this were a pleasure trip and that she could spend some time enjoying Paris. That was out of the question.

They drove on the *Avenue de la Grande Armée*, right up to and around the *Arc de Triomphe*, down the *Champs Elyseés* to the *Place de la Concorde* with the tall obelisk at its center. Henri then turned left into a steady stream of traffic on the Rue de Rivoli, made a dizzying series of rights and lefts and wound up on a narrow alley way called *Rue des Pretres-Saint-Germain-l'Auxerrois*, which Maggie did not even attempt to pronounce.

He pulled the Peugeot onto the sidewalk in front of a tiny building with glass front: *Le Relais du Louvre*, their hotel.

"Here we are." He got out, removed their bags and led her through the front door into a tiny but elegant lobby. A concierge seated at a desk in the corner stood to greet them.

"*Bonjour, Madame et Monsieur. Bienvenue. Je suis Lisette.*"

From that point on, Henri and Lisette settled the accommodations in French and Maggie just nodded and smiled, feeling a trifle out of control and not liking it.

Was it the language? Or because Henri just took over and handled everything?

Henri handed her a key and led her to a tiny elevator, so small they could barely get their bags in. She had no choice but to lean into Henri, sending her pulse into a sprint. On the second floor, he left his suitcase in the hall and opened her door. Then he rolled her bag in and handed her the key.

"Would you like to rest a while?"

"Absolutely not," she said. "It's nine in the morning and we've got a whole day of appointments and research. Let me just freshen up a bit and I'll meet you in the lobby. Five, no ten, minutes."

He smiled.

She closed the door and let out a deep sigh. If only he weren't so gorgeous.

✦ ✦ ✦

Their first stop: *Le Musée du Jeu de Paume*, the repository for confiscated art during the war. After the war it housed Impressionist and Post-Impressionist art. Finally in 1991 it became a gallery for contemporary art.

Maggie had e-mailed in advance and ran into what Henri called 'typical French bureaucracy.' But with the mention of Rudolf's name and position at the National Gallery of Art, she had succeeded in obtaining an appointment with the highest-level person at the museum, *le directeur*, Dr. Georges Lemercier.

When they arrived, the receptionist told them there was no record of their appointment and Lemercier was not available to meet with them.

Henri began a dialogue in French with the woman. Within a few minutes, the conversation escalated to an argument. The woman stood and shook her finger at Henri, who leaned over her desk and practically shouted.

Maggie was about to grab hold of Henri's arm when the inner door opened and a large man, in height as well as girth, perhaps aged sixty, stepped out. He looked at the three of them, demanded to know what was going on.

Maggie pushed past Henri and the receptionist and explained, praying the man understood English. Fortunately he did.

When he realized who they were, he turned and snapped at the receptionist, who in turn sat down hard on her chair with a snarl. Lemercier welcomed them into his office.

"Please sit. I'm sorry about that. I, er, forgot to tell Laraine you were expected." He shrugged. "I'm afraid I only have a few minutes to spare so please forgive me not offering refreshment."

Maggie shifted in her seat and glanced around the comfortable office of woods and glass, somewhat at odds with the historic building. *We came all this way for only a few minutes?*

"Then let's get to it," she said. She reminded Lemercier of the reason they were there. At Henri's earlier advice, she did not mention the name Klaus Rettke. *Le directeur* would certainly be familiar with Rettke's role in the despoliation of French art and might not be as forthcoming if he knew their relationship to him.

"The Occupation," Lemercier began, " was a very sad time in our history. This museum was the premier, how do you say, showcase for modern art-- the Impressionists, the Modernists, Picasso, Matisse, ah, it makes me weary to think how many precious works of art were lost." He shook his head. "If it weren't for the courage of Madame Rose Valland, the curator during the war," he went on, "I shudder to think what would have happened. All would have vanished, no doubt, into the nether regions of the Reich."

"Her name has come up often in my research," Maggie said.

"In nineteen-forty, Rose was assigned the very dangerous task of surveillance of the activities of the ERR. You know what that is?"

Both nodded.

"*Bon.* Her job was to keep a record of the destination of each shipment of looted art objects from the *Jeu de Paume*. Without her record, postwar recoveries would have been impossible."

"Is Rose still alive by any chance?" Maggie asked.

"*Non, non.* Rose died in 1980." He paused. "After the liberation of Paris, she was appointed curator of the French *Musees Nationaux* and in 1954 Head of the Commission for the Protection of Works of Art. She retired about 1968, I believe, although she kept up her work on the French archives for restitution."

Maggie's disappointed look prompted Lemercier to say, "However, she has a niece who was very close to her and is still alive. Claire Valland Domergue. She lives in Avignon. Perhaps she can help you. She knew a good deal about Rose's activities during the Occupation."

"Do you think she'd mind if we called on her?" Henri said.

Lemercier tapped his finger on his desk. "I will telephone her and ask, as a way of introduction. If I know Claire, she would be *très anxieux* to talk to you. She is most proud of her aunt." He leaned forward. "However, she is often traveling, so I cannot make promises."

"I understand," Maggie said, trying to keep the frustration out of her voice. *Why can't he call her now?*

"Monsieur Lemercier, would there be any way to look at the files Madame Valland kept during the German Occupation? We're interested in what happened to one particular Van Gogh painting."

Lemercier pursed his lips as if in doubt. "Her records are housed in a government office and only claimants who provide proof of identity and right of succession are allowed access."

She waited.

"However," Lemercier went on, "in this case, I think we may be able to make an exception, especially since you are trying to determine who has the right to succession, if indeed, the painting was stolen." He shook his head. "Stolen from the French *and* stolen from the Germans. *C'est ironique.* Let me see what I can do," Lemercier said. "I shall call you at your hotel and also let you know about Claire."

"*C'est trés bon, Monsieur,*" Henri said.

"I don't want to take up your time, Dr. Lemercier," Maggie said. "But I was always curious about Goering's role in the plundering of European art. How did he know so much about Post-Impressionist art?"

"Actually, he didn't know that much about art at all, Miz Thornhill. Goering employed a personal curator, an expert art dealer who made those selections for him. Selections to adorn the walls of Goering's country home, Carinhall."

"A personal curator?"

"*Oui.* Goering's visits to Paris were generally short so he left the art in this man's hands. His curator would attend auctions and visit the *Jeu de Paume* to examine the most recent confiscations from which he would select works to please his *master*. Like Goering, he was a true Nazi, a vehement anti-Semite and, generally, a despicable man." Lemercier stood, signaling he had other business to attend to.

They shook hands and said their goodbyes.

She turned before exiting and said, "Who was Goering's personal curator?"

"Hofer. Walter Andreas Hofer."

Chapter 19

True to his word, Lemercier phoned the next morning with directions to Claire's house in Avignon, in the south of France, and permission to examine Rose Valland's records. Claire had only that afternoon and evening available and then she would be off on a trip, so Maggie asked Henri to purchase tickets on the train for that morning. The sleek *T-G-V* would transform a six-hour drive to a mere two and a half hours. The bullet train. Maggie couldn't contain her excitement. The archives would have to wait until tomorrow.

They arrived at the *Paris Gare Lyon* with only minutes to spare and sprinted to catch the train.

"Here we are," Henri said. "Seats 22A and B."

"Just in time." She settled into a velvety blue seat. The train began to move and within minutes, Paris was behind them. Oddly, despite the speed, she could still enjoy the scenery. Pale green fields stretched as far as she could see and ramshackle barns dotted the meadows. An occasional human popped into view, an old woman, donned in colorful scarf and toting a bag full of fruit, children wrestling in play. But they were gone in seconds.

Henri lifted the armrest between them. Their arms touched. She didn't mind. Gazing out the window at the landscape, Maggie felt a jumble of emotions. Elation at traveling through France, nervous energy at what revelations Rose Valland's niece might shed, and an awkward shyness at being dependent upon Henri these few days. Yet in a way it felt comforting.

She'd been alone too long. Part of her wanted someone to lean upon. Another part wanted that fierce independence she'd fought for all her life.

She glimpsed a peek at Henri's profile and felt a twinge of sexual desire. Don't go there.

She steered her attention to the scenery and the sweeping verdant meadows dotted with distant ruins of castles and churches. Her thoughts tossed about from past to present like daffodils in the wind. With one breeze she was back in eighteenth century France, starving peasants rising up in revolution. Another breeze blew her back to today and the farm tractors working the fields.

She felt Henri intensely at her side but, ironically, she found herself thinking about Frank Mead and feeling guilty. As if she were cheating on him.

✦ ✦ ✦

Claire Valland Domergue greeted them at the front door of a two-centuries-old apartment building just outside the main section of Avignon. An attractive woman, white hair well-styled, possibly seventy-five, she was dressed, surprisingly, in a modern-day pantsuit with a silk scarf around her neck.

"*Bonjour, Madame,*" Maggie said. "Thank you for seeing us."

"Come in, come in," Claire said and led the way up a steep and narrow staircase to the upper apartment. "I am, how you say, sorry, but I speak English not very well."

"I will try to translate, if you will allow me," Henri said.

Maggie nodded, wishing all the more she could speak their language.

They walked into a large living room and Maggie almost gasped out loud. Windows from floor to ceiling opened out onto shallow balconies of decorative wrought iron. The view was a spectacular panorama of the River Rhone and a fortress-like building that dominated the opposite shoreline. Claire smiled and began to talk. Between her English and Henri's translation, Maggie worked her way through the conversation.

"That is the *Palais des Papes*, a fourteenth century palace built by the Popes as a secure home while in France. A mini-Vatican, you might say."

Maggie scanned the shoreline across the water. "Breathtaking."

"*Oui*," Claire went on. "Seven Popes ruled here from the early 1300s to the end of the century. They owned their own mint, baked their own bread, for which they were famous, by the way, and fortified themselves against the French.

"*Mais, si'l vous plait. Pardon*, er, but this is not why you are here." Claire ushered them to seats in the main parlor.

The three sat in a comfortable room of what Maggie assumed to be Provencal antiques: distressed light woods and fabrics of blue and gold. A teenage girl brought out a tray from another room with a coffee service and plate of pastries.

Claire poured black liquid into cups of *faïence*, a delicate china, hand-painted in pastoral scenes.

"Now tell me, how can I help you?" Claire said with a little help from Henri.

Fortunately, Claire understood English better than she could speak it.

Maggie summarized their mission. This time she had no choice but to mention Rettke, since surely Rose Valland would have known him. And to be truthful with herself, Maggie still, despite all logic, harbored a secret hope that Klaus was really *not* the monster history had portrayed. That Ingrid could rest in peace.

"*Mon Dieu.* Klaus Rettke? This is, is so extraordinary, I never--" Claire cleared her throat. "I never thought I would ever hear his name again."

"Are you all right?" Henri asked.

"*Oui, oui*, I just need to catch my breath." She paused. "Rose spoke of Rettke often, you see. He was the worst kind of Nazi--*un sauvage, un ogre, et un démon.*" Claire turned and pretended to spit on the floor.

With each word, Maggie's heart clenched tighter in her chest, that tiny hope fluttering out the window. She needed no translation.

"He cared nothing for people. He used them and tossed them away like orange peels." Claire wrung her hands as if trying to squeeze out the story. "Rettke." The name seemed to poison her mouth. "He took his job very seriously and was ruthless as a confiscator. He worked with Alfred Rosenberg, you know."

Maggie nodded. Thank God she hadn't told Claire about her friend's relationship with this hated man. She felt Henri's eyes on her but didn't meet them.

The older woman set her cup down. It sloshed in the saucer.

"Please go on," Henri said.

"Rettke and Rosenberg were the best Hitler had, or the worst, perhaps? Rettke himself, personally, brought many of the looted art pieces to the *Jeu de Paume*. He would photograph and archive them for the Fuhrer. That was how my aunt was able to keep track of--" Her voice fell off as the past crept in.

"Tell us about Rose," Maggie said, urging the conversation away from Rettke. She sensed, too, that Claire wanted to talk about her famous aunt.

"Ah, Rose. She was quite a heroine." Claire poured more coffee into her cup and began the story.

✦ ✦ ✦

Paris, France, Spring, 1943

Rose Valland hurried up the steps from *Le Metro*, grateful to be outside, even in the moist warm air of the city. Below ground she could not breathe and since the German Occupation of her beloved Paris, she'd developed a fear of being trapped within the maze of subway tunnels.

Le Place de la Concorde teemed with official automobiles and army vehicles of the Third Reich. Pssah. She wanted to spit. Barbarians. Cowards. When would it end?

A horn blared as she crossed the street and she was about to swear at the driver of a Mercedes Cabriolet when she realized whose car it was. Hermann Goering. Monster of all monsters. Rose held her tongue.

She entered the back door of *Le Musée du Jeu de Paume* and prayed that Goering was on his way to *Le Louvre*, not here. As usual, even at the early hour, the museum resembled the aftermath of a tornado. Trucks backed up close to the loading doors. Soldiers rushed about, carrying paintings, boxes, hoisting crates, passing inventories back and forth. Inside was no calmer. Angry voices carried above the bedlam and Rose felt herself jostled by the chaos.

"*Bonjour*, Madame," said a young French clerk who rushed up to greet her.

"*Bonjour*, Albert," she replied to her clerk of three years. "What have we to deal with today?"

Albert handed her a docket of papers, lists of paintings to document before they were packed and shipped to Germany.

"Here is the latest list of confiscations and one of removals. Twelve crates will be packed and shipped today."

Rose squeezed her eyes shut. How could she ever keep track of them all?

"Do you know their destinations?" she asked.

Albert shrugged. "Who knows? Somewhere in Germany."

She touched a hand to her head. How am I to maintain records? It is not fair. I cannot do this by myself.

"Madame, are you all right?" Albert said, face creased in worry.

Get hold of yourself. You are alone and you must do what you can.

Rose took the lists from him and crossed into the consignment room. Here the paintings were assigned numbers and packed into cases. The cases would then be trucked to the railroad station and loaded onto boxcars, perhaps never to be seen again. She wanted to cry. But there was no time.

During the last three nights, Rose had secreted archival film of the paintings taken by the ERR, duplicated it and returned it the next day before it was missed. This cache of photographs might someday help recover the precious art.

Rose stiffened at the sound of her name, spoken by a man she hated more than Goering. Klaus Wilhelm Rettke. *Merde.* A mean-spirited man who enjoyed sparring with her about the decadent art he had ripped from the hands of Jews.

"Madame Valland, I am so glad to see you this morning."

Rose didn't respond to the sexual overtones in his voice. She knew he was not attracted to her; no man was, for she was a plain and matronly woman. This was his way of reminding her of that. Worm.

"*Ja,* you see I would like to ask if you know anything about some missing film? I seem to be missing a canister of film of the latest confiscations." He leered, eyes on her breasts. "Would you perchance know where it might be?"

Rose's heart twisted in her chest. "I would not, sir."

He stared at her and made a smacking sound with his lips.

She wanted to scream and tear his throat out.

A voice called out, "Herr Rettke, here, I found it." A young German soldier approached holding out a film container in his hand. "It had fallen behind the desk."

Rettke took the film, smirked and started to walk away. He turned to Rose then. "How lucky to have found it, don't you think?"

Rose attempted a smile, but her lips were so dry they would crack if stretched. She gripped her notepad to keep her hands from trembling. She would not show Rettke fear.

How long can I keep up this façade? What if I'm discovered?

Her mind flickered to Simone, her friend and colleague at *Le Louvre*. Like Rose at the *Jeu de Paume*, Simone had been the curator of twentieth century art--pieces of the Impressionist and Post-Impressionist styles at the world's most famous museum. Several months ago, Simone had disappeared. Just like that. She did not show up to work one morning. No message, note, nothing. To this day no one knew where she was. Friends feared she had been placed in a war camp or as the Nazis referred to it, a concentration camp. Rose had never heard of anyone returning from a camp.

I could suffer the same fate. Vanish into the madness of the Reich. *Mon Dieu*. She had often toyed with the idea of giving up. What kind of spy was she anyway? A scared one. But each time she contemplated the consequences: all that precious art, her precious art would be lost to the world. How could she betray Degas and Matisse, Picasso and Van Gogh? *Non*. She had no choice. She was the one person who could save them.

Rose dropped her head and wiped a tear that welled in one eye, then cleared her throat and straightened.

He must not see my weakness.

"Please excuse me, *Herr Rettke*, I have much work to do," she said and traveled on wobbly legs down the hall.

"Madame Valland," a man's voice called.

She stopped abruptly then let out a breath. Publicly, Jacques Jaujard was *Musées Directeur*; secretly, he was the key man who kept the Free French government informed of its national treasures. He greeted her now as she exited the Room of Martyrs and led her to his office.

"Rose, I have news." He whispered. "Twelve railroad boxcars will be arriving to pick up the crates tomorrow. We must ready thirty-two cases by seven a.m."

"Thirty-two? The destination?" she asked, keeping her voice low.

"Who knows? But Doctor Buchner's name has been mentioned."

"Ah, so the Castle of Dachau, then."

Again she felt the lump in her throat. More paintings would be shipped into Germany to disappear forever.

"Perhaps," Jaujard said with a shrug.

Footsteps echoed on the tiles outside the office door. Rose drew in a breath.

"You must go, Rose," Jaujard said. "It is not wise to be seen together, the two of us. You cannot afford to get dismissed again."

She shook her head. "They will not get rid of me so easily."

"But they have before. What if this time it is for good? Who will handle the heating and facilities of the museum?" Jaujard said. "You are the only one here who knows about the preservation of art."

They looked at each other.

"We can't bear to lose you, Rose, but for other, more important reasons," he said as he took her hand and brought it to his lips.

She felt a flush race up to her cheeks. *Le Directeur* had never been so openly emotional with her before. This was about art, pure and simple. He cared as much as she for their prized national possessions, the paintings, sculptures, tapestries and other historic artifacts. They were France's legacy to the world. And it was up to her to keep them from being lost forever. A daunting task. Was she up to it?

A new shipment of confiscations arrived at the *Jeu de Paume* late in the afternoon. From the shape of the crates, the contents consisted of paintings of varied sizes. By six o'clock none of the crates had been unpacked. Rettke had ordered that they remain as they were.

Rose had to know why he was not removing the paintings from the crates. A tiny pinch of fear crept up her back.

"Pardon, Herr Rettke, shall I uncrate these so we may take inventory?" she asked.

"No, Madame," he said. "There is no need. They will be shipped directly to Germany." He strode away, boots slapping on the wood floor. Suddenly he turned. "Do not worry. I have the inventory." He grinned and waved a folder. As he walked away this time she heard him laughing.

Her heart drummed.

Bâtard. Bâtard misérable. Somehow I will make you pay.

If she had a gun right now she would shoot him in the head despite the consequences. The adrenaline rushed through her body and made her keenly sensitive to her surroundings. She forced her brain to slow. Think. You must have access to those paintings. No. Only to the inventory. But how?

Rose began to plan. She would steal the latest inventory from under Rettke's nose, photograph it, and return it without his ever missing it. Whatever she did, however, had to be done that night. The paintings and inventory would be gone in the morning.

Getting the dossier out was less trouble than returning it. Rose waited until Rettke was at last gone at nine o'clock that evening. She stole into the Room of Martyrs on tiptoe, slid the file between several others she carried and walked out. She then brought the file to her friend's home to print the photos in his darkroom. By midnight she had copies of each page of the four-page inventory of paintings. Cezanne, Renoir, Lautrec. Stolen from local collectors and gallery owners.

Rose recognized many of the names on the list because a number of these collectors had donated art to the museums. What would happen to them now? Would they be deported to Germany? Sent to prison camps? They were Jews after all.

At four in the morning, Rose walked the twelve blocks from her apartment to the museum. Aching from the exercise but more from the fear that tensed her muscles, she unlocked the back door of the *Jeu de Paume*. Not unexpectedly, she greeted a German guard who jumped to his feet from his sitting position and readied his gun. Dozing, no doubt, she mused.

"Madame?" he said.

Before he could question her, she said, "*Bonjour,* Private Schloss." She read the name on his uniform badge. "I could not sleep with all the work to be done. I thought I would come in and get an early start, *non?*" She smiled and the soldier, a mere boy, seemed at a loss for words.

"Shall I make us some coffee?" she whispered and winked at him.

He broke into a grin and nodded.

"*Bon.* I shall be back with some espresso."

"Espresso? You have some? It is so hard to find these days."

"Ah, I have my ways." She prayed no one had discovered her tiny tin of the dark powder hidden in her desk. "You sit a while. It is very early."

Rose moved at a rapid pace once the soldier was out of sight. She entered the Room of Martyrs and hurried to Rettke's desk where she stowed the dossier back to its original place. Then she practically raced to the door, peeked out and ran the rest of the way to her own office.

Sweating, she shed her coat and immediately began brewing coffee in the nearby kitchen. She did not wait for the pot to fill but poured one cup. Then she wiped her face with a dishtowel and tidied her hair before she hustled it down the hall to the guard.

"*Danke Schoen, Fraulein,*" he said.

Fraulein. I am French, you imbecile.

But Rose kept the smile on her face and said, "I will be in my office."

At that moment, the back door opened and Klaus Rettke pushed through. He stopped and stared at Rose, eyes wide. Then he snarled and she envisioned a Doberman pinscher gnashing his teeth.

Before she could say a word, he took her by the elbow and led her, tripping and stumbling, through the corridor into the Room of Martyrs and up to his desk. While she stood there, he rifled through the files and found the latest inventory. He skimmed through it.

When he looked up at her, she felt the sweat roll down her back. She decided to take the offensive.

"What is the meaning of this treatment?"

He pursed his lips. "What are you doing here at this time of night?"

"I have much work to do. I couldn't sleep, so I--"

"Liar." He said the word quietly, which frightened her more than a shout. From three feet away, she'd felt his hot breath spit out the word.

It took all her strength to remain composed but Rose stood her ground. "How dare you say such a thing. I have done everything in my power to help you and you call me a liar?"

"You? Help me? What do you take me for, Madame?" He spun around in a temper. "I have had enough of your insolence and your obstinacy. Your services are no longer required. Now get out. Get out of my sight."

Rose stood unmoving; anger clawed at her insides.

Rettke didn't matter. The Nazi pigs didn't matter. The whole world didn't matter. Only the art mattered. When her legs could move, she made an about face and marched to the door.

Chapter 20

Claire ended her story and gazed out the window, lost in memories. Her face was pale and her lips trembled, but she sat ramrod straight in her chair, arms folded in her lap.

Maggie spoke first. "Rose was very brave."

"She was." Claire cleared her throat. "And her reward was that she saved a great many paintings."

"How well did Rose know Klaus Rettke? If Rettke stole a painting, would Rose have known?"

Henri translated.

Claire looked at Maggie, brow drawn in a 'v'. "I don't know, but if he did, why would he not steal a Rembrandt or Vermeer? Why would he steal a Van Gogh?"

"I don't understand," Maggie said.

"Van Gogh was considered *entartete kunst*, er--" Claire put her hand to her mouth.

"*Entartete kunst* means degenerate art," Henri said. "If Rettke were stealing a painting, he would have stolen one that had value at that time and place. Why a Van Gogh?"

Because he liked it? Because he recognized its future value? Maggie leaned forward, knees almost touching Claire's. "Madame Domergue, you have been most kind. We cannot take up any more of your time. You must be tired." She stood. "Please, don't get up. We are very grateful for your information. Rose Valland was a heroine, indeed, and you have much to be proud of."

Henri translated, but it seemed Claire already understood. Her eyes met Maggie's and smiled. They said their goodbyes and left.

Maggie and Henri strolled toward the railway station, her mind turning Claire's words over and over in her head. Henri's cell phone rang. He talked a few minutes in French.

"That was Dr. Lemercier. We can visit the National Archives but only for a few hours tomorrow morning."

"Hopefully that's all we'll need."

They continued walking.

"Claire's story was interesting, *non?*" Henri said.

"Yes, but unfortunately, we're no closer to figuring out what happened to the painting. I guess even Rose Valland didn't know about Rettke's scheme," Maggie said. "Or if she did, she never made it public, at least not to her niece."

"*Alors*, we can check her records tomorrow and see what we can find."

They walked in silence.

"You know, I've been thinking," Henri said. "In a way, you are like Rose Valland."

"Me?"

"*Oui.* You are trying to save a great work of art, bring it out of hiding and share it with the world. Is that not like Rose?"

Maggie said nothing but secretly felt pleased. Mead had said something similar. It must be true, right? She smiled inwardly.

Henri stopped and took her arm. "You, too, are a heroine. Perhaps even now, you are in danger, from a ring of art thieves, cutthroats, murderers." He grinned and a lock of dark hair fell over his forehead. "Yet still you persist in your, er, quest for the truth."

"Oh stop. You've been watching too many movies." She turned and continued walking, taking in his words. Cutthroats? No. Art thieves? Possibly. Murderers? Most definitely. A new wash of fear spread over her body and in the warmth of the Provence sun, Maggie suddenly felt a chill.

✦ ✦ ✦

The bullet train pulled into Paris at eleven. Henri urged her to have a drink near the hotel. Maggie wanted to get her mind off Rettke and the painting for a little while . . . step back and regroup her ideas. A glass of wine might help her do that.

Henri did most of the talking and she learned a little about him: that he was an only child, that he studied at the Institute d'Art, that he loved Zydeco music, and that he was totally and maddeningly attractive.

"I think we need to go," she said, setting her third glass of *Pinot Noir* down.

He smiled and paid the bill.

They walked back and Henri took her arm in a protective way.

"Maggie?"

She turned to him.

"You are a very lovely woman."

"What?" Her stupid reply.

"I'd like to spend the night with you."

She mumbled something dumb again. Must be the wine.

She noticed her arm was still linked in his as they walked to the elevator in their hotel.

In the cramped lift, he took her face in her hands and brushed her lips with his.

Oh God.

When they reached her room, he took the key from her and unlocked the door. He was about to step in and she finally got hold of herself.

"No, Henri, this isn't a good idea."

"Ah, but why not? I am attracted to you and I think you feel the same? What is wrong with--?"

"Because this trip is business. I'm here to find out about the painting and also, possibly, something about my friend's murder."

"Did you not find out about Ingrid's grandfather today? And how he might have stolen the Van Gogh?"

"Yes. It's a good start."

He smiled. "You've never been to Paris, *n'est-ce pas?* The city of light, of love. I only thought that, well, we are together, it's only natural that--"

Maggie shook her head and tried to clear her fuzzy brain. So that's what all that *you're just like Rose-Valland-heroine-stuff* was all about. What a con. And I fell for it.

She took a breath and said, "Please, Henri, I'm tired. I need to sleep."

"Of course, I would not force you to do anything you don't want to. I understand."

She could see by the flash in his eyes that he did not. Great, now he's pissed off.

To his credit, Henri said, "We'll keep this strictly business, Maggie. I promised to help you and I will. *Bonne nuit, mon cher.*" He walked across the hallway and turned. "I'll come for you about eight. We can have breakfast and drive to the Archives."

Then he sprinted up the four steps to his room, fussed with the key and was inside.

Maggie stared at his closed door and for some reason that confounded her, she thought of Frank Mead.

Eight o'clock the next morning at a nearby café, Maggie babbled on as Henri ordered a basket of croissants and coffee. Her nervousness stemmed from last night. She remembered vividly his expression when she turned him down. He didn't seem upset now and she was thankful. Maybe he would try a new approach. What if he didn't? What if he gave up trying to seduce her? How would that make her feel? Oh for God's sake.

A few minutes before nine, they pulled up at the National Archives, an eighteenth century brick building, typical for French architecture of the period. The interior had been renovated for today's government offices, but only barely, and the once beautiful tile floors were badly scuffed.

At ten after nine, they sat across a small wooden desk from *Monsieur Claude LeBlanc.* He was a prim little man with thin, pursed lips and protruding brown eyes. To make up for his homeliness, he dispensed a smug and officious attitude.

Henri and LeBlanc carried on a three-minute exchange in French. Maggie crossed and re-crossed her legs. Finally, the government official got up and led them to a huge warehouse-like room with stacks upon stacks of metal file shelves. He pointed to a table and chairs.

Maggie kept up an incessant chatter waiting for the bureaucrat to return with Rose Valland's records. Why was she so anxious? Henri sat with his arms folded; she stood and paced, then sat and stood and paced, then sat. LeBlanc finally returned. He brought six boxes on a rolling cart and set them on the table, one by one. Maggie launched from her seat, opened the first and began skimming through files. Henri did the same to the second box.

She could see that most of the files contained lists of paintings, sculptures and tapestries that Rose had recorded: dates of entry and exit, destinations, artist name, artwork name, year of creation, etc.

"God, these are chronological not alphabetical. How will we ever find the Van Gogh?" she asked.

"By looking, not talking," Henri said as he continued to flip through the files.

Maggie shot him a glare but refused to be baited.

A number of files contained black and white photographs of the art pieces. She went through each but did not recognize the painting. Her mind dizzied with all the famous art works she encountered: Jan Vermeer's *The Astronomer*, Edgar Degas' *Portrait of Gabrielle Diot*, Henri Matisse's *Woman Seated in Armchair*. These were celebrated masterpieces, many of which had vanished.

"Listen to this," she said. "According to notes in Rose's files, a number of modern works were destroyed, burned or slashed in the garden of the *Jeu de Paume* on July 27, 1943. Paintings by Picasso, Klee, Miro, Ernst, and Masson. Unbelievable." She shook her head.

Two hours later, neither of them had turned up anything useful. She opened a third box. The very first file contained a large stack of photographs. This time the photos were of people, not of paintings. As Henri went through the catalogues of the artwork, Maggie sifted through pictures. On the back of each one were names and dates, meticulously inscribed in Rose Valland's hand.

In the photographs, she recognized a number of infamous faces: Hermann Goering, Heinrich Himmler, Paul Josef Gôebbels, Alfred Rosenberg, even

Hitler and Eva Braun. Many photos were of people she hadn't heard of, Otto Dietrich, Werner von Blomberg, and Walter Buch. Maggie examined the pictures. A caption, barely legible, disclosed the name of another face in one photo: Walther Andreas Hofer, Goering's personal curator. Could he be related to her ex-husband? A great uncle? Grandfather? She retrieved her magnifying loupe and held it over Hofer's face. Hard to tell. She set it aside.

As she continued sorting the images, she chanced upon a picture of Josef Steiner. The man Rettke mentioned in his diary. Maggie tried to recall. He owned an art gallery. It hit her then. Of course he looked familiar. He was the man in Ingrid's photo and in the Nazi film clip. She studied him more closely. Dark hair, deep-set eyes, handsome, yet far from Aryan looking. In fact, he looked either French or Jewish, but she had learned that the name wouldn't necessarily tell you nationality. After all, Alfred Rosenberg was certainly not Jewish.

Yet the thing Maggie noticed about Steiner was that he never smiled. Not in any of the pictures. In fact, he stood away from the others, stand-offish, as if he didn't belong, didn't want to belong.

"Henri," she said. "Do you know who Josef Steiner is?"

"No, who is he?"

Instead of answering, she lay the pictures down on the table and slipped out her digital camera.

Henri opened his mouth but she gestured a no to him. She clicked several pictures of Josef Steiner. She also shot photos of Walter Hofer then tucked the originals back in the file.

Maggie continued through the images until finally, she spotted Rettke. His arm circled Josef Steiner's shoulders. She held up the photo to Henri.

"Do these men look like friends to you?"

He squinted at the picture. "Hardly. This is Steiner? He looks like he's in pain."

"If you had a Nazi's arm around your shoulder, you'd be in pain too."

She set the photo on the table, aimed her camera again and snapped off several shots of the image.

"So," Henri said. "If Steiner was an unhappy participant with a band of Nazis, what was he doing in these pictures?"

A possible source for the answer came from an unlikely person: Frank Mead. His call that afternoon sent her to the Simon Wiesenthal Center in Paris and the Director, Joshua Diamond. Mead had contacted him in an attempt to locate a possible insurance claim but the connection had been so bad, he decided to let Maggie handle it in person.

"Gee, thanks," she said. She stood on a street corner facing *Le Louvre* as passersby brushed past her. Henri lit up a Players and waited.

"How come your connection was so bad but our connection is so good?" she asked Mead.

"Hey, technology, you can't trust it," Mead said. "The address is 64 *Avenue Marceau*. Should be easy to find for your guy."

"He's not *my guy*, Frank." She turned her back to Henri so he wouldn't overhear. "And his name is Henri. Don't worry, we'll find the office. Does this Mr. Diamond know we're coming?"

"He does."

"Does he speak English?" she said, remembering Claire and the uncomfortable conversation in French with Henri translating.

"He does," Mead said. "Better than me."

"Hmph."

"How are you making out there?" he said.

"Very well, actually. A lot of little pieces are falling into place."

"Yeah? Got a killer for me?"

"Uh, no. Not yet." She could hear a smile in his voice. "But listen, can I e-mail you a photograph to see if you can come up with an ID?"

"Sure. Got any information other than a photo?"

"The name. Josef with an 'f' Steiner."

"Wasn't his name in Rettke's diary?"

"Yes. Steiner evidently knew Ingrid's grandfather and some other big shots in Nazidom, like Hermann Goering. You'll recognize him."

"I will?"

"He's our fourth man, Frank. The fourth man from that Nazi film and Ingrid's snapshot."

"Right. Send it on in."

"So, how's my Rosie girl?"

"She's pretty darn good for a bitch, er, dog."

"Of course she is. Is she eating okay and--?"

"You mean does she miss you? She won't say, playing it close to the vest." He chuckled. "Eating like a horse, if you'll pardon the expression, and everything is coming out the other end in proportion."

"So, what do you two do when you're together?"

"Well, actually, we're always together. Remember the Canine Companions jacket? She goes everywhere with me and stays in the car if I'm on a case or something."

"Or something?" Maggie said. "You mean like on a date?"

"Yeah, like on a date," he said without missing a beat.

"Oh," she murmured.

Mead went on. "Hey, like I said, she comes with me everywhere."

She didn't fill the silence he left.

"Maggie, I've got work to do and this is one friggin' expensive call."

"Okay, sure, right," she said slowly. "Thanks for the info and, and for Rosie. I'll let you know what happens at the Wiesenthal."

She clicked her cell phone closed and tried to picture Mead and Rosie together. The image brought a smile to her lips.

Chapter 21

The Wiesenthal Center in Paris was housed in an unobtrusive office building on *Avenue Marceau*, not far from the Metro Stop at the *Arc du Triomphe*. Restless and eager for their appointment with Joshua Diamond, Maggie left Henri to peruse *French Fine Art* magazine as she wandered from one end of the long waiting room to another. She traversed the navy blue carpet, trying to avoid looking at the stark black and white photographs on the walls.

She couldn't help herself. War photos fascinated her. Even as a young girl, she'd always had a passion for history although, because of her relationship to a Civil War photographer, the Civil War was more in her area of knowledge than World War II . Now she studied a picture from a different war and it shot tremors through her limbs. The caption read: "A member of the *Einsatzgruppe* D prepares to shoot a Ukrainian Jew kneeling on the edge of a mass grave filled with the bodies of previous victims. German soldiers of the *Waffen-SS* and *Reich Labor Service* look on."

The victim seemed to have no expression on his face, no fear, no care. Perhaps he yearned for the release of death.

Maggie clenched her fists and turned to another: "Prisoner bunks in *Birkenau*." Fenced off areas in a muddy bog. She'd seen nicer stables. And finally, "Jewish children, the victims of medical experiments in *Auschwitz*," showed eight faces staring out blankly atop skeletal bodies, burned and blackened, pinched and bruised.

She squeezed her eyes shut. In the brief blackness, Ingrid's face flickered. Memories rolled in unbidden. Maggie's parents dead in a car crash when she was fourteen. Her aunt Sara moving from Vermont to care for her in Washington, so she could finish school. Meeting Ingrid in a support group for teens whose parents died suddenly and traumatically. Ingrid's parents, still in Germany, dying in a horrific train crash. At age thirty-one Maggie married Rudolf Hofer, handsome, intelligent, art-savvy. Cold, self-centered, egotistical. Only lasted two years and surprisingly that long. Also part of the photographic montage in her head were Aaron Beckman, murdered, his mother, a living reminder of the Nazi past. Then there was Alfred Rosenberg and Josef Steiner. His face, and now a name, was imprinted solidly in her mind.

Maggie uttered a sigh of relief when a voice interrupted.

"Hello, Madame et Monsieur?"

"Mr. Diamond?" Maggie held out her hand to a man, no more than five feet tall, curly gray hair and beard, with thick, no-rim glasses. She introduced Henri and was relieved to hear that the head of the Wiesenthal Center spoke excellent English although she detected a hint of a Slavic accent. Polish?

She and Henri followed Diamond through a long, narrow corridor lined with more graphic photographs of the Holocaust, into a tiny office at the end. The window looked onto the street; a busy newsstand perched on the sidewalk directly in front, so close Maggie could read the headlines on the latest cover of *Paris Match*.

"Now, how may I help you?" Diamond asked once they were seated across the desk.

Maggie described their mission.

"Tell me more about this painting," Diamond said. "That police lieutenant, er, Mead, gave me very little information on the phone. Bad connection."

She described the Van Gogh painting that was confiscated. "Would there be any records of who it might have been stolen from? Perhaps someone filed an insurance claim?"

Diamond rolled his chair in a semi-circle and opened a file drawer. "Now, there I may be able to help. We actually have information on many pieces of stolen art." He thrummed through several files until he pulled one out.

"Van Gogh, Van Gogh," he muttered as he ran his fingers down the page. "Ach, no, no. Odd but I find nothing, I'm afraid."

"Nothing? Not one file on Van Gogh?" Maggie had trouble swallowing her disappointment. "I can't believe it."

Diamond flipped through the folders again. "I will check again, but I don't see anything here."

"Could it be somewhere else? It's just not possible that there isn't--"

"Wait. There is another possibility." Diamond hurried to a different cabinet. Maggie held her breath. He opened one drawer, then another. "Van Gogh, Van Gogh. Ah, so. Yes, of course. An entire file drawer. I should have looked here first. Van Gogh, *Vase on Yellow Background*. Yes, here is a picture." He handed it to Henri.

Maggie snatched it out of his hands.

"This is it, the oleanders," she said.

Henri glared at her but she was busy gazing at the photograph. Exactly like Rettke's photograph. Exactly like Mrs. Beckman's forgery.

"What about insurance?" Henri asked. "Was the painting insured?"

Diamond ducked his head down and skimmed through each paper in the file. "Hmm, that is not always easy. Let me try something." He stood and left the room. Maggie sat down again, eyed the file on his desk then glanced at Henri. She leaned toward the folder but before she could get a peek, Diamond returned.

"We have another set of files on Holocaust assets. The American Association of Museums has put together a long list of criteria for investigating works that are claimed to be despoiled art. They also have inventoried some of the insurance claims that have been settled. So maybe, hmm." He flipped through pages in a file six-inches thick. "Van Gogh has his own separate file as you can see."

"That's all Van Gogh?" Her eyes widened.

"Yes, indeed."

"Not surprising. He was quite prolific," Henri added.

Diamond pulled out several sheets of paper with tiny black type on it. The director squinted at the words.

"It seems a five million dollar claim was recorded on this painting in 1945."

"Paid off?" Maggie said.

"Apparently," Diamond said, squinting at the ancient type.

"Who received the money?" Henri asked.

"I don't see a name."

Maggie's shoulders drooped. Damn, nothing is ever easy.

Diamond turned to a second page. "Maybe, maybe, just a moment."

Her shoulders lifted again.

"Ah, here."

She sat up and almost grabbed the papers from him.

"Yes," he said with agonizing slowness. "Paid on June 18, 1945 to one Jakob Steiner. An art dealer. Hmm. Five million dollars. A fortune in those days."

"Jakob Steiner?"

"Yakob. The 'J' is pronounced like a 'Y.'"

She reached into her bag. "Could he have been related to this man? Josef Steiner?" She pronounced Josef, Yosef, then handed Diamond the photograph and watched his face spring to life. His eyes shone and his mouth curled into a wry smile.

"Oh yes. He was related. Josef and Jakob Steiner were father and son. Josef, in fact, brought his son to Paris from somewhere in Germany after his wife died. It was, maybe 1933?"

"So he was German?" Henri said.

Diamond nodded. "German and Jewish."

"What happened to them after the war?" Maggie asked.

Diamond shook his head then looked back in the file. "I have no information on that. Sorry. You might try Holocaust archives. If they were remanded to a concentration camp, there should be a record."

"You seem familiar with this man, Josef," Maggie said.

"Ah, I most certainly am. He was a well-known art dealer and owned *Le Jeune Galerie*, known for its works of modern and Impressionist art. Big auction houses and individual collectors came from all over the world to his gallery." Diamond paused. "Of course, that stopped during the Occupation when—"

"When modern art was considered by some to be degenerate," Henri said.

"Precisely."

"What else can you tell us about the Steiners?" Maggie asked.

Diamond sat back, a crooked smile on his face. "There was some talk, no hard evidence, mind you, but some people were convinced--" His voice trailed off.

"Talk?" Maggie sat up in her chair and uncrossed her legs. "People were convinced about what?"

"That Josef Steiner was more than he seemed to outward appearances."

"Go on," Henri said.

Diamond clasped his hands and leaned forward on his desk. "Indeed. Josef Steiner was said to be more than a collector of fine art, more than a dealer in fine art, in truth, far more even than an art expert or critic."

Maggie bit down on her lower lip to keep from bursting out, "Who was he?"

Diamond steepled his fingers. "It is said Josef Steiner was one of the most infamous Nazi collaborators of the war."

A short, stunned silence followed.

Diamond rose. "I must bid you goodbye for now. I hope I have been of service to you."

They thanked Diamond for his help. Maggie turned to him, "Perhaps, Mr. Diamond, you could answer one more question. I would like to find out more about a man named Walther Andreas Hofer. Do you know who he was and what happened to him after the war?"

"Hofer, well, in part. He was Goering's own personal art expert." Diamond leaned on the back of his rolling chair. "There's very little, however, about him in our files. Only that he lived a long time after the war."

"Did he have a family?" she asked.

"A wife, maybe two children, maybe three." He shrugged. "I'm sorry, but he wasn't the focus of attention for us. You might try the National Archives."

"In Paris?" Maggie asked.

"Many records having to do with art theft would be there," Diamond said. "May I ask you a question?"

She nodded.

"Why does this man Hofer interest you?"

"I am, I was, that is, married to one."

Maggie stood outside the Wiesenthal Center in the glare of the afternoon sun trying to make sense of what she'd learned. Around her, horns blared and pedestrians brushed by, their lit cigarettes coming dangerously close.

Henri ushered her to a small café on the Seine and ordered cappuccinos as they grabbed a table outside on the street. Not far upriver sat the monarch of churches: Notre Dame Cathedral. Maggie could spot the tips of its spires.

Everywhere she looked, she caught glimpses of a famous monument or well-known street or building. The *Arc de Triomphe*, the *Champs Elysée*, *La Tour Eiffel*. And the museums. She felt breathless all the time. But while Paris had its historic, charming and romantic perspectives, the city of light also had its dark side. Paris was crowded, sooty and stunningly cacophonous. Street traffic could take responsibility for much of this. Even now, as Maggie watched, a bus attempted a wide turn and narrowly missed their table on the corner while *un flic* tried, unsuccessfully, to steer traffic down a side street. As the policeman waved to a car, a motorcycle slipped by his furious swearing and gesticulating and scooted down the street. The comical scene reminded her of an Inspector Clousseau movie.

Their coffees arrived and neither had spoken. Henri didn't press for conversation. She caught him looking at her from the corner of her eye and just sipped her drink.

Finally, he said. "So, where are you?"

She looked past him to the street vendors on the river walk. "Thinking about what Paris would have been like during the Occupation."

He nodded. "Deserted except for official vehicles. Lots of them. But barely any people on the street. They would stay home or at work not socialize like this." He gestured to the chatter around them. "It was a grim time. No laughter. Seeing a Nazi uniform would send the average person scurrying. There was no telling who they would stop and for what reason."

He reached into his jacket pocket and pulled out a pack of cigarettes. "Do you mind?"

She shrugged.

"When in Paris." He gave a faint smile, lit up. "Parisians were scared. Tough and proud, arrogant as usual, but frightened. Their home had been invaded. They had no rights. And worse, their art, the pride of their country, was being attacked, destroyed, and stolen."

"Until 9/11 I couldn't imagine the enemy on my home ground," Maggie said. "Now I understand."

"Americans have lived in isolation. Not anymore. The world has gotten much smaller thanks to your science and technology."

She smiled at the 'your.'

They sipped in silence.

"Josef Steiner was a collaborator," she said. "What did that mean, really, to someone in his position?"

"You mean as an art dealer or as a Jew?"

"Both."

Henri dragged on his Players, looked up at the sky. "It means he kept himself and his family alive and out of concentration camps by selling out to the Germans. By providing them with the art they wanted."

"But they didn't want his kind of art. They hated it."

"Some Germans, yes, and their orders were to expropriate the art, hide it or destroy it." He paused, peering into his cup. "*Mais*, not all Germans hated it. Many admired, even loved the Impressionists, Post-Impressionists, and Modernists. They could not say so openly, of course, or they would have been arrested or worse. Still, those that were cautious and cunning could plan for their future. They recognized the paintings would be worth something after the war." Henri waved to the waiter for two more coffees.

"Germans like Klaus Wilhelm Rettke," she said.

"It would seem so."

She stared across the street at the vendors selling postcards, key chains with dangling Eiffel Towers and replicas of famous art. Maggie recognized a *Toulouse Lautrec* poster even from a distance.

"I think the next step is *Le Jeune Galerie*, if it still exists," she said. "Steiner may have had the Van Gogh displayed there. . . perhaps that's where Rettke first saw it."

"Let me see what I can find out." Henri stubbed out his cigarette in an ashtray then spent five minutes on his cell. When he completed the last conversation he flipped the phone closed and said, "According to Jacques, a gentlemen who works there, the *Galerie* still exists and, in fact, is owned by a woman who worked under Steiner."

"Wonderful," Maggie said. "Let's go."

"He also said she might not be willing to meet with us."

"Why not?"

"It was a very difficult time in her life," Henri said. "Jacques wasn't sure she would want to relive those memories."

"That was sixty years ago."

"He is asking her right now, so we will see."

"If she worked for Steiner in the forties, she must be in her eighties now."

" Jacques explained that Collette Rousseau is eighty-four years old but looks and acts no older than sixty." Henri opened his cell phone at the first strings of a Bach Cantata.

Maggie drummed her nails on the table as Henri talked to Jacques.

Maggie tried to decipher a few words and to quell the anxiety that threatened to choke her.

Henri flipped his phone closed and smiled fully for the first time that day. "Madame Rousseau would be delighted to meet with us. In fact, she's just putting tea on."

Chapter 28

*L*e Jeune Galerie d'Art, situated in the heart of Paris' art district, *St. Germain des Pres*, was a simple glass storefront, partially shaded by a green and white awning. To Maggie, it was similar to galleries in Washington and New York--simple yet elegant. She moved closer to the window to get a better look. Ensconced on black velvet in the windows were paintings of a cubist nature by a contemporary artist named Amelie Madeleine.

Henri opened the door and Maggie followed him into the gallery. She appreciated the highly polished wood floors that balanced the austere white walls, covered with Madeleine's oils. Kiosks of smoked plexi held soapstone statues of unknown species. Human or animal forms, she couldn't tell, but Maggie presumed them to be creations by the same artist.

"Madeleine has become very popular in the States. MoMA in New York is considering hosting her show," Henri said.

Maggie didn't respond. Modern art didn't appeal to her, particularly this form, all lines, slashes and shapes, no relation to anything living or breathing. She preferred warmth and color, a work that didn't need hours of contemplation to decipher its symbolism. She preferred Van Gogh.

"*Bonjour*, Madame, Monsieur." A young man walked toward them and introduced himself as Jacques.

Henri spoke to him in French as Maggie toured the gallery, attempting to imagine how it must have looked sixty years ago.

"This way," Henri said. "Madame Rousseau is in the back."

Jacques led them to a tiny patio walled in by fences dripping in flowering vines. The air was thick with perfume and Maggie couldn't tell whether it was the profusion of flowers in the garden or the Chanel that wafted off Madame Rousseau as she glided toward them.

The eighty-something art matron delighted Maggie with her southwestern attire: fuchsia silk blouse, long woolen skirt of mustard gold and belt and jewelry befitting a wealthy Native American--turquoise and coral in thick silver settings.

"It's good of you to meet with us," Maggie said.

Her silent prayer was answered when Madame Rousseau replied to her in perfect English. "I am most happy to be of help. It is not often an old lady gets a chance to talk about the past. Kids today do not care much about anything that doesn't affect them directly. Do you not find that true in America as well?"

"Yes, it is very true. And," Maggie grinned, "I am flattered you think of us as kids."

Madame winked. "To me a kid is anyone younger than sixty. Please sit down." She pointed to some chairs then called, "Jacques, please, some refreshments for our guests."

Maggie and Henri settled in and both, in sequence, began explaining why they were there.

Madame's lined leather face went hard and her jaws worked silently.

"Josef," she said softly. "A decent man turned bad. Like so many back then." She spoke to the air. "Still, he had choices."

Coffee came and Jacques poured, offered cream and sugar then left the pot on the table. He escaped into the gallery without a word and closed the door behind him.

Maggie waited, sipping her coffee black, while Henri added cream to his. Finally, Madame said, "In order to understand Josef Steiner, you need to know a little of the circumstances in which he lived. Years before the French occupation, in fact." She set her cup down in its saucer preparing to begin her story.

"When the Nazis, Hitler, that is, came to power around 1933," Madame Rousseau began, "the art world was, how do you say, shaken up. By 1937 everything changed. Museum curators all over Europe were dismissed and replaced by Germans affiliated with the Combat League for German Culture. Culture, ha! They knew not what the word meant. This group began to coordinate small exhibitions of modern art for one purpose only: defamation. Propaganda exhibitions--*Schrekenskammern der Kunst*--which literally means *chambers of horrors of art*. The League defiled artists, art dealers, museums and collectors involved in modern art." She paused. "But it was only the beginning."

Madame raised the cup to her lips. She held it in surprisingly steady hands as she spoke.

"In the same year, '37, with one massive sweep across Europe, the Nazis confiscated more than 16,000, imagine, 16,000 works of so-called degenerate art, including works by *Wassily Kandinsky*. He was a favorite of mine." She clucked and shook her head. "They wiped out whole museum inventories in an instant. Those works not kept for a special exhibition were stored in warehouses or destroyed."

"Would you define degenerate art as the Nazis saw it?" Maggie asked.

Madame stood up. "No, no, don't get up, please. I need to stretch my joints." She moved to stand behind her chair. "Getting old is not for sissies." She smiled. "I think a famous American actress said that--Bette Davis."

Maggie smiled back.

Madame continued. "Ahh, you asked about degenerate art. Words and meanings seemed blurred then, that is, all blended together. Jews, Bolsheviks, Gypsies, mental defectives, were all synonymous with degenerate. But here, in essence, is the meaning: artists who worked in styles reflecting foreign influences; artists who painted works using color and design that did not replicate nature; artists who used forms that were geometric or contorted like the cubists, like Amelie Madeleine, our artist on show today. Or Picasso." She took a deep breath.

Maggie felt her face heat up because of her own personal dislike for modern art and her quick assessment of the artist Madeleine. She hoped no one noticed.

Madame took her seat and went on. "The Nazis felt that art that was not realistic, not depictions of the real world, was aimed at making fools of the hard-working German people."

"Meaning it was above their intellectual level," Henri said.

Madame shrugged. "In Hitler's own words: 'works of art that are not capable of being understood in themselves but need some pretentious instruction book to justify their existence, will never again find their way to the German people.' Now here is the irony." Madame leaned forward as if about to share a secret. "The most famous show of degenerate art was called *Entartete Kunst* and was on display in the Archeological Institute in Munich in 1938. It drew huge crowds, far larger than other shows of so-called legitimate art. *Entartete Kunst* drew over 20,000 visitors a day. Can you believe 20,000, waiting on long lines and cramming into those tiny spaces. The show went on a twelve-city tour and attracted over three million visitors in Germany and Austria by the time it finished in 1941."

"While the war was going on?" Maggie said.

The old woman nodded and sat back down in her chair, worn out from the emotional catharsis. But her eyes remained bright and Maggie could see she would continue her story in time.

Madame picked up the thread. "Unfortunately, the end result was that the visitors to *Entartete Kunst* were overwhelmingly swayed by the propaganda. They agreed with Hitler that modern art was confusing and needed explanation. It was perceived as elitist and mocked the sensibilities of the common citizen." She turned to Maggie. "The people were not to blame, really. They had all they could do to survive. Intellectual endeavors were on hold. So sad."

Maggie poured fresh coffee for them and let Madame catch her breath. The old woman smiled. "You are very patient, my dear, listening to me go on and on when you only want to know about Josef."

"Not at all. Your story puts everything into perspective and helps me to understand Josef a little better."

Madame displayed yellowed teeth, crooked and chipped--a contrast to her elegant attire and coiffure.

"So, now to Josef. He was a Jew who grew up in Germany. His family moved to Paris. Mother died young. Father was a professor of art at the Sorbonne, so Josef learned art and art history very early. He himself was not good at it, painting or sculpture, you see, but because he had a sharp eye and enjoyed meeting and talking about art, he naturally went into the art business. As a dealer. He opened *Le Jeune* in 1938 and did quite well financially."

"How did you meet him?" Henri asked.

"He hired me that same year he opened the shop. I was a mere girl but he took me under his wing and taught me about the Modernists. I was so thrilled to be here and I learned so much." She paused, eyes staring back in time. "Josef was a good man. Then, in May of 1940, the Germans marched into Paris. Month by month, year-by-year Josef changed, slowly, a little at a time. He became more interested in money than art, more interested in his name and reputation than helping young artists." Madame rested back in her chair and for several minutes didn't speak.

Maggie didn't press and she glanced at Henri whose eyes were riveted on the old woman.

"Then the worst came, the black days. Days of the Occupation, when Paris turned into a German state overnight." A wistful smile touched her thin lips. "Germans are a very clever people, you know. They understood that Paris was the center of art for the world. They knew from the beginning there was a gold mine here. Josef Steiner recognized this and planned for it. Prepared for the day when the Nazis would take his art, take his money, take his family and one day take him."

Maggie's throat felt parched and she took a sip of coffee, now gone lukewarm.

"So when the ERR was formed, Josef tried immediately to get into their good graces. Find his way into their inner circle, so he would be protected."

"Did he?" Maggie asked.

"For a while. Although you know, Jews can never be part of a Nazi inner circle."

Madame Rousseau looked from Henri to Maggie before continuing.

"There was one man, a leader in the ERR whom Josef played up to. This man was in charge of confiscating all degenerate art from the museums and galleries in Paris. He cared nothing for people and would just as soon shoot you in the head than have to step around you. A man whose meanness and egomania transcended even many of the Party leaders."

Maggie held her breath, knowing what was coming.

"Oh yes," Madame touched the side of her head with two fingers as if to keep it from aching. "He was on a par with Goering and Goebbels."

"You mean Klaus Rettke, of course?" Henri said.

The words were out, the name Klaus Rettke could not be recalled. Madame Rousseau gave a tiny nod and Maggie's heart ached for Ingrid.

"Maggie, my dear girl." Madame's voice brought her to the present. "Are you all right? You are deathly pale. I hope it is nothing I've said."

Maggie shook her head. "No, no. Of course not." She felt Henri's eyes on her. "I'm just trying to make sense of it all. Do go on with your story, please."

Madame fussed with her cup, accepting a refill from Henri. With a deep sigh, she continued.

"Monsieur Steiner, Josef, thought he was safe, immune from Gestapo treatment. Until that day. He and his son, Jakob, who was, let me think, about sixteen, just a few years younger than me at that time, were working in the office when Herr Rettke and his men stormed in." The old woman's eyes flared as she gazed back in time. "It was almost as if this were a game to Rettke, to prove to Josef Steiner that no Jew was immune to the Nazis, no Jew was safe." She paused. "Josef heard Rettke shouting at me and rushed into the gallery. Jakob followed. They argued, Josef and Rettke. But Rettke would hear nothing. He smashed a valuable statue and Josef went into a fit of hysteria, sobbing, screaming, stamping his feet. Poor Jakob, he tried to calm his father, reminded him of his weak heart but--"

"Steiner had a weak heart?" Henri asked.

"Yes," Madame answered. "He was taking many medicines, each day, three and four times a day, nitroglycerine, others, I don't know what." She paused. "Josef begged Rettke not to damage anything else, reminded him that he was under Reich protection, that he was their inside collector, their, er--" She could not come up with the word.

"Their collaborator," Maggie said.

"Oui. Collaborator. But that word was never said. Jakob never understood that about his father. I, myself, had blocked that word out of my mind. A terrible word even then. Josef was despised by the Jews *and* the Nazis. Yet, all he wanted was to stay alive and keep his family alive."

"What about you, Madame?" Henri asked. "Did you know about Josef?"

"Until that day, I thought Josef was a good and honest man, a bit eccentric, but then, I was a naïve girl. I didn't even know what the word collaborator meant. To me, Josef was Josef, a man who gave me a job and brought me into the art world. A world I embraced with all my soul back then . . . and still today."

"What happened that day?" Henri asked.

"Jakob tried to intervene between Josef and Rettke. That's when Rettke told the son his father was a traitor to his people. Jakob was stunned, didn't believe it. Josef struggled to breathe, the anger, the fear, causing him great physical stress. He demanded to know: Would he lose his art, his business? Would he and his family be sent to a camp?" Madame shook her head as if to clear the image. "And Rettke? He smiled. That's all, just smiled."

She fell silent and neither Maggie nor Henri pressed.

Madame picked up the story. "Then the terror, the, how you say, catastrophe. *Mon Dieu*. Within minutes, Rettke called his men in to confiscate all the works in *Le Jeune*. They marched through and tore the paintings off the wall, packed them in crates and stowed them in their trucks. It seemed like only minutes, yet it must have been hours, and they were gone. But by then it was too late."

"Too late?" Maggie said.

"Josef collapsed with a heart attack and Jakob tried to aid him." Pause. "I begged Rettke to let me call a doctor. He laughed, the swine."

Maggie stiffened.

"By the time he left, Josef was barely alive. He died in Jakob's arms moments later."

Maggie perched on the edge of her chair, her body stretched taut like a guitar string.

"Have any of the art pieces been recovered?" Henri asked.

"A few. Many, however, have vanished for good. Deplorable, very distressing. It still causes my heart to throb."

"What ever became of Jakob Steiner?" Maggie asked.

The old woman looked at her a moment, her brow furrowed. "I don't know. After the funeral for his father, he and his mother disappeared. Some say he escaped to America, but no one seems to know for sure. Years later I heard that the mother died very shortly after her husband, but never a word about the son."

"Is it possible he was taken to a concentration camp?" Maggie asked.

"I suppose, but not immediately. Later that week Jakob attended his father's funeral, as I recall. And I doubt that Klaus Rettke would have allowed that if the plan was imprisonment for Jakob."

"So, Rettke let Jakob go. I wonder why," Henri said.

"Perhaps he had another use for him? Perhaps Rettke planned to use Jakob like he did his father?" Maggie said.

"*Non,*" Madame said. "Why not just keep the relationship with Josef? It was perfect, fine-tuned. Why change that and risk testing out a sixteen-year-old boy?"

Maggie frowned.

A soft tap on the door and the young man, Jacques, entered with more refreshments.

Maggie turned to Henri again. He stared at her, dark eyes boring holes in hers. She turned away, uncomfortable.

Madame poured fresh coffee.

"What else do you remember about Jakob?" Maggie asked. "Anything at all. His school, his friends, hobbies. Sometimes the tiniest piece of information can be the key to a person's whereabouts."

Madame nodded. "Jakob, Jakob. Let me think. He was a handsome boy, brown-haired, blue eyes and not Jewish-looking, if you take my meaning? He looked more like his mother, who was an Italian Jew, Milan, I believe." She sipped. "He had few friends, spent most of his time when not in school in the *Galerie.*"

"And school, was he a good student? What did he study?"

"History and art, naturally. He was an excellent student, top marks." A nostalgic smile lit her face.

"What about friends? Did Jakob have friends that might have visited the Gallery?" Maggie asked.

"Occasionally. Yes. There was a girl, I think, Anna, Lena? I cannot recall her name." She set her cup down with a rattle. "I can see her in my mind, dark skin, dark eyes, French, I'm sure."

"Jewish?" Henri asked.

"*Oui*, at least I . . . wait, this girl . . . she had a brother. The brother, too, was Jakob's friend, his good friend. Name?" she spoke to herself. "What was his name? Edward? Edgar? *Non, non.* Too British. I believe his name was French. He was a Jew. Of that I am certain."

"How do you know?" Maggie asked.

"Because both brother and sister died at *Dachau*."

Chapter 29

M aggie let out a breath she didn't realize she was holding. Madame Rousseau had finished her narrative and suddenly seemed a tiny shrunken old woman. The past had aged her.

"Are you all right, Madame?" Maggie asked.

A tiny nod gave her the cue to go on. "I have one more question for you, if I may." Maggie rummaged through her bag and pulled out a small folder.

Henri leaned forward.

"This is a photograph that Klaus Rettke's granddaughter found. It is of a Van Gogh painting. Does it look familiar?" Maggie held out the picture and Madame adjusted the glasses on her nose.

"Ahh, *vraiment*. Van Gogh. *Oui, oui*, it is *The Vase With Oleanders*."

"Was it in the *Galerie* back then?" Henri asked.

"*Oui, certainement.* Displayed most prominently as you first walked in. Such a magnificent piece, we had many inquiries about it, would have sold it. . . ahh, *Vincent*." Madame touched a handkerchief to her mouth.

"Then Rettke would have seen it there," Henri said.

"Oh yes, no doubt. He saw it."

Maggie's mind raced at bullet train speed. Steiner had the Van Gogh at *Le Jeune Galerie*. Rettke saw it there. What happened next? Did he fall in love with it, covet it for himself? Did he loathe it but recognize it could be worth money, a way to ensure his future? Was it simply his job to bring it back to the *Jeu de Paume*, a directive issued by Rosenberg or Goering? In any case, he most likely had it packed with the others and shipped to the museum, perhaps to deal with personally later. He would have plenty of opportunity to dispose of the painting in his own time, his own way.

"Maggie?" Henri's voice interrupted her thoughts. "Do you have any other questions for Madame?"

"Van Gogh's *Vase With Oleanders* was one of the paintings confiscated that day?"

"Ah, *oui*, it was so."

Henri looked at her. "Anything more?"

"Oh, no," Maggie said. "I'm sorry. My mind was wandering."

"Of course, my dear." Madame Rousseau looked into her eyes then smiled and nodded. "Where Van Gogh is concerned, *Je comprende très bien.*"

Maggie believed she did.

They took their leave of Collette Rousseau and *Le Jeune Galerie* late in the afternoon. They stepped out into a warm evening, the sky a deep mauve. Maggie found herself staring at a large black limousine parked in front of the *Galerie* and she could visualize the scene in 1941. The limo transformed into a Mercedes Benz staff car of the Third Reich, black and polished to a mirrored shine. The door opened and Klaus Rettke stepped out . . .

She felt a hand on her arm.

"What are you thinking?" Henri said.

"Nothing," she said. "Just ruminating on Madame's words."

She began walking with no destination in mind. Henri walked at her side.

"At least we know where Rettke obtained the original painting," Henri said. "Still, we don't know what happened to Jakob Steiner, whether he died, escaped to America or--"

"I think we have more questions than answers now." She looked at her watch. "Henri, we have an hour before the National Archives close. Let's try to find out about Walther Andreas Hofer. Maybe we can find an answer to one question, at least."

"You know," he said. "You could just ask your ex-husband."

"Don't be silly. That's too easy," she said with a smile. Nothing was easy with Rudolf. Besides, if he were somehow involved with this case, asking him would be the absolutely worst thing she could do.

They headed for the Peugeot. Henri snaked his way into the rush hour traffic. Despite the heavy volume of cars, they made it to the *Archive Nationales--Musée de l'Histoire de France*, in ten minutes. Henri parked on a gravel lot nearly empty of visitors. He locked the car and they hurried to the main doors.

Maggie looked up at the massive building with a large square in the center. Similar to many structures in France, it was a dun-colored stone with impressive columns in the front and topped by the distinct Mansard roof.

"Beautiful," Maggie said.

"Originally it was built around 1700 for the *Princesse de Soubise* and remained a mansion of the family for many years--until the Revolution," Henri said.

"Ah, an aristocrat. Was she sent to the guillotine?"

"Perhaps." He smiled. "Like many historic buildings, however, it is used now by the government."

Inside, Henri questioned the clerk at the Information Desk in French. Within moments, Henri took Maggie's elbow and steered her to a staircase of pale marble with a stunning rosewood banister and delicate, scrolled iron work. At the top was a room fronted with wide double doors and Henri did not hesitate.

Maggie followed him in and listened again as he conversed with the clerk, a diminutive woman of middle age. The clerk smiled and blushed up at him.

That now familiar ambivalence struck her. She understood why the clerk blushed. Maggie was attracted to him too. Yet at the same time she couldn't quite trust him. Why? Maybe it had nothing to do with Henri. Maybe it was simply that she did not want a one-night stand.

The clerk stood then, interrupting her thoughts, and disappeared into the stacks of shelves behind her, returning moments later with a small box. Henri leaned over her desk and signed a form then picked up the box. Maggie followed him to a 15-foot long wooden library table lit by a dozen green desk lamps.

He set the banker's box on the table. "Records on Hofer."

She reached over and snatched off the lid, grinning.

"We only have forty minutes," he said. "Can you understand the French?"

"I think I can read enough to spot something significant."

He smiled. They got to work.

One by one they skimmed through the folders.

On the third file, Maggie snapped her fingers. "Here, listen. This one is in English. 'Walther Andreas Hofer married Marlene Ritter in nineteen forty, fathered three children, all sons and had one grandchild, also male. In nineteen forty-five, he emigrated from Germany with members of his family to reside in New York City, where he became an expert in modern art for Christie's Auction House. Hofer died in nineteen seventy-two.'"

She shook her head then turned back to the files. "There's got to be more." She began scanning through the pages again.

Ten minutes later, the library clerk approached and told them they had only five minutes to closing.

"We could come back tomorrow," Henri said.

"I don't think it would help. The information just isn't here." Maggie slipped the papers back in the box and sighed with frustration.

"That's it?" Henri said, rapping his knuckles on the table. "That's all we know? That Walther Hofer died in nineteen seventy-two?"

She looked at him. "Whatever happened to Hofer's grandson?"

That night at the hotel Maggie hunched over a tiny desk by the window in her room. Across the street was an eighteenth century ashen granite church mottled with bird droppings and surrounded by dying leaves. For a few moments, she tried to imagine what this street had been like three centuries ago when the church had been built. The closest she could come were scenes from *A Tale of Two Cities*. Uneven cobblestones mired with muck and mud, which inevitably wound on up everyone's clothes, particularly the ladies hems; slop dumped out of windows to the street below. Pedestrians beware.

Maggie flipped up her laptop and set up a new file. Before she talked to Mead she wanted to sort out all the data she had. She'd have to make certain assumptions to carry these facts to conclusions, however. But that was what a puzzle was about. Trying different pieces until the right ones fit. Ideas sparked around her brain. Perhaps she should bounce those ideas off Henri. She hesitated, wondering for the thousandth time whether her failed marriage caused her reluctance to get close to men. Maggie picked up the phone. It was time to take control of her life.

In five minutes she heard a knock on her door. She opened it to Henri and invited him in.

"I thought you were, er, tired," he said.

"There are more important things than sleep. Please have a seat." She pointed to the only chair in the room, while she grabbed her pad and pen, propped up her bed pillows and tried to get comfortable." I've been trying to put all this together in my head, but I need feedback from someone familiar with the case."

"The case," he said, smiling. "I'm flattered. Go ahead."

Maggie leaned back into the pillows.

"I was thinking about Hofer."

"Oh?" she said.

"It seems to me that even if Rudolf is a descendant of Walther Hofer, so what? I mean what difference does it make?"

"You think it's a coincidence?"

"I'm saying it doesn't matter. Do you think Walther knew something about the Van Gogh painting and left clues for Rudolf, who was, what five or ten years old when he died?"

Maggie blew out a breath. "You're right, of course. It's just too eerie to have this relationship pop up now."

"That I agree with. And perhaps you can talk to Rudolf about it when we return." Henri smiled. "Now, what do you want to talk about?"

"Let's start with some assumptions. First, we can assume that Rettke confiscated the Van Gogh painting from Josef Steiner at *Le Jeune Galerie*, based on Madame Rousseau's account today."

Henri nodded. "Rettke delivered it to the *Jeu de Paume* where much of the confiscated art started out. Then he somehow smuggled it out."

"To have a copy made."

"Why?" Henri asked.

"He recognized its value? Wanted to ensure his own future?"

"So he brought the painting to Hans Van Meegeren."

Maggie nodded. "But Van Meegeren made more than one copy of the Van Gogh and--"

"How do we know that?" Henri asked.

Maggie stopped. "Good question. We don't, for sure. But let's assume for now. Lots of things point in that direction."

"Go on." Henri took out his Players. "Do you mind?"

"No, go ahead." Maggie jotted some notes on her pad. "Now, let's say that Van Meegeren made two copies, gave both to Rettke and kept Steiner's original painting. Rettke returned one copy to the *Jeu de Paume* and kept what he thought was Steiner's original painting."

Henri lit a cigarette and puffed.

"Next assumption. Van Meegeren sold Steiner's original painting to Samuel Beckman. Beckman passed it down to his son Aaron, who discovered it was not an authentic Van Gogh *nor* was it a Van Meegeren."

"Ah, now your first assumption makes sense. Beckman did not have the original, nor did he have the Van Meegeren."

"Exactly."

"You know, Maggie, you are very beautiful when you are excited."

"Uh, right, thanks. Let's keep that train rolling." She kept her eyes on Henri. "Both Rettke and Van Meegeren had been duped. *Neither* man ever had the authentic painting." She bolted upright. "Wait a minute. Could Josef Steiner have had a copy made, knowing it might be confiscated? Even as a collaborator, he knew he couldn't trust the Nazis." Maggie curled her lips in a wry smile. "Never trust a Nazi."

Henri watched her but said nothing. "That's quite a leap."

"Let's say, for argument's sake, that's exactly what he did. Josef made a copy of the Van Gogh long before Klaus got hold of it."

Henri shrugged.

She went on, "Josef tells his son Jakob about the real painting and where he has it hidden. His last words to his son as he lay dying."

"Dying because of Klaus Rettke," Henri said.

She eyed him. "But maybe the final joke was on Rettke after all."

"Yes?"

"If Josef did, indeed, make a copy of the original painting, then Ingrid's grandfather confiscated a fake."

"A bit of payback, perhaps?"

"Ironic." She shook her head. "After the War, Jakob files an insurance claim for the missing piece of art. Five million dollars on the "fake" painting confiscated by Rettke. But Jakob keeps the real one and escapes to America. Now he has five million dollars *plus* the painting."

"And disappears," Henri said. "And we still don't know where he is, or who he is." Henri yawned. "Sorry."

Maggie looked at her watch. "It's almost midnight. We should pack."

Henri rose, stubbed out his cigarette in a glass ashtray on the desk. He moved toward her.

"Maggie." He reached a hand toward her face and his fingers burned a hole in her cheek before she caught herself. "It's late, Henri and we have an early flight."

"I'll help you pack."

The blood rushed in her ears and her heart hammered on her ribs.

She turned to Henri. Her cell phone sang out.

They looked at each other before she snatched it off the desk. She listened a moment, smiled.

"Frank, is that you?" Before she could turn, Maggie heard the door click. Henri was gone. Relief and guilt flooded through her. She dismissed both without a backwards glance and launched into conversation with Frank Mead.

Chapter 30

Frank Mead tried to listen to Delacruz on his cell, but was distracted by Maggie and Rosie enjoying a wet, sloppy reunion through his passenger window. The dog looked at him and whined. Damn, he would miss that silly mutt. He flipped the phone closed and leaned into the car.

"All right, Rosie, in the back." The dog obeyed and Mead grinned at Maggie's raised eyebrows. "She did most of the driving when you were gone." He went around and got in the driver's seat as Maggie slid into the passenger seat. Rosie stuck her nose between them and licked both alternately.

"I can't thank you enough, Frank," she said.

"She was a real pain in the butt." He broke into a broad grin.

"Hmm. Did she solve any cases?"

"Yup. Couple of cold cases now closed."

They both smiled.

"So I want to hear--"

"Let's hear what you--"

They smiled again.

"You first," he said. "What did you come up with in Paris that you haven't told me by phone?"

She angled toward him and as she thumbed through her notes put forth all the theories she'd worked out with Henri.

Mead listened, frowned.

"What?" she said. "You don't buy this?"

"The point is there's no evidence. How are we going to prove any of these, er, hypotheses?"

"By finding out *who* Jakob Steiner is and *where* he is."

He looked at her. "You think you know, don't you?" She tipped her head slightly. "I think Steiner is Emil Kahn."

"Why? Because you want him to be?" He paused. "You don't like him, do you?"

"Is it that obvious?"

"Oh yeah."

She looked out the windshield.

"Why do you think it's Kahn? Because he's an art expert? Why not Henri?"

"Henri?" She spun around to face him. "Why Henri? No, of course it's not just because Kahn is an art expert, but because of his age. Henri is too young to have--"

"Right, right."

"Frank, can you do a background check on Kahn? Find out where he came from, who his family was?"

"I'm ahead of you there. We did a background check. Kahn did live in Paris with his family. The Arthur Kahn family, Emil, the oldest son, all of whom were sent to Dachau and none of whom survived, according to German records."

"What? Are you saying Emil Kahn is dead?"

"Yup."

"For God's sake, Frank. You knew all along and you let me go on and on. Steiner is Kahn," she said to the windshield. "I knew it. I knew it."

Rosie snorted in the back seat.

"That's still a really big leap, Maggie."

She told him Madame Rousseau's story about Steiner's friends who died at Dachau.

"Madame thought the name was Edward or Edgar. But it was Emil," Maggie said.

Mead looked at her, said nothing.

"So when Emil's friend's family died in the concentration camp," she continued, "he assumed his identity. Why not? Who would know in this country? What better way to escape?"

"Supposing this is true, where does it leave us?" Mead said.

"Jakob Steiner files for five million in insurance because his daddy's painting is confiscated by Klaus Rettke. Then he assumes his friend's name, Emil Kahn, and emigrates to the U.S. He has a fine arts background thanks to daddy, Josef, so he pursues it here and voilà! A new life in a new land. Probably happened a thousand times in a thousand places in this country after the war."

They fell silent.

"And," she said. "Remember . . . Kahn, Steiner, left Europe not only with five million dollars but with the *real* Van Gogh painting that his father had hidden. Now he's not only committed insurance fraud, because the painting really wasn't confiscated by the Nazis, but he still has the original." Maggie slowed her words. "Steiner had a copy made . . . and not by Van Meegeren."

They both mulled this over.

"This whole scenario is nuts. If what you say is true, Ingrid's grandfather had a copy all along. And paid Hans Van Meegeren to unknowingly forge a copy of a copy."

"And if Van Meegeren kept the one from *Le Jeune Galerie*, selling it to Beckman as authentic, that explains why Beckman's copy was not a Van Meegeren."

"Then the real Van Gogh--"

"Is still and has always been with Jakob Steiner, aka Emil Kahn," she said.

Mead shook his head. "This is like trying to figure out Rubik's Cube in Braille." He rubbed his chin. "Can we put names on these paintings?"

"What?"

"You know, so we can keep track," Mead said.

"Go on," Maggie said.

"Okay. First painting, the authentic Van Gogh, belonged to Steiner. Let's call it *The Original*. We assume Steiner had the first copy made. Let's call that *Steiner's Copy*. Rettke confiscates *Steiner's Copy* from Le Jeune Gallerie then smuggles it out of the Jeu de Paume to get another copy made. This one is the *Van Meegeren Copy*."

Maggie nodded. "But Van Meegeren decided to make an extra copy, a *Van Meegeren 2 Copy*. He kept the *Steiner Copy*, thinking it was *The Original* and sold it to Beckman. That's how Beckman got a copy that was not a Van Meegeren."

"Right," Mead said. "Van Meegeren then gave Rettke his first and second copies. Rettke returned one and kept the other, which he thought was *The Original*, for himself. Let's say the one he kept was actually the *Van Meegeren 2 copy*." Mead gave a low whistle. "So where is this *Van Meegeren 2 Copy* now?"

Maggie shook her head. "Let's take it to the next step," she said. "Kahn, Jakob Steiner, that is, now has lots of cash, illegal mind you, and he has *The Original*, the genuine, honest-to-God Van Gogh, worth maybe $70 million. A private collector would pay that much for it, no questions asked."

Mead scrunched up his face. "So Kahn kills two people. . . why, for what reason?"

"To cover up his insurance fraud, for one," Maggie said. "Two, to keep the real Van Gogh hidden for future sale, or maybe he's even sold it by now. That ought to make the buyer pretty damned pissed off, if this all came out."

"And, since Kahn's concerned about his reputation," Mead picked up the thread. "He'd want to keep the world, certainly his family, from knowing about dear old collaborator granddad."

They looked at each other, both thinking that was a good reason to kill.

Mead tightened his lips. Maggie chewed hers. Rosie hiccupped in the back seat.

"Makes a wonderful movie," Mead said.

"Frank, we've got to get the proof. Can you get a warrant to search his house?"

"Under what pretense? Your Honor, we believe Dr. Emil Kahn might have a valuable painting hidden in his house. Maybe. Maybe not, but let's give it a shot. How about a warrant?" He snapped his fingers. "Of course. A warrant for probable hunch."

"Okay, okay, never mind. What about the gun?" she asked. "It's not a common piece. What if we find it in his house?"

"Yeah, all well and good, but not a compelling reason for a judge to let us search."

"But he--"

"Look, Maggie. You've got a reputable art expert, Ph.D., good citizen, no record. We are not getting a search warrant."

"So that's it? We're done? No way to get the son-of-a-bitch?" She threw up her hands.

They sat in silence for several minutes.

"What about tricking him?" she said.

"You mean entrapment? Forget it."

"There's got to be a way." Maggie stared into space.

"What happened to all the confiscated paintings after the War?" he asked.

"They suffered many different fates. Some stayed in Paris, some went to Germany, some went back to original owners, if they were still alive, although, very few, I would guess." Maggie swung around in the seat again. "What if we use Mrs. Beckman's name to get Kahn nervous? She tells us her contact in Europe has discovered this new painting, possibly the *Van Meegeren Copy*, the one from the Jeu de Paume. She wants me to do a tech analysis of it. We bring Kahn in as an expert for additional corroboration. But he never gets to see the painting, of course."

"Of course," Mead said. "Because the Beckman painting is the first forgery, not a Van Meegeren."

"Right, but he doesn't know that. I tell him that my technology confirmed that this painting is the authentic Van Gogh, which freaks him out."

"Great, now we've got a nervous, freaked-out killer on whom we don't have a shred of evidence. That ought to work fine." Mead slapped his knee.

"Well, it needs a little fine-tuning."

"It needs a total re-write. What do you expect him to do at this point, freaked out or not? Break down? Confess?"

"Maybe lead us to the real painting? If he hasn't sold it, he'd want to make sure it was safe and secure now that another painting makes claim to be genuine." Maggie shrugged her shoulders. "I don't know."

"Yeah, or he might kill you. Think of that?"

"At least I'm coming up with ideas." She sat up suddenly and got tangled in her seat belt. "Frank, take me home. Quick."

"Something I said?" He started the car.

"I need to get back to that photograph and my program. Kahn, Steiner, whoever he is, needs to believe that I'm making progress, getting closer to the answers." Absently, she petted Rosie's head, which appeared between the front seats. "We are not going to let him get away with murder."

Chapter 31

Maggie entered her apartment, which was hot and stuffy from being closed up for a week. She dropped the keys on the entry table and immediately went to open the French doors. Rosie raced out on her heels and the two enjoyed a few moments of quiet affection in the crisp autumn air.

After she gave her dog a few biscuits and fresh water, and had a pot of coffee brewing, Maggie turned on her computer and booted up her ARTEC program. As she waited, she poured a mug and reviewed the conversation with Mead. There was something about the paintings she couldn't put her finger on. Something that stuck in her mind and wouldn't shake loose. Had Rettke left a clue?

She set the cup down and picked up the copy she'd made of his diary, thumbing through pages and slowly fine-tuning her German. Nothing about a painting. Maggie reread for the tenth time Rettke's final words:

It is with great regret that I accept the truth. I shall never go home again. My Germany, my Berlin, is lost to me. The address at 395 Pichener Road is gone, but the memories of my childhood and the happy times with my family will live on.

Why would he list the address? Wouldn't Ingrid know it? She kept reading.

Perhaps, someday, my granddaughter, Ingrid, will seek out the home in which I was born, her ancestral home. It oftentimes is true that gazing back into the past, embracing it, understanding it, and finally accepting it, can and will influence the future.

She read and reread the final paragraph in Rettke's elegant pen. *Pichener Road.* Maggie jumped up and hurried to the living room. In a box on the coffee table were letters Ingrid had left behind. They were from her grandparents in Berlin. Now that Ingrid was dead, all of her possessions belonged to Maggie. She picked up an envelope, tried to make out the return address. Then another and another. All of the letters, in fact originated from *221 Gottke-Houghplatz.* Not *Pichener Road.* Was this a clue for Ingrid?

Maggie raced to her computer, closed her ARTEC program and got online to Mapquest.

Pichener Road, Pichener Road. Is it possible there's a Pichener Road in Washington?

She scrolled down the page. There it was. It seemed to be in the warehouse district. Was there a 395? She clicked a few keys. 395 was part of a public storage facility of many buildings, numbered from 200-600. Storage facility. Could Rettke have rented a unit to keep his belongings? Would he have hidden the painting there, still believing it to be the original? Would someone hide a valuable painting in a place like that? Why else would he have added this cryptic note in his journal, the note directed toward Ingrid? Maybe he was steering her to the painting.

She grabbed her cell and speed-dialed. It rang. Where was Frank Mead when she needed him? She ran out the door.

By the time she reached him by phone, her cab was pulling up to U-Store-It warehouses. Maggie threw money at the driver and jumped out. Mead drove up as she slammed the taxi

door shut.

"Number 395," she said and headed in between the buildings.

Mead followed. "You have a key?"

"What?"

"A key. Do you have a key?"

She stopped and turned. "No, I don't have a key. God damn it. I'll rip the lock out with my teeth if I have to." She headed down an alleyway, scanning the buildings for numbers.

"Great. Why I don't I call and get the manager down here. Make sure the unit does belong to Rettke and--"

She kept moving, Mead following. 395 Pichener was in front of them, the door latched with a combination lock.

"What's the combination?" he asked.

"How the hell should I know?" She spun in a tight circle. "Sorry. Just uptight. I don't know the combination."

"Let's get the manager here," he said then flipped the phone open. "While we're waiting, why don't you try a few numbers?"

"What numbers?"

"If this was Ingrid's grandfather's locker and he wanted her to find it, get into it, he'd use a number she'd know. Right?"

"Maybe."

"Come on, Maggie, what's her birthday, or his, or some other meaningful number."

She gave him Ingrid's birthday. He spun the dial.

"Nope. Rettke's?"

Maggie squeezed her eyes closed, trying to think. "Wait, I wrote it down from Ingrid's papers." She gave him the date.

"Nope."

"Damn it. We're so close."

Just then a short, dark-haired man approached.

Mead showed his badge and explained. "Who rented this unit?"

The man looked at his logbook. "Umm."

"Umm what?" Mead said.

"Umm, odd."

"Odd," Mead repeated. "Could you elaborate a bit?"

"Umm, well, I didn't rent it but the name is, well, er--"

"Well, spit it out, man," Maggie said.

"Hermann Goering."

Maggie blinked. "That's it," she said.

Mead asked the man a few more questions and sent him away. He called Delacruz to bring the crime team.

They both re-examined the lock.

"Try this number," she said, scrolling the browser on her smartphone. "Goering's birthday."

"No."

"What now?" she said. "Wait for the lock to be cut? I can't stand it."

"What about your ex's birthday."

"Rudolf? No way."

"You said he was friendly with Rettke. What have we got to lose?"

She stared at him, shook her head.

"Why would he use Rudolf's birthday? He didn't--"

"Maggie?"

"What?" she almost shouted.

"Calm down. It was just an idea."

She spun in a circle. "Twelve-ten-sixty."

He tried the combination. The lock popped. Mead slid the lock out of the hasp.

Maggie looked at Mead, stunned. Ingrid's grandfather used her husband's birthday? She had trouble swallowing.

Mead lifted the garage door and fumbled for a light switch on the wall.

She stepped in first.

The storage unit was approximately ten feet wide by fifteen feet deep and filled to the ceiling with old, musty furniture. Rolled-up rugs stood up in one corner, lamps in another.

Maggie hesitated, taking in the smell, the feel, the sight of the past. Her stomach hurt as it had more and more lately.

"Any paintings?" Mead interrupted her reverie.

She shook herself to the present and moved into the space. She touched a mahogany chest of drawers, pulled out the top one and the rest in succession.

"What about the rugs? Could it be rolled up in--?"

"I doubt it. It could get seriously damaged." Maggie brushed the dust off her blouse and scanned the room. "We'll have to move all this stuff out where we can really examine it."

Mead obliged. He carried several small pieces outside the garage door and then shined a flashlight into hidden niches.

Maggie searched the other side of the unit. "Looks like the last piece left is that one," she said finally and pointed to an armoire with curved side panels.

"That's an old wardrobe," Mead said. "Took the place of closets back then."

Maggie nodded. "See the curved ends, though. Like rounded doors." Gently moving tables, chairs and bric-a-brac, she reached the large piece. "Might be just enough room."

"For a painting?"

"A small, rolled up painting."

"Wasn't he worried it would be damaged if left rolled up so long?" Mead said.

"He certainly didn't expect to die and leave it permanently." Maggie made her way to the armoire.

"Here, let me," Mead said, pushing a chair out of the way. He reached over and with a gloved finger opened the end panel.

Maggie leaned in.

"There was something here--you can see it in the dust," he said. "It was a cylinder shape, like a tube or--"

"Noooo. Oh no. I can't believe it. It's gone." She flopped down onto a settee. Dust billowed into the air.

Mead poked around in the furnishings for a few minutes.

"Let's go outside. Air is rancid in here." He ushered her to the sidewalk.

"There's only one person who could have known about this. Only one," she said. "Rudolf. They were evidently close. He knew Rettke and Rettke used his birthday for the combination." Her words slowed and she realized she felt hurt at this. Why didn't she know Rudolf and Rettke were close? How much more did Rudolf not tell her?

"Maybe they had some kind of business deal going on? An art deal." Mead said.

"What else?"

"Perhaps Rettke trusted Rudolf to take care of the painting, find a buyer."

A van pulled up and Delacruz plus two crime techs got out.

Mead gave them instructions.

Delacruz stood with Mead and Maggie talking about the storage unit, when his cell went off.

"For you," the sergeant said to Mead.

Mead took the phone, listened, worked his jaws and looked at Maggie.

"Now what?" Delacruz said.

"More bad news, I'm afraid."

Maggie turned to him and their eyes met.

"Tell me," she said.

"Rudolf Hofer." Mead focused on Maggie. "He's been shot to death."

Chapter 32

Emil Kahn had barely fallen asleep when his alarm clock rang. Six-thirty. He rolled over and stared up at the ceiling in the shadowy room. Early morning light filtered in through the curtains of the bedroom and he could make out shapes. An armoire, a dresser, mirror, valet for his suits. He missed Serena, but at least he talked to her yesterday. Her voice soothed. What would she do if she knew?

He couldn't find the strength to move. Not yet. His body felt old, filled with cancer or some dread disease that made it heavy and cumbersome. How much longer could he keep up the façade? Soon. It would be over soon. And yet, trepidation crowded out this tiny ray of optimism. He wondered what his morning visitor wanted to see him about.

He folded his arm over his forehead and turned his thoughts to Henri Benoit and his insistence on meeting with him this morning. Urgent, he'd said. What could Henri possibly want? How much could he know? The alarm went off again.

Rolling painfully onto his side, Kahn sat up and massaged his stiff lower back. Then he stood and staggered into the shower. The hot water would help ease the aches for a while.

By seven-thirty, he was dressed in slacks and a golf shirt and had coffee brewed. Two cups helped him gain control of his nerves. Tremors had started anew in his right eye and his hands shook more and more often. Would Henri notice? Would it give him away? What about the police? What if they came to question him? But why would they? They had no reason. . . still, they might; they questioned everyone even slightly involved in a murder case, didn't they? The doorbell rang. Kahn clenched and relaxed his fists to relieve the tension then went to answer it.

"*Bonjour*, Emil," Henri said and walked past him into the living room.

Henri looked less than his best this morning. Jacket wrinkled, he wore no tie and his hair fell in waves around his face. Dark circles made his deep-set eyes deeper.

Kahn felt his spirits rise. He had to maintain the upper hand at all costs.

"*Café?*" He led him to the kitchen.

"*Oui, merci,*" Henri said.

Kahn refilled his own cup and poured a new one for his guest. He attempted to question Henri about his trip to Paris.

"*Allait-il comment votre voyage?*

Henri shrugged. "*Le voyage était bon.*" No more.

"*Avez-vous appris beaucoup `a Paris au sujet de la peinture de Gogh de fourgan?*" Did Henri learn anything of the Van Gogh?

"*Pas beaucoup,*" was the unsatisfying reply.

"*Et toi et* Maggie Thornhill *êtes devenus le long bon?*"

The two men took each other's measure. Kahn smiled, wondering if Henri had worked his charm on the lovely Miz Thornhill.

"*Très bien,*" Henri said. "*Très bien.*" But he did not smile back.

Emil set his cup down. "Now what was it you wanted to see me about so early in the morning? *Comment est-ce que je peux vous aider?*"

"*Mais non*, Emil," Henri said with a tight smile. "You have it all wrong." He sat down at the kitchen table and crossed his legs.

"It's not how you can help me. It's how *I* can help *you*."

Maggie had slept barely three hours all night. She couldn't stop thinking about the painting, Ingrid's grandfather, Emil Kahn, Henri and, of all people, Frank Mead. She didn't know why Mead kept popping into her thoughts, but there he was.

By the time she nodded off in early morning, she had convinced herself that Emil Kahn was Jakob Steiner, that he had cashed in his father's insurance policy yet somehow managed to keep the authentic Van Gogh when he escaped to America. When the fakes began to surface, he panicked, killed Ingrid, maybe even Rettke, although forensics couldn't prove he was murdered, and then Aaron Beckman. And now even Rudolf?

My God. Rudolf is dead. How is that possible? She lay in her rumpled bed, mind drifting to her ex-husband and the early days, the good days. The days when they first met, talked, laughed, made love. Now he was gone. A surge of anger welled in her. She kicked off the covers and stomped into the bathroom, slamming the door behind her. Rosie cried out and Maggie yanked open the door. The dog looked up at her with sad eyes. Maggie swallowed her bitterness and anger. She felt betrayed by those who had loved her. Betrayed and alone.

The tears fell. She kneeled down, put her arms around the dog and cried into her fur. Rosie licked her tears.

Finally, Maggie dragged herself to the kitchen, made some coffee and then returned to the bathroom and showered. Everything went wrong. She ran out of soap, the hot water turned lukewarm and the telephone rang when she couldn't get to it.

She dressed and checked her messages. Mead. She dialed.

"Hey, how are you doing?" he said, that same gentleness in his voice she had heard when Ingrid died.

"Just fucking great. Sorry. Here I go again, taking it out on you." She took a deep breath. "Did you find out what happened to Rudolf?"

"Shot, neat and quick. Probably the same gun as--"

"I knew it. It's Kahn, God damn him."

"Hold on. We don't know that."

"Where was Rudolf found?"

"His office, head on his desk."

Maggie drew in a breath.

"We checked his office and apartment," Mead said. "No painting or hint of a painting. No real surprise there. It's possible that Hofer hid the painting or locked it in a safe somewhere before he met up with the killer. Where would he stash it?"

"The museum has a safe," she said. "It's a huge room in storage that's secured by a high-security system. Temperature and humidity controlled. Some of the most valuable objects are kept there."

"I'll talk to whoever's in charge now."

"God, this is a nightmare," she said.

"Yeah, well, we'll check out the safe. But I think you're right. I doubt Hofer stowed it before he was murdered." Mead paused. "Maybe he was actually waiting for the killer, to cut a deal."

"So that means the killer has the painting." Maggie said, feeling a shiver of cold run up her arms.

"Maybe," he said. "It's just one scenario."

"Wouldn't someone have heard the shot? There are offices up and down the hallway."

"You'd think," he said. "No one we talked to at the museum did, or so they say. Not too many staff around, all scurrying to get ready for a show."

"Now what? I can't believe Rudolf is dead. Ingrid is dead."

"And Beckman," Mead said.

Maggie chewed on her lower lip, trying to quell the tears from starting. "Is a painting, even a Van Gogh, worth so many lives?"

Maggie was convinced that if she could locate the painting, ARTEC could prove its authenticity. She decided to use Mrs. Beckman's forgery to fine tune the program so it was ready for that ultimate test.

She photographed the fake and uploaded it into her computer. Side by side with the real Van Gogh image taken at the National Gallery, she then examined both images: the brushstrokes, the color density, textures, shadows and lines. She knew that an artist's aesthetic signature could be detected within the lines and curves of his work. If all else failed, there was fractal analysis, but that was time consuming and Maggie hoped she didn't have to go there . . . yet.

She stared at the two paintings. Mrs. Beckman's painting and the museum self-portrait were done by two different artists. Even she could see the differences, subtle though they were. She ran her hands through her hair.

If ARTEC worked, and she believed it did, she still needed to find the Van Gogh. She was certain that Kahn would have the answers.

Would he give them up? Not likely.

Maggie stood and circled the room, grappling with her thoughts. She walked over to the hall mirror and spoke to her reflection.

"Try the direct approach. Go see him, talk to him. Confront him with what you know. He'll admit he's Jakob Steiner, confess to the murders and take you to a secret room where he's got the painting hidden." She paused. "Then he'll kill you, cut you into tiny pieces, and bury you in the backyard. Which will serve you right."

She had to see him. Maybe she wouldn't accuse him outright, just lay out her theories and get his input. Test his reactions. Watch his body language. See if he sweats. Besides, he's not going to kill me in his own house. That would be totally insane, and insane is not what Kahn is. Desperate, perhaps, but not crazy.

She scurried into the bedroom, opened her night table drawer and retrieved the gun that Mead had given her. She stared at it a while then tucked it into her shoulder bag. She felt safer.

"I'm the one that's insane."

Rosie opened her mouth wide and yawned.

Maggie resolved not to call ahead. It was still early morning and Kahn was bound to be home. She dropped Rosie off at Vanessa's and hurried away on foot.

On the Metro ride to Kahn's house she rehearsed what she would say, somehow make her visit seem plausible. Kahn and his ego would undoubtedly be happy to give her advice about ARTEC, Van Gogh, life, death, whatever.

She walked the two blocks from the Metro and just as she turned the corner she stopped short. Henri Benoit strode down the steps of Kahn's house, lips compressed, eyes narrowed, and took off in the opposite direction.

Maggie side-stepped behind a large elm and focused on the Frenchman as he disappeared around the corner. There was nothing unusual about Henri visiting Kahn. They were friends, colleagues, at the least. Yet it bothered her. Something about the timing and Henri's troubled visage.

She chanced a few steps when a voice caught her attention. She backed up. Emil Kahn burst through his front door, cell phone to his ear, eyes almost feverish. The door slammed behind him and he never turned back. She watched him descend his front steps, quickly for an old man. He struck out in the same direction as Henri and vanished around the corner.

How was she going to confront him now? More important, what was his almighty hurry? Perhaps Kahn's worried, fearful that his game is up. That's it. Or is that merely my imagination? Still, Maggie couldn't let go of it. Kahn would attempt to escape, run away, like he did so many years ago. He'd be gone forever. And with him, the painting.

Anxiety simmered in her gut like carbolic acid. She chewed on a thumbnail and studied Kahn's residence. Older home, colonial, two stories, probably with a basement. They all had basements. Nicely kept, but not pretentious. Yard needed some work. A burglar might break in and look for silver or electronics. But it didn't look like a house that would have a seventy-million dollar painting on display.

Suddenly, it clicked. That was exactly the reason it might be in the house. Because no one would guess the truth: the painting was hiding in plain sight.

Maggie cast her eyes up and down the street then walked up to the front door. She tried the bell, in case a wife or housekeeper was inside. No response. God. Now what? Suppose Kahn came back. This was illegal entry. Even Mead couldn't get her out of this one. In fact, he'd be so pissed off, he might not want to. Her hands started to sweat and she felt the urge to urinate. What the hell was she doing? Breaking and entering.

What if the painting was here? The real painting? And Rettke's copy. She thought back to the three people who were killed for this painting and couldn't suppress a shudder. Suppose Kahn was planning his getaway right now. Perhaps he was at a travel agent purchasing tickets to who-knows-where, right at this moment. She should call Mead. No, that would take time. Precious time. She patted her bag and felt the heft of the revolver. A breath oozed out of her mouth.

Maggie gathered her nerve, reached into her pocket and pulled out surgical gloves, which she always carried in case she was called in on a crime scene. She snapped them on, not an easy task with her jitters. She held her breath, tried the front door knob. Locked. She walked down a side alley, glancing over her shoulder several times. Too early on a Saturday morning for most folks. The windows were closed but maybe not locked. She tested one. Locked. And another. Same. She stopped moving when she came to a gate that led to a small garden. Lovely. Kahn's own secluded space in the city. She flipped the latch. Again she surveyed the area then walked to the back door. The screen door was locked.

By now sweat dripped down her forehead and dampened her hair. She made her way further around the house and came upon sliding glass doors. She pushed on one and it slid open with a tiny squeak. Her heart started thrumming and she told it to shut up. Aware that she was royally screwed and maybe dead if anyone came by, she inhaled sharply and stepped inside.

Blood rushed in her ears and she had troubling listening for any sounds. She wiped the sweat off her upper lip with her forearm. God, I'm going to leave my DNA everywhere.

A clock ticked somewhere in one of the rooms. She peered around. The room she entered was a den with bookcases, L-shaped sofa and end tables. She tiptoed through the hallway. Her fingers touched the digital camera she had stashed in her pocket.

Daylight provided all the light she needed. She stole into the kitchen then the dining room and living room, examining the paintings on the walls, which appeared to be prints, and checking cabinets where something might be hidden.

She found a room that was certainly Kahn's office and dug through the paper stacks on his desk. Nothing unusual. She glanced at his appointment book. Henri's name did not appear in it for this morning. Odd. Surprise visit? She fingered books on the shelves, opened cabinets and closets, peeked behind pictures on the wall.

Next, she climbed to the second floor. Each creak and groan of the old steps made her blood bubble. She searched the three bedrooms, each furnished with antique European pieces, Persian rugs and lacy curtains. As her Aunt Sara would say, "From the old country."

Her shoulders slumped in frustration. Was she wrong about Kahn after all? A flutter of despair rose in her throat.

Back downstairs she stood in the entryway, massaging her temples with her fingertips. Birds chirped outside the windows as the city awakened to mid-morning. She turned back to the staircase. That's when she noticed it, half-hidden in the handsome wainscoting. A door.

To the basement.

Chapter 33

Frank Mead kicked back in his swivel chair and mulled over Maggie's theories. She was so sure Kahn and Steiner were the same man. He, on the other hand, wasn't. Maybe he'd visit Emil Kahn and get a new read. See what the good doctor had to say. If he really was Steiner, would he be rattled or was he too sure of himself?

Mead picked up his cell, punched in Kahn's number, but disconnected before it rang. Instead, he tried Maggie on her cell. He wanted to untangle this convoluted trail of paintings before he tackled Kahn. Or at least try.

She picked up on the second ring.

"Maggie, yeah, listen, I wanted to . . . what, wait, what?" He couldn't have heard correctly. "Say again. You're where? I can't hear you." He scrunched his face up. "What're you whispering for ?" He shut up and listened. "You are kidding, right?"

She hung up on him.

Mead clipped his phone to his belt and sprinted through the office door. Twenty minutes later he was parked across the street from Emil Kahn's house.

The day was clear and crisp, not a cloud in the sky. Perfect day for a break-in.

Mead stepped out of his Beemer and looked around. An old lady walked her Sheltie across the street. He walked to the front door and rang the bell. No answer. He ambled up the alleyway, hands in his pockets, trying to look casual. Anxiety burned the hole in his gut deeper. He popped three Tums, found his way into the garden and spotted the open sliding door. Shit.

He stuck his head through and listened. Nothing. What the hell was she thinking? And what was he doing, following her off this precipice? If he got caught, at the very least he could be busted down to a beat cop, at the worst . . . *that* he didn't want to contemplate. He felt sweat bead on his upper lip and swiped it with the back of his hand. What choice did he have? He could arrest her for B and E, or he could try to get her out of this mess.

He stepped into the room and warily made his way through the house.

"Maggie?" he said, voice low.

A tiny sound caught his attention. Downstairs. He located the door to the basement and opened it as gently as possible. The lights were on below. He tread lightly one step at a time, hoping the stairs wouldn't squeak. They did.

"Maggie?"

When he reached the bottom he found himself in a family room. Sofas, chairs, big screen TV and kids toys strewn around: a blue and red tricycle, a giant stuffed panda, and wall to wall bookcases packed with paperbacks. He picked one out: *Stellaluna*, a kids' story about a bat. Mead shoved it back in place. Where the hell was she?

"Maggie?" No answer. Was she hurt? Unable to respond?

He noticed two doors on the opposite side of the room. He drew his gun instinctively and tiptoed to the first, his breathing strained. He yanked the door open. Clothes swayed on the pole. He pushed them aside and looked. Empty.

Next he tried the second door. Same routine. This time he found a laundry room.

He snatched out his phone and pressed Maggie's number, waited as it rang. He could hear it ringing nearby; he zeroed in on the sound. It was coming from the other side of that bookcase.

She answered on the third ring.

"Where the devil are you?" he said, anger roaring in his ears.

"Step back," was the reply.

"What?"

"Move away from the bookcase."

He did. The bookcase swung out into the room.

"And you thought this only happened in the movies," she said, negotiating the narrow space.

"Yeah, *Young Frankenstein*. What's going on?" he said. "Do you realize how much trouble you could--?"

"Come with me."

She walked back through the opening angled between the wall and the bookcase. He tamped down his anger and followed.

Lights came on in a room that wasn't a room. It was a museum, an art gallery. Paintings hung on the four walls, perhaps a dozen. Each was bathed in warm spot lighting. Bronze and porcelain sculptures stood on marble pedestals.

"Holy shit," he whispered.

He faced Maggie Thornhill who was beaming as if she'd just won the lottery.

"How did you find this room?"

"I thought I heard something like a humming sound coming from behind the bookcase. Then suddenly it clicked off. So I took a closer look." She smiled. "I'm a photographer. I observe things. I noticed that the edge of the built-in bookcase didn't quite meet the wall. Light was coming through. At first I figured it was poor craftsmanship. Then the click and the humming began again. It reminded me of the humidity system at the museum, you know, to keep the artifacts from drying out. I decided to have a closer look. I ran my fingers over the shelves and found a switch. Voilà."

He just shook his head.

"They're real, Frank, every single piece of art in here. I'd stake my life on it," she said.

"Your life might be at stake," Mead said.

She ignored him. "Kahn's own private collection. There it is. The Van Gogh." She pointed. "In the flesh, er, the oils."

He blew out a long breath, his wrath subsiding as he realized what she'd discovered.

"You think that's the original?" He moved closer to the painting.

"I'm sure of it," she said. "Also, somewhere here, he's got the copy Rudolf had, a Van Meegeren. Probably still rolled up."

"My, my, my," was all Mead could say.

"Frank, what do we do now? Can we get a search warrant? How can we--?"

"Hold on, whoa, whoa. You come busting into this guy's house and now you want me to make it legal? What am I, a miracle worker?" He paced.

"Frank, don't you see what's going on here? Kahn is Steiner. This proves it. You've got to--"

"I don't *got* to do anything." He held up his hands. "Listen, Maggie, think. All these works could very well be legitimate. Kahn may have bought them, collected them for years. Then all we've got is your breaking and entering."

"And yours."

"Right, that's just fucking great. Do you know what this could do to me? You know how long it took me to make Lieutenant. I could lose my job, everything I worked for, I could--" he sputtered, unable to finish.

"I'm sorry, Frank. I didn't think--"

"Exactly, goddamn it, you didn't think. Now what? Any brilliant ideas? We can't use any of this evidence, you know, none of it, nada, zilch." He slapped his forehead.

"Please, take it easy. You're right, I admit it. But it's done and it can't be undone. We have to turn this to our advantage." She moved toward him. "I'm sorry, Frank, really. I don't want to be responsible for you losing your job, for God's sake."

He looked at her, his heart ratcheting down a notch at her anguish. "Awright, awright. Let's figure this out."

"Look," she said. "All these works of art may very well be legit. But not the Van Gogh. Not that one. He collected insurance on it sixty years ago."

Mead swung around to study the infamous painting.

"Still Life: Vase With Oleanders," Maggie said. "With his signature bottom left."

"Jesus," Mead said.

"I'm going to shoot these digitally so we can check their authenticity." She reached in her bag and brought out her camera. "All of these are stolen. I can feel it in my bones."

"Yeah, well from your bones to a judge's ears."

Maggie hurried around the room, snapping pictures. She turned to him as she stowed the camera back in her bag. "What now?"

He fixed her with an exasperated look. "I could arrest you."

"Very funny."

"Do you see me laughing? If I arrested you, all this," he waved his arms, "would become an open investigation."

She stared at him.

He stared back. "I could report suspicious activity in the house and as an officer of the law it would be my duty to check. Once I'm in, I'm in, and anything I find that appears to be an illegal enterprise would be subject to an investigation. Legal investigation."

"What suspicious activity? Me? But how would you have known I was here? I just walked in, didn't break any--"

He took her arm and ushered her up the steps, shutting the light off behind him. "Come on."

Mead walked to the back door with Maggie in tow. "Like so." He opened the back door, stepped out and punched a windowpane from the outside in with his gloved fist.

"Yikes," she whispered.

"Now lock the back door and come back out through the sliding door." She did and closed it behind her.

"Go home," he told her. "I'll handle it from here."

"Frank, whatever you do, don't let that painting out of your sight. We can't lose it now, when--"

"I hear you." He wanted her to stay but said, "Get out of here. Now."

Mead watched her walk away and prayed he could save both of them.

✦ ✦ ✦

The crime team crawled over the basement and art gallery collecting evidence. Mead was on his cell when he heard voices in the other room. He flipped it closed and took several deep breaths. Confrontation time.

"What is happening here? How did you get in?" Emil Kahn ranted as he entered the room, cheeks blistery red, eyes bulging.

"Please, sir, calm down. Let me explain." Mead took the old man by the arm and led him to a chair.

"Do not patronize me. I do not need to sit. I need to know what in blazes is going on. What gives you the right--?"

Mead held up his hands. "Dr. Kahn. I came by to see you this morning, to ask you some questions about--"

"What questions? Why do the police need to ask me questions?"

"Please, sir. You're an art expert, right? I needed some information about a painting, the Van Gogh, well, you know which painting." Mead cleared his throat. "When you didn't answer, I thought you might be out back. I walked down the alleyway. That's when I saw the broken glass."

"Broken glass?"

"Evidently someone smashed in your side window. When I came into the house to see if the perpetrator was still on the premises, I saw the door below the staircase ajar. I figured you might be hurt or in trouble. I checked the downstairs, saw the bookcase moved, and, well, here we are."

Kahn blanched.

"Doctor, why don't you sit down?"

"No, no, I must see, downstairs, the painting, I mean my paintings."

"Can you make it down the steps?" Mead asked.

Kahn pushed him aside and limped down the lower stairs, sheer fury lending him strength. Mead walked behind. Kahn reached the bottom and gazed around the room. He touched the edges of several frames and ran his hand over a bronze statue. "*Mein Gott.*"

"What did you say?"

"Nothing, nothing."

"Doctor, it would help us if you could tell us whether anything is missing."

Kahn blinked.

"This looks like a valuable collection," Mead went on.

"Indeed," Kahn said. "These are very valuable works, Lieutenant. Paintings and sculptures I have collected over the years. All perfectly legitimate, I assure you, and I have the papers to prove it."

"I never asked if they were legitimate."

Kahn fell back, stricken. "But, I--"

"I don't doubt you, sir. I'm sure they're real. May I ask, though, why they aren't kept more secure? If anyone wanted to steal works of art, wouldn't they target collectors, experts, and assume they have private collections?"

"Perhaps. But in my opinion, a fancy high-tech security system would be infinitely more dangerous, would give away the fact that there were valuables in this house, you see. Look around you, Lieutenant. Does this look like a house where millions of dollars in art work would be hidden?"

Mead shook his head, not in agreement, but in astonishment. Was Kahn so naïve, so foolish to believe his own words?

The crime team distracted Kahn, and the old man's eyes were on them. Mead saw his chance.

"By the way, sir, there's a blank space on the wall there with a spotlight shining on it. Looks like a painting hung there at some time. Did you take it down?"

Kahn whirled around. His lower lip began to quiver.

"No, noooo, *Gott*, please. It's gone, my precious painting, gone." Tears filled the man's eyes.

"What painting is gone?"

Kahn squeezed his eyes shut in answer.

"Doctor, is it Van Gogh's *Vase with Oleanders*? Is that the one that's missing?"

Kahn's eyes opened slowly. He said simply, "Of course not. I never owned a Van Gogh. Never."

"What painting is missing then?"

"A Degas," Kahn whispered. "A precious Degas."

Mead nodded. Maggie had been right all along.

Chapter 34

Emil Kahn closed the door on the last of the crime lab team. Mead had left an hour before but the technicians had taken their bloody time. Did the cop believe him about the missing painting, that it was a Degas? He didn't think so. For an uncouth and, no doubt, uneducated member of the police department, Frank Mead worried him. Those eyes--boring into his, searching, seeking, suspicious. Ach. What was the matter with him?

Kahn leaned his body against the door for fear he might collapse. The weariness soaked his bones. Death might not be so bad. Then he envisioned Serena and the children and snapped himself to control. He had an important task to take care of, one that would take all his strength.

Adrenaline steadied him. He moved to the couch in the living room. Pulling out the middle cushion, he unzipped the cover and shoved his hand into the soft foam pillow. His fingers scrabbled around, finally touched metal. He almost cried in relief. The police had not searched thoroughly after all. There had been no search warrant, only a suspected crime that Mead reported. He withdrew his Walther PP.32 and caressed it to his chest. He checked for ammunition. Then he slid it into his jacket pocket and shrugged on his jacket.

Kahn knew who had the painting, the only person who could possibly have taken it.

✦ ✦ ✦

Maggie drew her shoulder bag close. The camera inside contained the digital photographs of Kahn's hidden treasure of paintings. She was sure that this Van Gogh was genuine but she had to find out whether the other pieces were stolen or confiscated art works.

If Kahn is Steiner, all of these could be lost works from World War II. Who to ask? She could e-mail the photos to Lemercier in Paris. But that would take an extra day with the time difference. What about someone at the National Gallery? A lump tightened in her throat when she thought of Rudolf. No. The staff there is in total disarray with Rudolf dead.

She finally settled on Henri. As Rudolf's curator and art connoisseur, he would recognize the stolen works.

Maggie stepped to the corner and hailed a taxi. Sitting in the cab, she realized the sunshine had vanished, a leaden sky in its place. The wind blew scraps of trash around. Any minute it would rain.

She reached into her bag for an umbrella and was instantly reminded of what it carried. Mead's gun, a semi-automatic 9 milimeter Glock. It made her feel safe. Like Mead did. She recalled Mead's words, something to the effect that either *he* would stay to protect her or *his gun* would. She'd chosen the gun that night and wondered now if that had been a mistake. The idea of making love to Frank Mead had a definite appeal of late.

Maggie shook away the notion and turned her attention to the weapon in her hand. She stroked the cool, smooth metal; her fingers inched their way up the barrel. Forgotten until now, she felt oddly comforted by it.

In front of Henri's apartment door she fought her way through a whipping wind. Maybe she should have called first. What if he wasn't alone? God, she'd be mortified if a cute young thing opened the door.

She gave a tentative knock and tried in vain to untangle her hair.

The door opened. Her hands dropped to her side.

"Maggie. What a surprise." Henri hesitated before allowing her in.

"Sorry to intrude, but I was hoping you'd have a minute to look at some pictures. Is this a bad time?"

"*Mais non*, please. Looks like it might storm." He half smiled. "I have some coffee, if you like."

"Thanks." She untied the belt on her raincoat.

A glance around the apartment told a different story about Henri than she'd been prepared for. Antiques rather than modern, heavy oil paintings rather than Impressionist, and Schumann rather than jazz in the background. How little she knew him.

Henri straightened his dark red turtleneck and led her into the living room, two steps down from the entry hallway.

"Sit down, please." He handed her a mug of coffee. "It's strong, beware."

"Henri," she said. "I expect you've heard about Rudolf?"

"Yes. I am so sorry, Maggie. I know you were getting divorced but still, it is hard to lose someone close to you."

"Two someones." Clearing her throat, she said, "How did you find out? It wasn't in the papers yet."

"Ahh, through friends at the museum. They have closed the gallery today, in memoriam, you know."

She lowered her head.

"What pictures do you have for me?" He rubbed dark stubble on his chin. She realized suddenly that he wasn't really all that handsome. His nose was large, his eyes small, not blue like Frank's, and . . . what was she thinking? Mead had certainly gotten under her skin.

She pulled out the camera. "Can I load these onto your computer? I'd explain but it's just as easy to show you."

"Oui, over there." He stood, walked past her toward a desk in the far corner of the large room. He clicked a few keys on the laptop on his desk and gestured to the chair.

She sat.

He lit a small brown cigarette. Strong, European.

Maggie plugged in her camera then she set up a new folder in the C drive and began the download. Several photos popped up on the screen as they both waited. She could hear him inhale deeply behind her. The smoke and the smell gathered around her head and reminded her of Paris.

"What am I looking at?" he asked.

"Photographs taken in a gallery of a private collector," she began. "The police want to know whether these could be works stolen during the war."

"Who's the collector?" He drew several quick puffs on the Players.

"I can't tell you that. It's part of an ongoing investigation."

"You mean *the* ongoing investigation."

She didn't answer.

Henri pulled a chair up beside her and crushed the cigarette into a glass ashtray. He leaned over to get a closer look at the photos in the thumbnail she had created. He enlarged each one and took his time studying them.

She watched as Henri clicked on photo by photo, and back again.

"Maggie, are these from Rettke's collection?"

"What? No. What makes you say that?"

"It just makes sense. You finally located Rettke's cache, the art he confiscated during the war, yes?"

"Absolutely not," she said.

Henri suddenly gasped. "The Van Gogh. It is here? The genuine?"

"I don't know if it is the real one. That's why I'm here."

The *Vase of Oleanders* glimmered in blues and golds on the large flat screen.

He turned to her, face drained of color.

"What is it?" she said.

"It's just a shock to see the painting, now, again, in another setting. It cannot be the real one." His voice sounded hoarse. "Who's collection is this. You must tell me."

She shook her head. "I'm sorry, but I can't." She paused. "What makes you say this is not the real painting?"

"I, I don't know, for certain."

"Do you recognize any of the other works?"

He didn't answer.

She touched his shoulder. "Henri?"

He bristled.

Maggie kept her eyes on him as he focused on the screen. His jaws worked silently.

A knot of anxiety began to form in Maggie's throat. She was sure he knew more than he was telling. The nagging suspicion that she'd felt about him in Paris came back in full force, sending her stomach into a back flip. Something wasn't right.

As if in confirmation, the doorbell chimed.

Chapter 35

Maggie clicked a key on the computer and the screen went black. Henri opened the door and she half-expected to hear Frank Mead's voice. Instead, it was Emil Kahn's. She blinked twice as if to clear her mind.

Before Henri could complete a *"bonjour,"* she heard Kahn's deep-throated, "Where is it, Benoit?"

"Where is what, Emil? And what is this *Benoit*? You never call me that," Henri said. "Come in, please, don't--"

"What have you done with my painting? You took it and I want it back. Where. . . is . . . it?"

Henri swiveled to Maggie as if she had the answer.

Kahn's face morphed into a rigid mask when he saw her.

"What are you doing here?" Kahn said.

"Nice to see you too," she said.

"Emil, please, come in." Henri reached for the older man's arm.

Kahn looked from Maggie to Henri then seemed to make up his mind. He stepped into the apartment, hair ruffled, coat collar crooked.

Henri pushed the door closed and the wind whistled to a stop. "Please, sit."

Kahn descended the two steps into the living room. His eyes narrowed but he said nothing as Maggie stood across from him.

"Let me get you something to drink, maybe--" Henri offered.

"Why is she here?"

Henri stiffened and his lips tightened into a thin line. "Because we are friends, Emil, just like you and I are friends." He picked up the pack of Players from the side table and lit one. "Why are you so distressed, what is wrong? And what painting are you referring to?"

"I think it would be better if Miz Thornhill were not here. This is between you and me."

"Ah." Henri looked at Maggie. "I have a feeling she already knows what this is about. *Oui?*"

Maggie's mind flashed through her options, landed on one: the truth, or at least the truth as she knew it. But what if she was wrong? What if Kahn wasn't Steiner? She had no choice.

"It's about the painting," she began. "It's always been about the painting. Vincent Van Gogh's *Vase With Oleanders*, missing since World War Two. The one Ingrid was murdered for."

A soft moan escaped Kahn's lips.

"Wait a minute," Henri said. "Let me get this straight, Emil. This painting, the one Rettke had photographs of, the one you've been trying to authenticate, you think that I have it? This is crazy. How can I have it?"

"Do you take me for a fool, Benoit? You found the painting and stole it from me, from my house. You've known all along, haven't you?" Kahn said. "I want it back, you thieving scum, you--"

"Emil." Henri closed the gap between him and Kahn. The two men stood face to face and despite Kahn's height advantage, Henri seemed to wield the power. "You had the painting? The genuine Van Gogh, all along? All this time? How did you get it, where . . . wait a minute. Those photos you downloaded," he turned to Maggie, "was that the Van Gogh?"

"What photos?" Kahn said.

"You said it was a collector, *oui*, a private collection." Henri turned to Kahn. "*You* are the collector. You've had the painting all along." He swore in French under his breath.

"Henri, please," Maggie said. "I'll explain the photographs, but I think Emil needs to do some explaining as well."

Kahn's eyes bulged. "You have pictures of my painting? You were in my house." This was not a question. "With that police lieutenant." He leaped across the room, suddenly spry for his age, forcing Maggie to retreat a few steps.

"Son-of-a-bitch. Of course, now it makes sense. My God. You discovered my gallery and took pictures of my collection. How dare you," Kahn sputtered. "Those precious works, they're mine. Rightfully mine. I bought every one of them, with my blood, with the blood... of my father." Words suddenly failed him. He backed away from her and pulled a gun from his pocket. "It cannot end this way. Not after so many years."

"*Mon Dieu*, Emil, *s'il vous plait*," Henri said, holding out a hand.

Maggie's fingers crept toward her bag on the couch.

"Don't move," Kahn said, voice raw.

"Let's talk this out, Emil, please." She kept her voice soft. "There's no need for that. Please. Put the gun down. Let's get out the truth, once and for all." She looked into Kahn's watery eyes. "Isn't it time?"

"Please, sit, Emil, let's talk about this," Henri said.

"You two first. Sit," Kahn said.

Maggie sat near her bag. Henri lowered himself onto the arm of the sofa, his body touching hers.

The old man sat on the closest chair. His hand never loosened on the gun, however, and his back remained ramrod stiff.

"Someone please tell me what's going on," Henri said.

"Since you seem to know everything, my dear, why don't you tell him?" Kahn relaxed his grip on the gun, letting it rest on his lap.

Maggie aimed her words at Kahn. "Your real name is Jakob Steiner. Your father was Josef Steiner. He owned an art gallery, *Le Jeune Galerie*, in Paris during the war. Josef was, in fact, an expert in the Impressionist style and a collector. Also, sadly, he was a Nazi war collaborator."

She knew it was the truth.

Kahn squeezed his eyes shut and Maggie thought he might faint. All the arrogance had drained out of him. When he opened them, however, a fire had rekindled.

She went on. "Before your father died, he told you of the Van Gogh painting. He'd had a copy made by some unknown artist, *not* Hans Van Meegeren. This copy wound up in Aaron Beckman's hands." She took a breath. "Josef Steiner hid the original from Rettke and the ERR so they wouldn't be confiscated. The painting Rettke actually commandeered was a fake, a copy from the very beginning. The irony, though, was hidden from him, perhaps until he died." She slowed her words. "I wonder if Rettke ever knew the truth at the end." She took note of Kahn's twisted smile.

"Josef then took out an insurance policy on the real painting," Maggie said. "If and when the Nazis turned on him--he was sure they would, after all, he was a Jew--at least his family would be protected."

"Is this true?" Henri asked.

Kahn remained silent.

"So," Maggie kept on, "you collected five million dollars and escaped to the States with the authentic Van Gogh. But you did well in this country with the insurance money and you didn't need to sell the painting. Not right away. You planned to sell it eventually to a private collector, no questions asked, no publicity. No one need know that the painting was one confiscated from its rightful owners or that you'd already cashed in on the insurance. Committed fraud. " She paused. "Seventy million dollars. Isn't that about what it's worth? Not a bad legacy to leave your kids and grandkids."

Maggie glanced up at Henri who shook his head as if bewildered. She turned her eyes back to Kahn and the gun he held loosely in his hand now. It took him a few moments to gather the energy to speak. In the silence, she slid her hand into her purse and found her cell phone; she flipped it up, tried to find the speed dial for Mead and pressed it. She hoped.

"Everything you say is true," Kahn said. He spoke so softly, Maggie strained to hear.

"The Nazi bastards killed my father. He was a good man until they corrupted him. You understand, don't you?" Kahn said to no one. "I couldn't let my family know their grandfather was a collaborator. It was a disgrace, worse even than going to a concentration camp, worse even than death."

"And the insurance?" she asked.

He blew out a long breath. "After the War, the Jews who survived tried to get their valuables back, put the pieces of their lives together. They filed for insurance. Most of them got it. I did the same only I still had the real painting. No one knew. I had never confided in a soul. Not even my mother,

God rest her soul. When the insurance money came, I took the name of my dear friend, Emil Kahn, who died at Dachau. I came to this country."

He slouched, spent. "Serena, my poor dear wife. What will she do? Don't you see? I had no choice. They left me no choice. I was compelled to keep the truth hidden."

"Emil," Maggie said softly, "you killed three people to protect your secret. Three people who had a right to live. How will Serena feel about that?"

Kahn sprang up in his seat, gun poised again. "What? Wait, what did you say? Three people. I did not, no. Not three people. Ingrid Rettke, yes. She knew about me. I'm sure of it. . . yes . . . she knew or would've known soon. And then she'd let the truth out." Kahn's face shone with sweat and Maggie feared a heart attack was imminent.

"How did Ingrid know about you?"

"That Nazi swine, her grandfather, of course. I would have been happy to kill him as well, but he, well, he beat me to it. Monster."

"And Aaron Beckman?" she said.

"Yes, yes, he had learned too much. He was getting close to the truth. Ach." Kahn shook his head, eyes feverish. "But I never. . . I never killed anyone else, a third, you say? Who is dead? Who?"

Maggie just looked at him.

Kahn waved his gun at the room. "Tell me. Who else was murdered for this painting?"

"Rudolf Hofer," Henri said.

"No, no. I did not kill Hofer." He drew in a slow, deep breath and met Maggie's eyes dead-on. "You must believe me."

She looked at him long and hard. And believed him.

The only other possibility, however, made her heart ache. Whichever was true, her fate would be the same.

She composed herself as best she could for inevitable death.

Chapter 36

The room seemed to shrink in size. Maggie knew Kahn spoke the truth. But the alternative was far worse.

"It was you," she said in a hoarse whisper to Henri. "You killed Rudolf."

Kahn sat up, gun gripped tighter in his hand. "Henri? You? My God. Why?"

Henri broke into a thin smile. "Emil, Jesus, use your head. I did it for both of us. Hofer threatened our partnership. You couldn't take care of a young, strong man--much too risky. *Alors*, I did it for you, for us."

"Wait," Maggie said. "Partnership, what partnership?"

Henri pulled out his cigarette pack, took his time lighting a cigarette and drew in several puffs. He crossed the room to stand by Kahn, who was sitting stiffly in his chair.

"Emil and I have been in business for a long time. Through his contacts and mine, we have managed to locate confiscated art and sell the pieces through private collectors. Each of us would vouch for the other, authenticate the painting, even fake the provenance, if necessary. We've had a very successful relationship, *non?*" Henri touched Kahn's shoulder and the old man flinched.

Maggie's muscles were tense to the point of painful and adrenaline raced through her veins. She thought she could fly if she had to.

"But you were holding out on me, dear friend," Henri went on. "You never told me you actually had in your possession the prize of all paintings: the *Vase with Oleanders*. No, you kept that one a secret. Did you think I wouldn't find out? Very foolish." Henri sucked in the smoke. "And then you came along, Maggie. Your ARTEC program, *oui*, it is quite impressive, your damned science too convincing. It would lead the police straight to Emil because he was their expert. Inevitably it would lead to me. I couldn't let that happen."

Kahn shrugged Henri's hand off his shoulder and stood up. He faced the Frenchman, gun pointed at his chest. "You are wrong about me, Benoit. I killed because I had to, no other reason. I never would have killed Hofer."

"Ah, so killing Ingrid Rettke and Aaron Beckman was all right under your high moral standards, yes, but why? Because her grandfather was a Nazi? Because she could jeopardize your plans? Because Beckman would have exposed you? But not Hofer? What a hypocrite you are." Henri took a step closer to the gun. "We are still in this together, Emil, you and I. There is no escaping. The truth will bring us both down."

Kahn took a step back. "The painting. You knew about my gallery and went back as soon as I left the house. You broke in, that's why the police said there was a burglary. Yeesss, of course. I was right, I knew it all along. You took the painting. Damn you. Where is it? It is mine, rightfully mine. My father died for that painting." Kahn towered over the Frenchman and seemed oddly powerful for a man in his eighties.

Henri took advantage of the old man's rage. He ducked his head and rammed his body into Kahn's, sending both men crashing to the floor. Henri landed on top of the old man and twisted the gun out of his hand. He aimed it at Kahn's head.

"Stop," Maggie screamed. She scrabbled for Mead's gun in her bag, felt the cool metal. "Drop the gun, Henri," she said. "Drop it. Don't make me shoot you."

Henri swiveled slowly to look at her, Kahn inert beneath him. "You can't shoot me, Maggie. Look at you. Your hands are shaking so bad you might shoot yourself. Have you ever shot anyone? Ever killed anyone?" He smiled. "You won't shoot me."

He stood. She backed up.

"Give me that gun before someone is hurt." Henri held out his hand.

Her left eye caught movement. Kahn had staggered to his knees. Before Henri could react, the old man seized his arm and wrestled him for the Walther.

Maggie aimed her gun at Henri, but the men wrenched and struggled and she couldn't get a clear shot. Instead she raced back to her bag and grabbed her cell. She pressed 9-1-1 but before she could speak, her legs were kicked out from under her. She toppled to the floor and her gun flew out of her hand. The two men struggled against each other. She could sense Kahn weakening. Somehow she rolled to her knees. The Walther went off in an ear-splitting roar. The bullet scudded by her head in a whoosh of flaming air.

She imagined she heard Kahn yelling but her eardrums reverberated. Then another blast from the gun and she went deaf, the world silent as a 1920's film. She fell backwards. When she looked up she saw it coming. Too late. Henri's fist collided with her face. The pain sucked her into a stygian hole--first light. . . then stars. . . then pitch blackness.

When she came to, Maggie lay on the floor. She moaned as her fingers investigated her damaged face. The right cheek flamed with agony. She couldn't see out of that eye. A viscous liquid dripped into it. Her fingers came away red. She lifted her head too quickly and suddenly she was puking. Puking and crying at the same time. Her stomach roiled and knotted, then finally eased. She crawled a few inches and bumped into a body. With her good eye she recognized Emil Kahn. He stared up at her, but the light had been extinguished from his eyes by the bullet in his chest. A large blood-stained circle soaked his white shirt.

She listened for sounds, but her ears wouldn't cooperate. Where was Henri?

Maggie pulled herself up with a brief surge of strength but immediately collapsed into a chair. She held her head, a hollow ringing from the blasts, and watched blood drip onto her blouse. The pain in her cheek and jaw sent the room into a spin.

Where was Henri?

Through a film of blood and tears Maggie could make out someone edging toward her. She managed to stand but swayed as the room swayed.

"Where do you think you're going?" Henri said, his voice coming to her from the depths of the ocean.

"It's over, Henri. Kahn is dead."

"*Mais non, mon cher.* He is not dead. . . yet. I am afraid that Emil Kahn must kill one more person."

He slid on leather gloves and Maggie thought she might throw up again.

"Here is how it went down, as they say in Hollywood," Henri said. "Kahn came here to find out where his painting was. He threatened to kill me if I didn't give it to him. When he saw you he was surprised and confused. I tried to protect you by jumping him, but it was too late. His gun had already gone off. I fought him, wrestled the gun and in the struggle he got shot. Too bad, you were already dead. Sad ending, *non?*"

Her throat closed.

"It's simple, really. You know too much, Maggie. About me, about Kahn, about our little art scam. Once you are gone, Kahn's story dies with him. I can go back to my work at the museum and the auction houses. True," he mused to himself, "I will need to cultivate some of Emil's clients, you know, so they trust me as they trusted him. The world will be sad to lose such an accomplished art connoisseur, but I think I can take his place." He offered a pained smile.

Her face throbbed and she could feel her eye swelling shut. Slowly, she searched the room with her good eye.

"Are you looking for this?" He held up Mead's gun.

"You can't get away with it, Henri. The police, the DA, no one will believe you. Two bodies here in your apartment. No way. The crime lab team will find evidence, forensic evidence to prove you did it, fingerprints, trace--" She caught her breath then added, "Mead won't buy it. And he'll never let it rest."

"Ah, the bulldog cop. I guess I'll have to risk that." His features curved into a bittersweet smile. "Ah, Maggie, what could have been between us." The Walther was in his hand again.

A rush of adrenaline brought a sudden clarity of thought. "You're forgetting something, Henri," she said. "The reason Kahn was here tonight."

He glared at her with the same sickly smile.

"You can't kill me. I have something you want."

"What could you possibly have that I want?"

"What you've been searching for. . . what you've coveted for a lifetime. . . what you've killed for."

It was her turn to smile. "Van Gogh's *Vase With Oleanders.*"

Chapter 37

Henri held the Walther pointed at the floor and smiled.

Fear, on top of her injuries, made it hard for Maggie to breathe. She tried to speak but the words were stuck in her throat. Emil Kahn's body lay near her feet. She forced herself to avert her eyes lest she cave into a hysterical heap.

Henri spoke instead. "*Je ne pas la lui faire*, Maggie. Rudolf Hofer found the painting--the one Rettke had hidden for all these years. Once Hofer was disposed of--"

"You mean once you killed him."

"The painting is now in my possession."

"You're wrong," she said. "You forgot something."

"Oh?" His smile tightened.

"Hofer didn't have the real painting because Klaus Rettke never had the real painting."

Henri said nothing, just looked at her, his face tight with a grimace of a smile.

She licked parched lips. "Ingrid's grandfather confiscated a Van Gogh *copy* from Josef Steiner. Remember what Emil said? Steiner had the original Van Gogh copied while he kept the real one hidden for his son's future. Josef Steiner duped them all: Rettke, Samuel and Aaron Beckman, even Hans Van Meegeren, who would have been mortified to know he forged a copy of a copy." She paused. "And now he's duped you."

Henri licked his lips. Minutes that seemed like hours elapsed.

Maggie tried to ignore the pain in her head and cheek. She could feel her eye swelling to the size of an ostrich egg. Through her good eye she watched Henri's face as he pieced together these new facts.

"Kahn had the painting all along. *Bâtard.*" Henri's face flushed and his mouth worked but no words came out. He did a turn around the living room, gun still in hand.

"Then why was he here? Did he think *I* stole the painting from his house? Of course he did. *Méprisable bâtard.*"

"Emil kept the painting in his basement gallery," Maggie went on. "Had you never seen it there?"

"Basement gallery? What basement gallery? What are you talking about?"

"I thought you were his partner."

"We conducted business at auction houses or museums. I know nothing of this gallery. *Merde.*" Henri spoke several angry sentences in French. Then, "Those photographs, they are the paintings in his secret collection?"

Maggie's head was spinning and she thought she might throw up again.

"Answer me. Those photos, they are paintings that belong to Kahn?"

"That's right," she managed.

"Where's the Van Gogh?" Henri hurried to the computer and picked up the copies. "There's no Van Gogh here."

"It's there," she said. "Look on the computer."

Henri set the Walther down on the desk and began scrolling through the images on the flat screen.

Maggie leaned against the couch and with her hand felt something hard and cold. Mead's gun. Her fingers closed around it. The room seemed to tilt at an odd angle. She tried a few deep breaths to keep from passing out.

"*Mon Dieu, mon Dieu,* it is here," Henri said. "The Van Gogh. The original? It is the original?"

"A legacy from Josef Steiner to his son."

Henri dropped his head in his hands.

"You killed Rudolf for nothing. For a copy. Damn you."

"Shut up. Shut up." Henri reached for the gun.

"For nothing. You killed him for nothing." She was looking through tear-filled eyes.

"Listen to me," Henri said. "Kahn came here looking for the painting. Why was it not in his gallery? You took it? You confiscated his painting?"

A laugh bubbled out of her mouth. She couldn't contain it. "What do you think?"

Henri growled, a dangerous low-throated sound like a wounded animal.

But I don't have the painting. She tried to think but her mind reeled in confusion. *Where is the Van Gogh?* She'd seen the painting, knew it was there. She'd taken a photograph of it. Henri was holding the proof in his hands. But wait a minute. She knew *she* didn't have the painting. If Kahn didn't have it and she didn't have it, where the hell was it?

More important, no matter where it was, she had to convince Henri that she did, indeed, know its location.

Henri lowered the gun and sat on the couch across from her. "How did you know about Emil's collection? About the painting?"

"I broke into his house."

"You what?"

"I wanted to find some evidence that he killed my friend. Is that so crazy?"

"Go on."

"I found his gallery in the basement, his secret collection of art. When I saw the Van Gogh, I knew it was the genuine work. I didn't want to risk losing the painting, so I took it. It's small, easy to hide." She exhaled, took another breath. "I left the empty space there for Emil to find. To see what his next move would be." She paused. "I didn't expect him to come here, though. I certainly didn't know about your illicit dealings with him."

She leaned forward, ignoring the heart that was ready to jump out of her chest. "Listen to me, Henri. We could pull this off, you and I."

"What do you mean?"

"I have it worked out." She rubbed her forehead. "First, we call the police."

He laughed.

"No, wait. What have you got to lose? We call the police, tell them the truth. The truth up to a point."

"And what truth is that?"

"That Emil came here, threatened you, you accused him of the murders and--"

"Yes?" Henri said, tightening his grip on Kahn's Walther.

"He fell apart. He knew he was trapped, had no way out. He didn't want to face the shame of his family finding out he was a killer, or that his father was a Nazi collaborator. Emil was simply overwhelmed by guilt. He shot himself in despair." She stood, clutching the gun in her pocket and dizziness threatened to knock her down. She forced herself upright. "I can corroborate the whole story, since I was right here. The police will believe me, Henri. Mead will believe me."

Henri lowered the hand with the gun. "Go on," he said quietly.

"Then, when the air clears, the story dies down, we get the painting. I can take you to it. With your contacts, you can sell it for millions and the two of us can split it, go our own separate ways."

"Why should I trust you?"

"Because you want the painting. The seventy million dollars."

Henri pursed his lips and said nothing.

Her heart ticked like a bomb. She sank back down on the arm of the chair. Please, God, please.

"All right, Maggie," Henri said. "Perhaps I can trust you for thirty-five million dollars, *non?*"

She quelled the nauseous sensation in her stomach by swallowing over and over. She told him, "Put the gun near Emil's hand, Henri, just the way it fell. We've got to stage the scene so the police don't suspect anything but suicide."

"And you know about crime scenes, don't you?"

"I've photographed a few ."

He did as she directed. He wiped the gun, pressed Kahn's fingers onto the grip for prints, then gingerly placed it beside Kahn's right hand. Henri stood and looked down at the body. He turned to her. "Tell me, Maggie, where is the painting?"

"It's safe, Henri, I promise."

Now, she had to act now. She pulled out the gun from her pocket and pointed it at him.

"Again?" Henri smiled.

"This time my hand is not shaking, Henri. Step over there and sit down," she said. "Sit down."

He did. "So you don't have the painting after all, do you?"

She didn't answer, just reached for the cell phone in her bag. She flipped it open and gave it a voice command to call Mead. Before she could speak, Henri leaped forward and lifted the coffee table off the floor. It came at her like flying debris in a hurricane.

Her gun went off almost instinctively, but by the time she recovered from the surprise, Henri was on top of her, pushing her to the floor.

Maggie fought to hold onto the weapon and the two rolled. She tried kneeing him in the groin but the awkward position she was in didn't give her the leverage. She bit his hand and tasted blood. He yelled and backhanded her. Still she held onto the gun.

Her arms ached from fending him off and she couldn't get a grip on the trigger. They crashed into the couch then a chair. They spun and tumbled. Over and over. Maggie screamed and it echoed in her head. But her strength was fading. Somehow, Henri stood over her, *her* gun in his hand.

I'm dead. I'm dead. She moaned and rolled to her side. *Like Hell.* She let out a howl and kicked out at Henri's shin. He came down with a shriek. She whirled around on her knees and with every ounce of breath left in her body, head-butted him.

A gunshot sounded then another.

There was a thunderous pounding on the door.

"Open up." Mead's voice, loud, menacing. "Maggie, you in there? Benoit? Open the damned door."

She heard a resounding crash and the door splintered open. Footsteps in the background, bellowing voices, furnishings toppling, total clamor. Another gunshot?

When she looked up from her position on the floor, she saw Frank Mead cuffing Henri. She smiled and the scene went black.

Chapter 38

Her eyes opened to intense pain. She closed them, opened them again. The pain eased a bit. Her mouth tasted like the Mojave and her tongue felt swollen to the size of a tennis ball. When she could finally focus, Frank Mead was the first countenance to come into view.

"Fra. . .nnk."

"Yeah, it's me."

"Where. . . am I?"

"Hospital. How are you doing?"

"Gr. . .eat. Wa. . .ter, please?"

"Here, try this." He put an ice cube on her lips and she sucked it greedily. "Easy."

She blinked a few times, trying to remember what happened. "I didn't, umm, Henri didn't shoot me?"

He shook his head.

"What, what were. . . the shots I heard. . . then?"

"I shot Henri."

Silence.

"Is he dead?"

"Unfortunately no. Just grazed his side."

"God."

"Some water now?"

She nodded, struggled to half-sit.

He gave her some water through a straw. She fell back.

"Thanks."

"For what? Water?"

"Saving my life."

"Hey, that's my job."

She touched her eye and winced. "Ahh, what I must look like."

"You're color coordinated."

Maggie looked at him through her swollen eye. "What?"

"You know, black, blue, a hint of yellow--"

She groaned and tried to cover her face.

"Don't be silly, Maggie. You look beautiful as always."

She tried a smile. "That's a lotta' blarney."

She pushed herself up onto her elbows. "Frank?"

"Lay back there. What?"

"The painting. Where is it? What happened to it?"

He raised an eyebrow. "Painting?"

"Where is it, Frank, please?"

"Oh, you mean the Van Gogh? That painting. It's absolutely safe and secure. Trust me."

"Frank, where . . . is . . . the painting?" She ran out of breath.

"As I said, safe and secure."

They looked at each other for a long moment until he finally said with a smirk, "I wanted to get a reaction out of Kahn. Leave a nice blank space on the wall."

"You took it. I knew it." She shook her head. "So, where is it?"

"In the trunk of my car."

Maggie opened her mouth but a nurse poked her head in. "You need to go now, sir."

"Time for you to rest," he said to Maggie.

She reached out her hand. "Wait, Frank, how long have I been here? Rosie, what about my poor Rosie?"

He took her hand in both of his and squeezed it. "Not to worry. She's already with me, sends a slobbery kiss. In fact, she's in my car guarding the painting." He grinned. "I'll bring her to visit later."

"Frank, aren't you going to pass along that slobbery kiss?"

✦ ✦ ✦

To Maggie, the world was right. The sun perched on top of the Capitol Building as she and Frank Mead walked along the Smithsonian Mall toward the domed edifice.

The blue of the sky matched his eyes and polo shirt. He wore casual Dockers and no jacket.

He looked good to her.

She wore a summery short-sleeved blouse with khaki pants and no jacket. Too bad her face still showed dark bruises, even a week later.

At least I can see through this black eye.

Three days of summer had descended early on Washington, and, blessedly, it was humid-free. Both of them wanted to soak up the dry warmth while it lasted.

Maggie felt a sense of peace she hadn't felt in a long time. Peace centered around a deep and lasting sadness. Sadness about so many deaths. Such a horrible waste. All about greed.

Sadness that Emil Kahn, aka Jakob Steiner, had suffered so much at the hands of the Nazis--that his life was forever tainted, his death, tragic.

And then there was the Van Gogh painting. She hoped it would eventually go to Kahn's wife and family. After all, Jakob's father, Josef had bought it legitimately. What he did, what his son did, after that, well. . . The resolution would be a long time in the courts.

And most of all, she felt heartsick about dear Ingrid. Maggie would miss her, did miss her terribly. At least Ingrid would never know the truth about her grandfather, his infinite cruelty, his brutal role in the ERR and the third Reich. She'd be spared that shame and grief.

For now Maggie looked forward to resuming her classes this semester and to a new course she planned to design for the spring: *The Role of Digital Photography in Analyzing Works of Fine Art.*

She looked at Mead's profile. Strong, aquiline nose, square jaw, fair hair a little long around the ears. He turned to her and smiled. She smiled back.

"You know," she said. "I was thinking."

"Uh oh."

"Do you think we could've gotten away with keeping the painting?"

"You mean *stealing* the painting?" he said.

"Uh, yeah, I guess. You know, find a collector, sell it, no questions asked, collect *beacoup* bucks." She stopped.

"And what? Run away into the sunset?"

"Something like that."

He stopped walking and turned to her. "Would you run away with me, Maggie?"

She smiled. "I don't know. Yet."

"Fair enough." He took her hand and they continued up the Mall.

About the Author

With a Master's Degree in Science and more than 28 years as a science museum director, Lynne Kennedy has had the opportunity to study history and forensic science, both of which play significant roles her novels. She has written three other historical mysteries, each solved by modern technology. *The Triangle Murders* (formerly called *Tenement*) was a finalist in St Martin's Malice Domestic Competition, 2011 and Winner of the Rocky Mountain Fiction Writers Mystery Category, 2011. The Triangle Murders also won a B.R.A.G. Medallion Award for best Indie Mystery in 2012.

Her novel, *Time Exposure*, was a finalist in St. Martin's Malice Domestic Competition in 2012.

She blogs regularly and has many loyal mystery writer and reader fans. Visit her website at www.lynnekennedymysteries.com

65162939R00150

Made in the USA
Charleston, SC
18 December 2016